WK OCT 2017

A Division of **Whampa, LLC**
P.O. Box 2540
Dulles, VA 20101
Tel/Fax: 800-998-2509
http://curiosityquills.com

Cover Design by Ricky Gunawan
http://ricky-gunawan.daportfolio.com

ISBN: 978-1-62007-124-3 (ebook)
ISBN: 978-1-62007-125-0 (paperback)
ISBN: 978-1-62007-126-7 (hardcover)

Table of Contents

Prologue. 6
One. 11
Two. 20
Three. 26
Four. 34
Five. 41
Six. 47
Seven. 54
Eight. 61
Nine. 66
Ten. 72
Eleven. 78
Twelve. 83
Thirteen. 90
Fourteen. 94
Fifteen. 98
Sixteen. 103
Seventeen. 105
Eighteen. 109
Nineteen. 118
Twenty. 125
Twenty-One. 133
Twenty-Two. 137
Twenty-Three. 144
Twenty-Four. 146
Twenty-Five. 151
Twenty-Six. 159
Twenty-Seven. 165
Twenty-Eight. 170
Twenty-Nine. 178
Thirty. 182
Thirty-One. 188
Thirty-Two. 197
Thirty-Three. 203
Thirty-Four. 211
Thirty-Five. 221
Thirty-Six. 229
Epilogue. 239
More from Curiosity Quills Press 246

For my parents, who had the good sense to give birth to me in England, where the sense of humor is far more ridiculous than anywhere else in the world.

For Penguins all over the world. ♥

And for my cat, Mr. Bojangles, who inspired and urged me to write the story in the first place.

May he rest in peace.

Prologue.

The gentleman stepped up to the podium and straightened his tie. He looked out at the several hundred students whose eyes all rested upon the gentleman's athletic build. An athletic build he was quite proud of, at that. He was a renowned gentleman, scholar, professional assumptionist and part-time religious expert. His theories and social experiments were famous the world over, and as a result, he was invited to the best parties and most prestigious events. He was happy. New theories were getting harder to come up with, and it had been at least a year and a half since his last lecture at Oxford University, but here he stood, once again on the brink of high expectations, with not one but three new theories to present.

The students were honored to have him as a guest speaker, and the other professors had waited for this lecture for several months, many of them having abandoned their families, moved across the country, and re-shuffled their schedules to make time to listen to what was expected to be a world-shaking lecture. Members of the national and international press arrived two hours earlier to get the pre-lecture buzz from the students and faculty. Things like *profoundly excited* and *would trade my left testicle to see that man speak* were uttered.

The auditorium sat in silence, poised on the edge of their seats, notebooks at the ready, recording devices fully loaded, their studious brains humming, fully prepared to be inspired.

The gentleman shuffled his notes and got right to the point.

"Ladies and gentlemen," he said, "I realize that I need no introduction and so, I will get right to the point."

Several students quickly wrote that down in case there was some hidden meaning to be uncovered later.

"Today, I have three new theories for you and they will be presented here for the first time."

Thunderous applause roared throughout the auditorium. Several people lucky enough to get a seat stood up and applauded harder.

The gentleman breathed in his last breath of true success.

"My first is a modern proposal of sorts; at first glance it may seem absurd, but as we all know, first impressions can be deceiving."

A few respectful chuckles arose from the audience.

"I believe that this modern proposal will benefit the world if taken seriously and pondered to the utmost." The gentleman cleared his throat, shuffled his papers once more, and launched into it with hasty abandon. "I present to you A Proposal for Global Public Nudity!"

When expectations had been so high that people reorganized their entire lives in the fond hope that their anticipations would be more than met, it came as quite a disappointment when not only were those not met. But instead, those expectations were drugged, tied, gagged, placed in a bag, driven out to the middle of God knows where, and buried in a twenty-foot-deep hole which was then covered with concrete.

Almost everyone in the room stopped breathing, and only a few people remembered to blink.

The gentleman mistook the looks of shock and awe as surprise and delight and continued enthusiastically.

"Firstly, designer labels and fashion have ruled our lives for long enough. The re-introduction of the tube-top should have been a clear signal that the industry can now manipulate us to wear whatever they feel is necessary for daily living. And furthermore, can charge whatever ludicrous prices they deem suitable. How many girls have come home from school crying because their best friend has the new designer label? It is a ploy. A well-thought-out ploy to separate us from our hard-earned wage. If we instigate global nudity, then the war over who is cool and who is not according to fashion becomes obsolete. No one needs to buy *skin*. We are all born with it; it's waterproof, durable, and available in a wide range of colours."

No one wrote anything down; everyone had enough trouble concentrating as the once renowned gentleman on stage quickly and carefully fed his career to the sharks.

"How many people hide their true self and figure behind the many shades of fabric that hang in the millions of department stores around the world? Like the army, that is mere camouflage. Fat people pretend to be thin. Females with a self-perception of less-than-adequate bosoms dress themselves up to appear a little more well-endowed than they actually are. Thin, ugly, small, repellent males are simply handed the ability to cover their true selves with designer shoes, shirts, pants, and so on, only to be later discovered by some poor unsuspecting female, or male, that he is less than he appears. The inhibitions that have clouded the minds of the general populace for so long would be stripped down to reveal the truth, and only the truth.

"What follows is a short list of some of the absolute advantages of Global Public Nudity.

"Parents will no longer have to endure the hassle of teaching their children the delicate art of tying their shoelaces. There will be no shoelaces to tie.

"Breastfeeding will become a communally shared experience, much like asking for directions or helping an elderly lady across the busy street. There will always be a wide number of *portable milk outlets* available, especially in busy places like malls or Starbucks.

"Global public nudity holds a great deal of advantages for men, also. No longer will a suffering male have to wait for a celibate fiancée to display the goods. *Playboy* will become a thing of the past, therefore cutting down on the clutter of magazines that shroud the bathrooms of many homes.

"The ever-present zipper problem will be abolished, as there will no longer be a vicious cutting device hanging around the groin section of the male body. But the greatest advantage to males will be the decrease in time that taken for women to get ready for work, a date, dinner, a movie, etc., etc.

"There will be a sharp decrease in the amount of emotional stress caused by elderly people exposing themselves in public places. The act of exposing oneself will no longer be an issue, as everyone will be totally stark naked.

"In conclusion, I realize that some of these points may initially appear as nothing more than barefaced cheek, an insult to society. But I assure you, these points are logical and viable and would instantly solve many of the problems that plague the world as we know it today. So I propose that we *strip* away our inhibitions and bare to the world our true selves," he finished with a flourish.

There was no applause, no standing ovation. If the university had allowed crickets to be present at the lecture, they would have been the only sound heard.

The gentleman mistook the looks of pity and disappointment as eager interest and spellbound curiosity, and so he quickly launched into his second theory, which involved aliens not only building the pyramids, but also inventing the mango chutney-curried chicken-mayo-dried cranberry sandwich. He managed to get through the majority of the theory before the Oxford security guards intervened. The mango chutney-curried chicken-mayo-dried cranberry sandwich theory was the last nail in the coffin of his career. As the security guards dragged the gentleman off stage, his last words were, "No, wait, I also have a theory about the devil, the dead not dying, Santa Claus, his elves, and a penguin!"

But no one heard him. They were all too busy laughing.

In many ways, he was wrong. Global public nudity would be amusing, somewhat entertaining, and probably really disgusting, not to mention completely absurd. Aliens did not build the pyramids. Slaves built the pyramids while under the overpowering influence of large men holding even larger whips. But on certain points he was absolutely correct. Had anyone bothered to listen to his theory about the devil, the dead not dying, Santa Claus, his elves, and a penguin, they would have eventually found out that he was right on the money.

One.

There were deals, and then there were deals. And this was a deal. The signature sat, burning comfortably, on the dotted line. Then, while the Prince of Darkness gleefully packed his clothes, the document was on its way to the administration office via the Underworld Postal System for filing. He didn't really like the demons in the administration office; they were low even by his standards.

Decisions, decisions. Whether to take the blue underwear or the orange?

It had been so long since he'd been allowed to get away from it all and really commit to some good old-fashioned deceiving. And to walk on the Earth again, that would be truly fabulous. The last time he'd possessed a body must have been at least three thousand years ago. Reflectively, though, he really hadn't had the best of luck with possessing people.

He shuddered as he packed his knitted doilies and remembered the whole Adam and Eve fiasco. That had been his first real possession. He'd been aiming for Eve but missed by a few feet and ended up in that stupid snake. He'd had to slither round for a good few hours before he got the hang of how to move, and then had to deal with the constant compulsion to eat eggs. It almost wasn't worth the hassle. Everything turned out okay in the end, introducing sin to the Earth and all, but he'd found the whole episode a rather trying ordeal.

No matter how many times he steeped in a bubble bath, it still took him weeks to shake that slimy, scaly feeling.

The Devil looked in a mirror and stared at the grim, distorted figure before him. *Sad. I really have to start getting more sleep.* Maybe he'd take up a relaxation program when he got back from the Earth, something to improve his quality of life. Tai Chi: that's what he'd do. He'd go down to the dungeons and find some ancient Chinese souls who could teach him Tai Chi. After he'd tortured them for a while.

I'm forgetting something. The Devil picked up his going-away checklist and a pen.

-Pack clothes . . . check!

-Clean bathroom . . . check!

-Turn off coffee maker . . . check!

-Send Deal made with God stating Devil may walk the Earth for One Week document down to the administration department . . . check!

-Give bone-chilling speech to the new arrivals . . . check!

-Leave instructions with one of the demons on how to feed the fish . . . .

That's it. He'd forgotten about his fish, Percy. The Devil walked out of his apartment onto the high rocky precipice that served as a sort of porch and looked down at his rather overly warm kingdom.

Demons wandered hither and thither, dragging tortured souls around with them. The Devil grimaced; it was so hot down here, and it wasn't even a nice dry heat, the humidity was unbearable. Soon enough, he'd be able to breathe the lovely fresh air that the human race so easily took for granted. The thought cooled him ever so slightly, and a small cloud of steam rose from his body. He stretched out his black, tattered, leathery wings and shouted out over the cavernous kingdom, his dark voice bouncing off the jagged rocks.

"Listen to me, all you inhabitants of Hell. For those of you who are new, there will be a public flaying of lawyers at six tonight. Make sure you bring something for the potluck dinner or you will not be allowed to enjoy the festivities. And if anyone's seen Azeal, could they please tell him I'd like to see him immediately in my quarters? That is all!"

The Devil re-folded his wings and stalked back into his home. He playfully tapped on the fishbowl where Percy the goldfish swam happily around without a care in the world, except that he could never understand why his water always stayed so warm.

There came a sharp rap at the door, to which the door grimly responded by swinging open to reveal a short, stumpy, egg-shaped demon with only one leg and half a wing. Even his horns looked like something created by using a toilet paper roll and lots of sticky tape. His yellowy-green eyes darted suspiciously around the room.

"Ahh, Azeal, do come in," motioned the Devil as he made kissy faces at Percy, who felt somewhat confused as to why this large, ugly, black mass kept making faces at him.

Azeal hopped in, started to lose his balance, flapped furiously with his half a wing in order to straighten himself and then proceeded to fall over. The Devil shook his head sadly and made a *tsk tsk* kind of sound with his forked tongue.

"I really have no idea how you ever survived through the Crusades. Maybe survived is a bit of a strong word. You did lose your leg and the vast majority of your wingspan."

Azeal, not possessing the ability to speak, simply made a rude noise and pushed himself back up on his one leg.

"Now listen carefully, Azeal. Percy is very special to me, and if you should accidentally kill him, I'll have you flogged 'til the rest of your wing falls off. Understood?"

Azeal burped loudly and grinned a maliciously stupid grin.

The Devil rolled his eyes.

"His feeding instructions are next to his bowl, along with his food. I'll be back in a week. If any pressing matters arise, the Second Coming, that kind of thing, you'll be able to reach me on my cell. Got it?"

Azeal farted and left it at that.

"Good," said the Devil. It suddenly became very clear to him that the clock on the wall was trying to tell him something.

"Oh my, is that the time? I'll be late." And with a great flapping of wings he ranout the door, knocking Azeal over in the process. The Devil popped his head back through the doorway.

"Azeal, did I mention that I'd have you flogged if you messed up?"

Azeal jumped to his foot and bounced up and down a couple of times while making distressed choking noises.

"Good." The Devil grabbed his suitcase and took off at a sprint.

The Gates of Hell looked dark as ever as the Devil ran up to them. The excitement was really getting to him and he could hardly stop himself hopping from one foot to the other.

One of the two large guards at the gates of Hell stepped up to the Devil.

"Pass, please."

"What?" said the Devil, brimming over with disbelief.

"I said pass, please. Bit deaf, are you?" replied the guard.

Fire began to burn in the Devil's eyes. "Do you know who I am?"

The other guard suddenly came running forward and pushed the first guard back. "I'm so sorry, boss," said the second demon guard. "You see, that's Stan, he's new here. Won't happen again."

The Devil raised himself up to his full height and spread his wings in a terrifying arc. Then he folded them up again and burst out in a fit of laughter.

"I really can't be mad at you today. Going to Earth, you see, approved by God Himself. Ha! Idiot. Do be a good boy and let me out."

The two demons pulled open the unbelievably large, iron gates to reveal a long line of people waiting to get in. Part of Hell's policy clearly stated that everyone had to stand in line for at least five years before entering.

These pitiful fools, and they thought standing in line at the supermarket was bad. The Devil grinned an evil grin and sprinted off toward the end of the line, which disappeared into a set of double doors marked with a large pink neon sign that said *Exit*. And then underneath, in smaller, less bright neon letters: *Fat chance*.

The Devil ran through the doors without a care for the poor dead people on either side of him.

"Move it, coming through, get out of the way you insolent fools!"

The way out of Hell was a little more difficult than getting in. Getting in required that a person be ignorant, redundant, or evil, and preferably dead, or so unbelievably cursed by God that there wouldn't ever be a chance of being redeemed. The Devil's situation was that of the latter. But by the recent agreement with God Himself, the Devil had been granted a temporary pass to get out of the Fiery Inferno and walk around for a whole week. During which he would wreak unspeakable havoc and attempt to add to the growing line of people waiting to get into Hell.

The passage into the world consisted of a long, dark tunnel that stretched endlessly up into seemingly nothingness. People generally fell down the tunnel. It was an extremely rare occasion that anyone went back up it. However, the Devil had done this before; he knew the drill.

He unfurled his dark wings and prepared for the flight up. Oh, he couldn't wait to see the body he would possess. He'd had a nice one picked out for quite a while now, a reclusive millionaire, young and healthy. The contract stated that he would have to inhabit a body the moment he reached the Earth, and the Devil knew it was just a matter of throwing himself into the right person. He flapped his wings, kicking up dust and debris, focused, then prepared for takeoff. He was pumped. He was ready. And so it came as a complete surprise at that point when a three-hundred-pound man in a white vest and boxer shorts with little hearts on them fell from the tunnel above and landed on the Devil's face.

The fat gentleman got to his feet. "Bloody hell! Where am I?"

The Devil arose from the ground and folded his arms.

"Well, you're dead, aren't you? And I'm assuming that in life you were somewhat of an asshole and consequently, here you are. Torture

15

for eternity," the Devil pointed a long, bony finger toward the end of the line, "that way!"

The fat man, somewhat confused, replied, "Uhh, yeah, thanks," and waddled off toward the line.

The Devil shook his head, unfurled his wings once again, and with a great big flap worthy of an American Bald Eagle, flew up the portal. Everything always went a bit blurry around this part; going from one reality to the next was never easy. It always gave him the kind of feeling that his insides were turning outside. The Devil loved the feeling. And as he rose higher and higher, going faster and faster, heading for the end of the tunnel, he smiled at how easy he'd found it to strike such a simple deal that would allow him to take human form and destroy lives.

The end of the tunnel was nigh as he rushed toward a bright blue light. Then, nothing but frantic oblivion. All was dark.

The Devil opened his eyes and took a deep breath. *Ahh, fresh air.* It would appear he was on the floor. He tried to stand up but, as he did so, he didn't really move all that much higher. What was the problem here? His surroundings were simple: a couch, a TV, a lovely coffee table with some fine bone china.

The Devil stretched as his senses came into play.

A door opened off to his side and a pair of legs in badly wrinkled stockings appeared and dropped a plate of food in front of him.

The Devil looked down at the plate of brown mush and then up to see a little old lady grinning down at him.

She opened her mouth and cooed.

"Aww, who's a cute puddycat, Fuzzbucket?"

The Devil mustered all his strength and cried, "What?"

What actually came out was *meow*.

I don't believe it. I'm in a cat! How the hell did I end up in a cat?

The Devil didn't know what to do. The Devil, the Prince of Darkness, Beelzebub, the Deceiver himself, trapped in a cat for an entire week. And not just any cat: a cat called Fuzzbucket. He suddenly had a strong urge to systematically clean himself, and being in complete shock and not knowing what else to do, went ahead and did so.

Down in the depths of Hell's Administration office, a lowly demon examined the contract she'd just received to file. She made a *tsk tsk* sort of noise and shook her head as she read the fine print through a magnifying glass.

Please Note: If by any chance the above noted chosen body is unavailable due to death, dismemberment, or divine intervention, the party of the second part (being Lucifer, the Prince of Darkness) will waive all possession rights and will be deposited into a body of the party of the first part's (being God) choosing.

The demon lifted a large metal stamp and branded the word *received* into the contract with a satisfying *hissssss.*

The evening air was close and the heat, relentless. It beat at every passerby in the small town of Obidos, located somewhere in the west of Portugal.

Sweat escaped from every available pore on the body of Raymond Miller as he wandered down tight, quaint streets.

He loved Obidos at this time of year. Not so much for the heat, as no one really loved the town for its heat. But because Obidos was so quiet, hardly anyone around, no tourists, just the locals. The locals left him alone; they didn't like the strange visitor who appeared out of nowhere for a few weeks every year and then vanished without a trace. It became a favorite pastime of the locals to stand completely still with a fixed frown whenever Raymond would appear on the street. They would watch him walk down the street, moving only their heads until he disappeared into a shop or around a corner. Shopkeepers wouldn't talk to him except to tell him how much he owed them. They would answer any pleasantries or questions with a severe *umph,* all the time frowning like their lives depended on it.

They didn't like Raymond because he didn't follow the tourist trend. He always turned up out of season, and he kept himself to himself, not to mention he'd built a ghastly, great big mansion on the outskirts of town.

Raymond was in fact a billionaire who had quite methodically worked out when the off-season occurred for every beautiful place on Earth. He would travel round all year to these places, then build a house where he could stay for a couple of weeks, and that was his life, day in and day out. All he ever wanted was a quiet life, and when his one-hundred-fourteen-year-old grandmother died, she left Raymond, her only living relative, all her money. Although on the surface a quiet and very innocent-looking lady, she had made her money by running drugs from the United States to Japan. She was a little old lady with too much time on her hands, and she liked traveling to the Orient. Or that's what all the security people at the airports thought as they helped her off the plane and even carried her drug-filled luggage for her. Her drug-running name was *Silent Grasshopper*. Raymond had no knowledge of this, as she told him that she won all her money on the lottery, and so he remained blissfully unaware.

Raymond had been an Olympic swimmer before the inheritance, and although he remained in good physical condition, he no longer swam. When he got the money from his grandmother, he decided to follow up on his high school dream to do absolutely nothing. He traveled around the world, spending the vast amount of money he'd acquired. He partied occasionally, hired women to satisfy his carnal pleasures, hired people to cook for him, but really did nothing of any importance. If he vanished off the face of the Earth, the only person who would miss him would be his bank manager, who talked to him every few days and who could have been considered to be Raymond's only friend.

As Raymond walked out onto the bridge that crossed the local river, he stopped and admired the sunset. He could see a couple of children playing soccer at the other end of the bridge, a little too close to the road, he thought. There really wasn't that much traffic in the town, so there was probably nothing to worry about. At least, that's what Raymond thought right up until he saw the bus.

The bus driver's name was Dante and he was on the last route of the evening. He was, however, currently preoccupied with the sudden appearance of what appeared to be an orange object descending from the sky. Dante was so enamored with the strange object that he failed to see the young boy who ran out into the road after his run-away ball.

Raymond started sprinting before he even knew why. The urge hit him in the form of one simple word that felt very strangely as if someone had spoken it directly into his head. *Run!*

Everything happened very quickly. Raymond reached the boy just in time to push him out of the way; he looked up at the last minute to see an orange swirly thing plummeting toward him.

The orange swirly thing, consequently, was the last thing Raymond Miller saw in his life, as a millisecond later he was hit by the bus that killed him.

Moments later, the soul of Raymond Miller came face to face with a disgruntled-looking man dressed in a black robe standing next to a large neon sign that pointed *up*.

Two.

Death was not having a good day. Incidentally, Death did not normally go by the name Death. Especially when traveling; there would often be random outbursts of either laughter or panic. He often adopted the name *Arnold*. However, at this particular point in his existence he couldn't have cared less and committed himself to simply being called Death.

Death wasn't just having a bad day, he was having a tragic day. The kind of tragic day that made people wish they could just crawl into a ball on their couch with a tub of ice cream and watch several episodes of some equally tragic TV drama. And furthermore, he wasn't dealing with it all very well.

Most people had regular nine to five jobs, five days a week, sweeping the streets, working in an office, providing overly greasy food to nations that were nowhere near starving, etc. Death did not. Death's job consisted of seeking out those individuals who were about to leap off this mortal coil and guide them to their next destination, which usually consisted of simply up or down. He didn't kill anyone, he didn't swing a fiery sword, and he didn't rain down fire and brimstone. Although he did own a fiery sword; he kept it at home in the closet because he was afraid he might cut himself. Death had always been the more paranoid of the Angels. Ironic, considering popular opinion stated that he was easily one of the most terrifying, spooky, and mysterious Angel archetypes. Even the other Angels agreed.

For years, Death accepted his job as being an essential part of God's plan. Over time, the passage from this world to the next became a little easier, and the direction of up or down was often marked by large shiny sign posts with big neon arrows so there was no confusion, but lately he had begun to get a bit fed up with it all.

The whole situation culminated just a few hours previously at a local Irish bar, conveniently situated in Ireland, where Death had stopped for a quick drink. The Irish made good beer, and Ireland was on the way to Greece, which happened to be his next stop. A quick drink turned into a couple of quick drinks, and then a couple of slower drinks, and continued to escalate until two hours later when Death found himself outside that same pub screaming mindless obscenities at a lamppost. Apparently, it looked at him funny when he had been kicked out of the pub and he was rather insulted by it.

The reason for his abrupt removal from the bar was due to some specific comments made by one of the locals.

In the midst of all the drinking, Death struck up some light conversation with the friendly gentleman sitting next to him. He later looked upon that as his first big mistake of the current century.

The gentleman's name was Mickey. A lot of Irish people tended to be named Mickey and they all seemed very fond of alcohol and bombings. Death used his angelic powers to get a brief glimpse into Mickey's mind, unsturdy as it was. Mickey, as it turned out, was a gamekeeper at a local farm about an hour's drive from the pub. He was meant to be at home with his angry wife but called ahead and told her that he had to visit a sick friend. He did that often.,Not because he had a lot of sick friends, but because he had an angry wife. She always got even angrier as Mickey was always off visiting his sick friends. This turn of events turned into a vicious circle over the past few years and drove Mickey's wife to the fine art of bomb making. Unbeknownst to Mickey. His wife, at that very moment, had been putting the finishing touches to her latest masterpiece which was to be shipped out that very night.

Death and Mickey exchanged the usual pleasantries, the conversation became bombarded with many slurred words, and Death even slipped off his barstool a couple of times.

Anyone who ever had the misfortune of hearing an Irish person speak would know that they were not the easiest of species to understand. Adding a fermented vegetable concoction to that mix created something akin to the sound a cassette tape recorder would make if it taped fifty squawking seagulls and then played it back at high speed in reverse. Even then, it'd only be slightly close to the true drunken Irish language.

"So, whadyadafararrleavin?" asked Mickey.

Thankfully, Death, being what he was, easily translated drunken Irish.

"What do I do for a living? Funny you should ask," replied Death. "I guide people to the afterlife when their physical and spiritual presence on this Earth is no longer required."

Death watched as drunken confusion washed over Mickey's face like the sea approaching high tide. This was a common occurrence, and completely intentional, as Death's appearance was not entirely normal, and he found that an easier way to keep people calm. In fact, Death's appearance was almost stereotypical of the old Grim Reaper characters featured in sixties horror movies. He wore a flowing dark robe, was practically faceless, and had thin white hands. Once upon a time, he used those skinny white hands to clutch a scythe so he could be easily recognized, but during the Great Heavenly Survey of 1753, a 700-page enquiry for the recently deceased, the scythe became obsolete, as results from the recently deceased showed that the scythe depicted a far scarier Angel of Death than was absolutely necessary. Too, his black robe then changed to an extremely dark burgundy colour so he didn't look quite as scary. Just to be on the safe side, an Angelic Defense Mechanism made sure that any living human who saw Death would not be able to remember ever meeting him after Death disappeared from sight for more than ten seconds or so.

"So," Mickey said, "yawarkferverbankthin?"

Death rolled his eyes and tried hard to concentrate on his beer.

"No, I don't work for the bank." He seemed to recall going through a similar situation not so long ago when he had been mistaken for a lawyer. That seemed to be happening more and more these days.

"Werdedyigurtschoo? Oxfarwaset? OrmebeCambridge? Onlyyalakverytelligent." Mickey smiled a self-satisfied smile.

Death could see the direction this conversation was headed. He just shook his head and downed the last of his beer before ordering another one. He turned to his neighbor and attempted to smile politely, which wasn't an easy thing for a practically faceless Angel to accomplish.

"I'm going to try and explain this to you slowly as I know you're far more intoxicated than I am. The fact that you haven't commented on my lack of face or dark robe or the cold tingly feeling that travels up and down your spine every time I speak substantiates your severe intoxication. I'm the Angel of Death. Sent by God Himself to guide the souls of man to the next life. Is it really that difficult of a concept to grasp?" He turned back to the bar and accepted the fresh pint from the bartender.

Mickey looked worried, as if he'd offended the dark stranger. His glazed eyes searched for an answer and then enlightenment dawned upon his face. "So, is tha much muni n tha?"

Death looked Mickey up and down, decided that he couldn't wait until the day that he could guide this poor soul off the Earth, and went back to his beer.

It took all of ten minutes, another round of beers for the lads, and an offhand comment by a young man named Seth to push Death over the point of no return. Seth, a local farm hand, had never really gone to school, but had the most amazing talent of breaking a situation down to its most basic components. Plus, his parents were

English, so he was the one person in the bar who didn't sound like a cassette player that was stuck on reverse play.

The conversation continued to cover the finer points of Death's employment, and everyone had been doing a great job of keeping their drunken faces straight and showing feigned interest right up until the point when Seth made his comment. That same comment was the reason that Death ended up outside that same bar a little while later, screaming at the surprised lamppost. The lamppost wasn't used to being shouted at for no reason and wasn't happy about it.

"So basically," Seth said, as innocently as possible, "what you're telling us is that you're some sort of a doorman in the afterlife? Like old Jimmy Barns used to do at that fancy hotel in Dublin, showing people where to go, opening the door for them, getting them a taxi, kissing their ass? Is there much money in that?"

Well, that was it. The crowd literally fell about the place laughing.

Mickey, as reserved a character as he was, ran to the bathroom before he peed himself.

Death did not take the reaction very well. He fell off his chair for the final time and let go of any remains of patience that he had left.

Everyone quieted down as Death continued to shout at the bar patrons, telling each and every one of them exactly when and where they would be the moment that they died. He didn't actually know offhand, he was just guessing, but that was the only thing he could think of on short notice that might scare them.

The bar was stunningly quiet. Death could almost smell the victory. In fact, he was very close to smiling, until the bar patrons burst into another round of laughter and Paddy the butcher was the one who ran to the bathroom

At that, the bartender decided the funnily dressed stranger had caused quite enough entertainment and should be kicked out before he got rowdy. The group of drunken Irish men all cheered as the Angel of Death got thrown out of the bar. Questions like "Dayaworkdinapartis?" and "wuldyabevailabultaperfarmatmedartersbirthday?" followed him out the door, along with more rounds of laughter.

An hour later, after he had grown tired of shouting at the lamppost, and the mailbox proved unresponsive, Death decided that he'd had quite enough.

He'd talked the whole thing over with God just a month ago, but the talk had done no good. God was infallible and omnipotent (not to be confused with the word *impotent*, which is a common disorder found in older men), and therefore knew when, where, and how everything in the entire world was going to happen, throughout the existence of all time. When Death tried to plead his case, God, knowing how this whole thing was to end, simply sat there with a whimsical smile on His face. Death asked what he should do and God just patted him on the head and told him that it probably wasn't worth worrying about. Then He wandered off whistling happily to Himself.

That actually succeeded in calming Death down for a while, but lately things had just been getting worse and everything all sort of culminated when he realized that he was somewhat of a glorified doorman and that he was standing on a lonely street in the middle of Ireland shouting at a lamppost. But the thing that really bit into him, the one thing about his job that had been burning up inside of him, was that when he guided people up or down, not once, not even once in a thousand years, had anyone said so much as a thank you.

And so, after a lot of alcohol, provoking by the local townsfolk, and a long conversation with a suspicious-looking cat, Death, The Angel of Death, The Grim Reaper, The Guide to the Afterlife himself, decided that he'd had enough. And right there on the spot, he quit.

Three.

Detective Nigel Amadeus Reinhardt felt nervous. Everyone got nervous. Women got nervous when there were spiders around. Men got nervous when there were women around. This little predicament covered neither of those situations, yet Nigel continued to be nervous. With good reason. Nigel currently found himself hanging upside down over the edge of a seven-story building, and the only thing preventing the well-known effects of gravity was a large man named Big Ernie.

Big Ernie was named Big Ernie for one simple and obvious reason. He was big. Not big, as in *I wouldn't want to sit next to that overly large man on a long plane journey because his girth would eventually crush me* big, more like *I wouldn't want to sit next to that overly large man on a long plane ride as he looks like he could remove my head with his bare hands* kind of big. That was not his only asset; he also happened to be a tremendous flute player and volunteered at the old folk's home on the weekends. Not something he particularly enjoyed doing, but his Mum, Big Priscilla, said he had to do it to build character. Aside from the flute playing and assisting the old people to get to the bathroom, Big Ernie also worked for a loan shark. Something he kept from his mother, as he knew she had a fear of sharks. The loan shark's name was Norman but everyone called him Itch.

Itch was half the size of Big Ernie but twice as loud. Local opinion held that Itch sounded very much like one of those small, fluffy white dogs, the kind seen in heavily guarded, gated communities where rich people brag about golf scores and their new Persian rug.

Big Ernie liked working for Itch for two reasons; firstly, Itch paid him very well, and secondly, Itch often let Big Ernie hold people upside down off the edge of tall buildings. Sometimes he hung them upside down over short buildings; it generally depended on the location they happened to be in. He enjoyed this very much and was quite happy to dangle Detective Reinhardt in this position for as long a time period as required.

Despite the awkward situation and the general nervousness associated with the current situation, Nigel took everything rather well. Outwardly, he appeared almost calm. That gift got Nigel through school, college, and then university virtually unscathed. No matter what the situation, no matter how traumatic, he could simply stuff his hands in his pockets, nod confidently and knowingly, and ask people if they'd like a cup of tea. That usually caused people to believe that he knew something that they didn't, and so they left him alone.

A bird flew past the suspended Nigel and thought it a bit peculiar for people to be hanging off buildings, especially so close to lunchtime. That same bird was later shot up the bottom by a deranged old lady who had recently been deceased.

The ability to remain calm during a crisis proved to be a remarkable survival tactic that also got him through the Police Academy Criminal Psychology Program. And this same skill landed him a good position at the local police station in northern London. That, and an extremely high IQ. This skill, however, had nothing to do with the unfortunate predicament in which he now found himself. Anyone who ever had a vague acquaintance with Nigel would say that despite all of his good qualities, there were two areas in his life where he showed immense weakness: gambling and girls; the latter bordered on a psychological problem and the former was a worldwide crisis that no one would ever solve. Nigel had only ever loved one girl. As bad luck would have it, that same girl broke his heart and left him emotionally buggered up.

A telepathic message suddenly originated from somewhere in London. The message flew from its origin in search of someone specific to connect with. The message had a bit of trouble finding its intended recipient because, at that precise moment, that particular person was hanging upside down off a building. The phrase *beware the elf* suddenly ran through Nigel's head as the message found its destination. He thought that to be quite strange. Itch was fairly short, but by no means an elf. Nigel dismissed the thought and blamed it on the altitude and all the blood in his body rushing quickly to his head.

Coincidentally, the reason for Nigel suddenly reaching new heights was due to his gambling problem, a problem that he successfully managed to hide from his co-workers on the force and his superiors due to the fact that he'd be fired on the spot, professionally humiliated, and discharged in disgrace from his position if the truth were ever revealed. True, he would be a great loss to the department; true, he'd miss the job; and looking back, he should probably just have forgotten about gambling altogether, but he couldn't. It was too much fun, it gave him a rush, and he was, plainly and simply, addicted. Dealing with psychopaths and general loonies day in and day out simply wasn't enough to occupy his mind. Tracking down serial killers was almost a mundane task to Nigel. But pulling down that handle and watching the fruit spin, that was truly an awesome life-fulfilling experience. Hitting just one more time to see how close he could actually get to twenty-one without busting, that was a pure thrill. Watching the ball go around and around at the roulette table, mind-blowing.

Another bird flew by, and the thought briefly entered its mind that London may not be the best place for it to be living. Too many strange folk. This same bird was later crushed by a man sitting on a desk. But for now, it began to make plans to move to a warmer climate where people didn't hang off buildings quite as much. Maybe Greece, or it had been told that Venice was nice at this time of year.

Itch paced back and forth along the edge of the building. Itch was short and chubby but had a mean streak that stretched for a mile. Some days, two miles.

"So," Itch said, "how does it feel to be hanging upside down off the edge of a building, detective?"

"Quite refreshing, thank you for asking," replied Nigel. "I've been a bit on the sluggish side these past few days and these last couple of minutes have been a real eye-opener. Really, thank you from the bottom of my heart."

Nigel grinned and attempted to continue remaining calm by placing his hands in his suit pockets, something that looked more awkward than calm. A gentle breeze caused Nigel to sway ever so slightly.

Big Ernie decided he should put his two cents in.

"You're behind on your payments, my friend!" he said. Big Ernie wasn't all that smart, so Itch compiled a list of menacing one-liners that he could blurt out at the customers anytime he felt the need.

Nigel tried to adjust himself a little and straightened his tie.

"Yes, I realize that, and I promise I'll have the money to you by Sunday at the latest."

"Is that the best you can come up with?" said Itch. "You owe me a total of fifty thousand pounds! If you don't have the money right now, how do you expect to get it before Sunday?"

"It'd be in your best interest to pay us," said Big Ernie.

"Yes, I realize that, Big Ernie, thanks for reminding me. The way I see things, you have two options. The first would be to have Ernie here—"

"Big Ernie," corrected Big Ernie.

"Yes, sorry, Big Ernie, absolutely. Like I was saying, the first would be to have Big Ernie here let go of me and see whether or not I can figure out how to defy gravity in under three seconds."

The wind picked up a little more, causing Nigel to sway and Big Ernie to switch arms.

"The second option, and the one I highly recommend, is that you don't drop me off this rather tall building, and you let me live at least until Sunday so that you can get the money that you are owed."

Itch stopped pacing. "And how exactly do you plan to obtain this money, as I have it on good authority that you are completely broke and don't have a penny to your name?"

Nigel brushed a speck of non-existent dust off the lapel of his jacket and looked up at Itch.

"That's hardly your concern, is it? You see, all that matters to you is that you have the money, all fifty thousand pounds, in your hands by Sunday. If, for example, I didn't happen to have your money by Sunday, you would then be free to fling me off any building you like. Now, if I were an Australian flying squirrel, getting flung off a building of any sort would be quite all right as I could just glide my furry little body to safety, correct?"

The question caught Itch off guard, and he felt that he was beginning to lose control of the conversation, so he answered quickly, just to make sure he was still involved. "Yes, I suppose that would be correct."

Nigel continued with what most people would refer to as reckless abandon. "That's right. But, as we both know, I'm not an Australian flying squirrel, nor am I small or fuzzy. If flung off a building, I'd probably just end up dying. In which case you wouldn't get your money, and I would never again be able to make a large gamble that I couldn't afford, which in turn would cause me to borrow money off you that I would then have to pay back with interest, right?"

Nigel could sense Itch's brain fighting with itself in complete confusion. Inflicting confusion was another of Nigel's gifts, and one he was quite proud of, although it really served no meaningful purpose aside from providing cheap entertainment and, if in the right situation, convincing a loan shark not to throw Nigel off a building.

"Hang on a sec," said Itch, "what was that bit about the squirrel again?"

"Okay, you've got me. How about this? We just agree that I pay you all the money back on Sunday?"

Itch thought about the proposal for a second, and then decided that he must have won the conversation after all. "The whole amount by Sunday or hanging off the edge of buildings will be the least of your problems."

"I don't want to hurt you, Nigel, but I will if I have to," said Big Ernie, who had missed the entire conversation.

Itch glanced at Big Ernie to quit the one-liners, but the large man looked like he was having too much fun.

"And I appreciate that, Ernie, really I do," said Nigel. "All the money by Sunday, I promise. You can trust me."

Itch stepped away from the edge. "I don't trust you as far as I could drop you. But you have until Sunday."

Big Ernie lifted Nigel back up onto the ledge and dropped him on the rooftop. Nigel jumped to his feet, brushed off his suit, and ran his hands through his hair. He smiled politely.

"Don't suppose I could interest either of you in a quick cup of tea?"

"Thanks, but we have three more people to hang off buildings today, and it looks like it's going to rain later, so we'd better get to it," said Itch politely.

"Suit yourself. Nice view up here." And with that, Nigel turned and left.

As he walked down the stairs, his heart slowed a bit, and he smiled at the fact that he hadn't been dropped off the building. He did, however, think that the time had come to pay these men back. He wasn't in the habit of borrowing money, but he had needed the fifty thousand for a trip to Vegas. He met Itch and Ernie through some contacts on the street and although he knew their business was completely illegal and technically he should arrest the pair of them, he just couldn't do it. They weren't a bad pair, really, and they knew far too much about him. If he arrested them, then his secret problem would no longer be a secret. But he wasn't worried; he knew how to get the money.

Nigel exited the stairwell and walked calmly through the lobby of the building.

He thought about where he had been going when Big Ernie had lifted him off the street. The station received a call this morning from a Mrs. Jones on Front Street who claimed that her cat had been possessed by the devil. Ordinarily, dispatch would send a uniformed constable to follow up on the report, but something horrific from a past investigation had stuck with Nigel. Something he'd put out of his mind until Mrs. Jones' phone call.

Around a year ago, a disgraced priest had taken to chopping up certain members of his congregation. New Scotland Yard took a few weeks to put two and two together, and once they discovered the answer was clearly four, they then multiplied it by twenty-seven, added one-million-seven-hundred-thousand-three-hundred-and-ninety-one, then divided the whole thing by Pi, which came out with the answer five-hundred-fifty-thousand-seven-hundred-and-thirty-nine-point-nine-one-one-nine-five-five-four-one-one-one and so on. That number was then taken and each separate numeral was assigned a binary language character that was in turn inputted into a child's Fisher-Price music box and played backward. The result was a rendition of *What's New Pussycat* as sung by Tom Jones that caused several middle-aged female members of the police force to remove their underwear and fling the items at the music box. Unfortunately, the result of the investigation meant practically nothing in terms of the case at hand. The powers of New Scotland Yard that be decided that the Mathematical Cryptography Department was not the correct team to solve the murders and quickly dispatched Nigel to resolve the situation as fast as possible.

It took Nigel three hours to figure out the killer was none other than the victims' priest, Father Jensen. Nigel and a squad of uniforms showed up at Father Jensen's house.

At first glance, the house appeared empty.

After a thorough search, Nigel fell upon the disturbed priest in the attic. Funnily enough, at his time of discovery, Father Jensen sat on the floor half-naked, rocking back and forth and humming the tune *What's New Pussycat*. After several hours of interrogation, which involved Nigel asking questions and Father Jensen drooling uncontrollably in between cryptic answers, Nigel concluded that the priest had begun to question God about a great many things. Apparently, what finally drove him mad was the fact that God had begun to answer him, and they weren't the answers he expected. Instead of claiming to talk to God, he claimed to have started talking to the Devil who encouraged him to cut members of his congregation up into small pieces.

As two uniformed police officers dragged the priest from the interrogation room, he turned and looked Nigel dead in the eyes and said, "It's the cat. He'll come in the form of a cat and you can't stop him, no one can!"

Since that time, Father Jensen was committed to a lovely mental hospital where he occupied a rather nice, off-white, padded room. The last report Nigel received stated that Jensen had given up talking to both God and the Devil and had instead taken up the fine art of counted cross-stitch.

And so Mrs. Jones' phone call had twitched Nigel's interest. He looked at his watch and decided to get a coffee before going to meet the possibly deranged Mrs. Jones.

Cat possessed by the devil? It's going to be one of those days.

Four.

The alarms had been going off for some time and Celina McMannis, Assistant Robotics Engineer at Majestic Technologies, London, was fed up. She had been playing with her fiery red hair for a good five minutes in a last, forlorn effort to ignore the blaring sounds emanating from the speakers mounted on the surrounding walls of the lunchroom. It wasn't working.

She always knew the Santa Claus Project was a bad idea, but no one had listened to her. Artificial intelligence just hadn't been tested enough to be put into real practice, especially on such a large scale. Celina flicked through her notebook, filled with little sticky notes with little schematic drawings on them. Several pages contained complex drawings; other pages contained doodles of doggies, for no other reason than Celina had a fondness for doodling doggies.

One page had a picture of a heart with an arrow through it and the initials *CM+DR* sketched in the middle. That being the last remnant of a failed relationship with one Dean Richards, who turned out to be a complete moron who eventually met the nasty bit at the end of Celina's short fuse. Celina's temper had given her a certain reputation; some people said she failed to have a fuse at all.

Dean Richards ended up paying a substantial amount of money to be inducted into the witness protection program where he lived out his days as a semi-happy urine analysis technician under the assumed name of Monty Niggle. The reason for such extreme action came after he made the horrible mistake of sleeping in Celina's bed. Despite Dean's slightly unfavorable body odor, Celina probably wouldn't have minded him sleeping in her bed; however, the woman sleeping next to Dean, whose most striking feature was that she was not Celina, did cause some discomfort. The discomfort was largely aimed at Dean's testicles, which were rendered completely useless for six months after. Revenge and retribution, in Celina's opinion, were not only a dish best served cold, they also came in anything up to four courses. The infliction of temporary impotence upon Dean Richards was merely the appetizer. Dean decided that he wasn't going to stick around for the main course.

When Celina finally gave up the search for Dean, she decided to swear off men for an indefinite amount of time and threw herself into her work. She applied for several positions; the most lucrative and interesting proposition came from Majestic Technologies. The company claimed to be making an enormous step forward in the field of artificial intelligence and not only that, the owner of the company, a billionaire industrialist, had offered her the job in person.

The alarms stopped.

"About time," said Celina to the empty cafeteria.

The project took five years to be fully developed and then another year to build the blasted little buggers. She sighed to herself and continued twirling her hair as she always did when she was impatient.

The Santa Claus Project was the brainchild of a man named Neville Bartholomew Snell Jr III. The same Neville Bartholomew Snell Jr III who offered her the job in the first place. Aside from being a billionaire, Neville also had a bad habit of buying everything humanly possible, including those sharp knives seen on late night TV. After a lifetime of spending, he decided that he would like to leave something behind. Something so the people would always remember him.

"Silly old fool," said Celina quietly.

Using a dozen ingenious scientists, the very latest in computer robotic design technology, and a group of teenage special effects technicians, the old fool had developed the Santa Claus Project: a unique and groundbreaking undertaking destined to reshape Christmas and make vast quantities of money for people who were already rich. And maybe bring small pockets of happiness to greedy children. That was the plan. That was not going to be happening anytime soon. Or even at all, for that matter.

Celina got up and wandered around the large lunchroom. She tested one of the exit doors. Still locked. Her cell phone chose that very moment to chirp to life. Thankful for someone to talk to, she happily answered.

"Celina McMannis speaking." A disdainful sneer fled across her face looking for somewhere to hide. "No, I didn't rent that movie. Why would I rent a movie called *Good Loving in the Amazon*?. . . . Well, I'm sure it is very good, I'm sure you watch it every chance you get, but I just don't think it's my kind of movie. . . . I don't care if it's on my account, I don't have it!"

She ended the call with a slight beep and decided that there was a major flaw with cell phones. Any other phone could be slammed down when the user was angry, but with a cell phone, the only option was to get worked up, scream and shout, threaten war and pestilence, and then *beep*, the call was over. The sheer inadequacy of the cell phone made her angry and she threw it across the room where it landed amid the remains of a barely digestible tapioca pudding in the large cafeteria garbage bin.

A mirrored wall had been built into the lunchroom to make it look flashier. The employees used it to look at other employees while they ate their lunches. Celina looked in the very same mirror and wondered if she should start exercising again.

She had a slim figure with broad shoulders, the kind of body torn between playing rugby and dancing the ballet. Oh, how she wanted some yogurt. That was the reason she'd wandered into the lunchroom in the first place.

I'm probably going to get shouted at for this, all for my love of yogurt. She shook her head sadly.

Celina had overheard one of the guards during her rush to the cafeteria. The last thing security saw on the monitors before the power went off was a black shape climbing the high, electrified security fence. And then everything had gone to hell. Alarms started going on and off; the electric doors began locking and unlocking themselves at will and had great fun doing it.

Having the paranoid disposition of believing she was responsible for everything that went wrong, Celina decided to slip out of the control room, hide in the cafeteria, and get some yogurt while she was at it. She hadn't counted on the automatic locks trapping her inside the cafeteria or the vast amounts of yogurt that completed failed to be in the fridge. And so here she sat. Wishing she had yogurt.

"I wonder if this has anything to do with the elves," she said aloud to the empty room.

"Pull!" shouted Neville Bartholomew Snell Jr III.

Splash went the Mexican into the pool.

Thanks to an automated alarm warning system, Neville knew about the security breach at his Majestic Technologies lab just outside of London. He knew very little about the event details, but one thing he knew for sure was that he was definitely not sending the police in there. Not with his top-secret project in the works. The situation was frustrating.

Neville was a marvel of a human being, from the standpoint of most outside observers. Many people threw a tantrum when angry, some sat quietly and fume, others reacted violently, some had outbursts, a lot shouted and screamed, a few broke down and cried. But not Neville. Neville had more interesting and extravagant ways of dealing with his anger. Being one of the top ten richest men in the world gave him the profound right to act completely weird and get away with it without question. When poor people acted weird, they were simply written off as weird and often arrested. Rich people who acted weird were not weird at all. They were eccentric.

"Pull," shouted Neville again.

Splash went the second Mexican into the pool.

Neville originally made his money from a large glue factory in southern Brazil. The factory was supposed to be making a super-strong glue that would place as a fierce competitor for every other glue on the market at the time. The air-conditioning on the factory floor gave out two hours after production started, and the relentlessly hot Brazilian weather heated the vats of glue too high, rendering it completely useless as high-strength glue.

An astoundingly ugly gentleman from New York, whose face always looked like it was at war with itself, had just come up with an ingenious plan that would revolutionize the office stationery and memo-taking industry. He discovered the concept quite by accident while he was on a blind date. A mutual friend had set him up with a rather nice woman whose only fault appeared to be an embarrassing and messy snorting sound she made every time she laughed, which was something she did often, mostly to cover up uncomfortable silences.

The date wasn't going especially well, and when the ugly gentleman excused himself to go to the bathroom, it got worse as a piece of toilet paper firmly attached itself to the bottom of his left foot. Upon returning to his table, he found the woman gone and the other restaurant patrons and staff laughing at him due to his lack of date and his addition of stick-on toilet paper. A particularly ill mannered waiter sauntered up to him and with a gallon of cynicism said, "Get the message, you're a loser."

The restaurant patrons who had been politely tittering to themselves burst into all-out laughter, causing the ugly gentleman enough embarrassment to last a lifetime.

It was during that moment of pure embarrassment that his brain gave out on him, and all he could think of was *message*, *paper*, and *stuck*. No one suspected a thing, and the moment never really became common knowledge, but that was the instant the sticky note, a very clever pad of paper used to relay messages or reminders to anyone by sticking them all over the place, was invented.

The ugly gentleman encountered only two problems while inventing the now-famous stationary: 1) no money. He solved this by suing the restaurant for severe emotional damage, the settlement of which was rather substantial. And, 2) as hard as he tried, he never could get the glue consistency just right, until one day, he ran into a weird man who owned a Brazilian glue factory, and the rest was history.

Neville sold the ugly man defective glue which worked great for sticky notes, and in turn the ugly gentleman paid Neville vast amounts of money, turning him from just being weird into being superbly eccentric.

"Pull," shouted Neville. Although the security breach at Majestic seemed suspicious, Neville decided the best course of action was to await further information regarding the situation.

Splash went the third Mexican, as the fourth Mexican climbed into the medieval catapult.

"Beatrice?" said Neville.

"Mr. Snell," replied Beatrice, who just happened to be a six-foot former body builder with a Harvard business degree, legs like tree trunks, and Neville's personal assistant. His real name was Matthew, but Neville insisted on calling people by whatever name he felt they should have at the time. No one argued; he was just eccentric, after all.

"Beatrice, I think we'll wait and see what happens with the situation in London. Keep me updated," and then as an afterthought, he added, "but, just in case worse should come to worst, put the lawyers on yellow alert." The thought of Celina McMannis trapped in the building did concern him a little but the thought was fleeting; she'd turned down his advances one too many times anyway.

"As you wish, sir. Should we keep firing the Mexican cleaning staff into the pool, sir, or have you had enough?"

Neville had many strange ways of dealing with his problems and more somber moods. Firing members of his staff from a medieval-style catapult into his swimming pool was one of his favorites and always seemed to brighten him up. Today, it was the cleaning staff's turn, a group of Mexican men and women who worked hard to abolish every speck of dust from Neville's many mansions and, in turn, were paid handsomely.

"No, I think that's enough for today. That last one got some good height, didn't he?"

"Yes, sir," said Beatrice, "very good height indeed." Beatrice waved a hand toward the Mexican staff who quickly disbanded and went back to their duties.

An assistant gardener working for Neville once questioned the head gardener as to the safety issue surrounding the firing of human beings from a catapult and the sanity of their boss. The head gardener simply reminded the assistant that they all received good wages and an excellent benefit package, and as to the sanity question he replied, "Well, he's just eccentric, ain't he?

Five.

Nigel spent a good part of the morning hanging upside down off the edge of a building.

Celina spent the better part of her morning locked in a deserted lunchroom.

Both individuals were blissfully unaware of the sudden and frightening waves of information flying from satellite to satellite far above their heads, transmitting the news around the world.

A lone journalist in the darkest southern regions of Brazil was the first person to pick up on the subject of the news. It came as quite a shock to him in much the same way it had to the world that woke up to the fact that people all over the place, even in Manchester, had simply stopped dying. The regional newspaper in Brazil received the news from the same shocked journalist an hour or so after the first several occurrences. The national newspapers got the reports mere minutes after that. Information shot out of Brazil at an astonishing rate and crisscrossed reports of similar happenings all over the world.

By breakfast time, the media moguls everywhere made even larger fortunes spreading the information and searching for theories. Some said that it was a miracle, an act of God. A group of Australian scientists believed they had inadvertently found the cure for death while experimenting with a new nerve gas on a group of ducks. The group of nervous ducks disagreed and quacked accordingly.

Religious fanatics around the world, believing that the Second Coming was upon them, went wild. Many of them formed study groups, others danced in the streets, ministers began scheduling church meetings, and somebody woke up the Pope.

The Sons and Daughters of the Lemming Order, an over-dramatic and sensational religious cult, were about to achieve ultimate enlightenment by committing suicide. The plan was to race through the local coastal village shouting and screaming about their impending enlightenment and how very upset everyone else should be that they were not going to be achieving it, and then run off the nearest extremely high cliff to certain death. They were all considerably shocked to find that ultimate enlightenment consisted of them lying on a bunch of sharp rocks protruding from the ocean below a very high cliff.

A group of American scientists tried their very best to give some scientific explanation for the event but for the life of them couldn't think of anything.

A Belgian media mogul named Boris dubbed the all-newly-common occurrence *The Lazarus Effect*.

The real reason for the sudden amount of people waking up in large refrigerators or on their deathbeds was not anything to do with science, or nervous ducks, and had nothing do to, really, with a direct act of God. The real reason was due to an unusual happening in a small pub in Ireland the night before, involving a young man named Seth, a lot of fermented vegetable juice, a disgruntled lamppost, a talking cat, and the Angel of Death. Strange combinations produced strange results. That result, however, sent the entire world into a light chaos. As of around eleven the previous night, no one in the entire world had died.

Sure, people were still passing away, but they would be gone for only a few minutes before coming back and declaring that there was really not much happening on the Other Side, and, despite a collection of shiny directional signs with lovely large neon arrows, they didn't know where to go. So everyone had been turning round and going back the way they had come.

It would appear that Death just wasn't home anymore and if he was, he wasn't in any mood to be answering the door. Actually, that statement was truer than anyone actually knew. Death wasn't home.

At the precise moment that the news went international, Death was sitting on a quiet beach in the Bahamas trying to decide what flavor of margarita he should try next. He already had a nice collection of little paper umbrellas sticking in the sand next to him and he was determined to build a bigger collection.

After the incident at the pub, after shouting at the lamppost, after the mailbox proved unresponsive, Death didn't know where he should go. He wanted to quit but he just couldn't take that final step and actually do it.

"Kiwi and orange please," said Death to the thong-clad waitress.

The waitress turned and headed back to the bar. After a few steps, she forgot what the strange-looking gentleman in the dark robe had ordered. Then she thought it a bit peculiar that he wore a dark robe in such a hot climate. Then she totally forgot that she had just taken an order, that she had just talked to anyone, and began to wonder why she was thinking about dark robes in hot climates, and for absolutely no reason she could fathom, a dark tingly feeling ran down her spine. She walked over to another gentleman who wanted to order a drink and took his order instead.

This had been happening to Death all day. The problem with being an angel is that, as a defense to the heavenly realm, anyone who saw an angel or talk to one would later forget the encounter completely, leaving only the slightest echo that anything ever happened. The only exception to the rule was messenger Angels, where memory retention was rather important. And so the waitress was constantly forgetting Death's drink orders. This made it difficult to just sit and relax, as he had to keep walking to the bar and getting his own drinks.

On his little visits to the bar, Death would complain about the waitress to the bartender, who in turn shouted at the waitress for a reason that he suddenly couldn't remember. It then took Death a few tries before the bartender could hold the drink information in his head long enough to actually make the margarita.

Death thought back to the night before.

While he had been standing outside the pub in Ireland, he'd begun to think that quitting might not be one of his best ideas. That was, up until that nice cat told Death that he deserved a break and asked had he ever considered visiting the Bahamas.

Despite the fact that the cat was just a cat and not only that, a talking cat, Death found him very convincing. In fact, the conversation with that cat landed him where he was now, staggering like a baby giraffe up to the beach bar with the beautiful Bahamian sun reflecting off the radiant, clear blue water behind him.

Death ordered another margarita from the bartender, this time with a green umbrella instead of a blue one, as he wanted to balance out the colours in his collection.

Oh what freedom, to be able to choose my own colour of umbrella.

The small TV mounted in the corner above the bar featured an overly broad man with fake-looking hair who introduced himself to be Martin Hitchcock and attempted to report the news. Not that anyone in the Bahamas cared what happened with the rest of the world, but the news was reported nevertheless, just in case anyone in the Bahamas suddenly decided to care what happened in the rest of the world, which probably wasn't sunny and didn't serve margaritas as tasty.

The subject Martin Hitchcock reported on was very serious. Death decided to pay attention to the news broadcast for a while, for the simple reason that he could.

Martin Hitchcock shuffled his papers.

"The top story again, dead people all over the world got up and walked around today." Martin Hitchcock adjusted his tie and shuffled his papers again for dramatic effect.

Death dropped his fresh, new margarita into the sand and stared open-mouthed at the TV, which was difficult, as theoretically, he didn't have a mouth.

Martin Hitchcock shuffled his papers once again, removed a sheet and, using the ancient art of origami, folded it into a swan before placing it next to him on his desk and then continued.

"Those occurrences began a little after eleven last night and have continued to shock the nation and indeed the world. The local government agencies have released a notice advising any relatives of the recently deceased to contact their local authorities as chances are, they're not entirely dead yet."

Martin Hitchcock then launched into some possible scientific explanations, but by that point Death had already passed out.

Jeremiah the goldfish swam around in his glass fish bowl in his little, uptown London apartment. Due to his three-second memory span, he found it very easy to entertain himself. He would swim across his bowl and see a castle.

"Oh, a castle," he would say to himself. He would swim around the bowl, come back to the same castle and say, "Oh, a castle!"

He could entertain himself like that for hours at a time, sometimes days. Things had been increasingly difficult for him lately, though. Strange thoughts and pictures would pop into his head at random times throughout the day or night, even when he slept. He would forget those three seconds later, but it would appear that he had been receiving premonitions. Not that he knew what a premonition was, and even if he did, he wouldn't remember it after three seconds anyway.

He tried making notes of them, using the little coloured rocks at the bottom of his bowl, but he was never quick enough to get whole words out before he forgot them. So all he ended up with were a few letters that didn't make sense to him. But what he found, although he couldn't remember finding them, was that he could take these thoughts that popped into his head and throw them out of his head, out of his bowl, and send them hurtling out of the apartment.

Sometimes he could even direct the thoughts at people. But after he'd sent the thoughts or pictures out of his head, he would forget that he ever received them and he never really knew who he sent them to, anyway.

"Oh, that's strange, there's a castle here," said Jeremiah.

All this started about two years ago and had been steadily increasing until he was at the point where he would get frustrated. But then he would forget being frustrated and everything would be fine again.

"Oh, a castle," Jeremiah said to no one in particular.

Six.

Jiffy's newspaper stand existed when dinosaurs roamed the Earth, or at least that's what he told the kids who tried to steal candy from his little shack on the corner of Marylebone Road and Albany Street, next to Regent's Park. Whether the statement was true or not is a secret that probably died out with the dinosaurs.

"And I'll still be here when they come back an'all," he would shout as the children ran away.

Jiffy retired at the age of sixty-five and lasted all of two hours as a retiree before returning to work, claiming that living with his wife was a hell of a lot more stressful than selling papers from the crack of dawn to the dead of night.

When Nigel was fresh on the force, he was called out to Jiffy's newsstand twice a week due to constant reports of candy theft and dirty little buggers nickin' his walking stick when he wasn't looking. Nigel and Jiffy became fast friends, and even when the thefts were finally alleviated, Jiffy would still call twice a week so that Nigel would bring him a coffee and they could chat for a while about this or that.

Jiffy, an elderly man who despised youth, refused to admit that he had ever been that young and foolish. He often tried convincing people willing to listen that he was born, had been a toddler, then skipped the teenage and young adult years to mature into the five-foot-three-inch old codger he was today.

Nigel had come to see Jiffy as someone who was always up-to-date with the news, a streetwise gentleman who had seen the best of times and the worst of times and couldn't give a crap either way.

Jiffy had come to see Nigel as a friendly copper who brought him coffee.

Coffee was exactly what Nigel was on his way to pick up when he began to notice a slight change in the demeanor of London's people on this dreary, almost drizzly, morning. The homeless people weren't walking around muttering to themselves as they normally did. The average Londoners walked around with their heads down, not making eye contact with anyone and trying very hard to pretend that the world around them didn't exist. Today, everyone travelled around in excited little groups. People were actually talking to each other, which was practically unheard of in parts of southern England. The world around Nigel had changed, and he wanted to know why. He stopped in the little hippy-run coffee stall in the centre of Regent's Park and bought himself a coffee and one for Jiffy. If something funny were going on with the world, then Jiffy would know about it.

Nigel found the newsstand in the usual spot and Jiffy happily accepting money from people as they bought the morning newspaper. The difference today was the abundance of people buying papers and staring wildly at the front cover, pointing and exclaiming.

"Amazing isn't it? Who would've thou—"

"—always knew this would happen—"

"—bloody weather—"

"—yaknow, my aunt Ettie passed away last year, I'm thinking of digging her up just to make sure because if all this—"

"—act of God—"

"—nervous ducks, I heard—"

"Nigel!" exclaimed Jiffy.

Nigel stopped his eavesdropping and handed Jiffy his coffee with a smile.

"Aw, thanks, lad, couldn't half use it today with business what it is an'all."

"What is all this, Jiffy? I must be out of the loop," said Nigel, feeling a little left out.

Jiffy gave Nigel the kind of look that only the old can give to the young, as if everything they said is completely ridiculous.

"Well, it's the news, innit? The worldwide phenonem-phemoneon—thing."

Nigel shook his head. "I'm not with you."

Jiffy leaned heavily on his walking stick and snatched a newspaper from a surprised-looking man about to purchase it. He stuck the front page in Nigel's face and waved it about a little for emphasis. The headline in large black print stared back at Nigel: The Dead Live!

All other news for the day seemed inconsequential due to the severe outbreak of not dying. Nigel skimmed the newspaper while Jiffy spilled his coffee and swore as only old people could. He finally got bored with verbally abusing his own customers and turned his attention back to Nigel.

"Are you going to buy that paper or what?"

"Sorry, Jiff, this is all new to me. Fascinating, isn't it?"

"You youngins' always walking around with your bloody eyes closed, I suppose you were out on the pull all night?" asked Jiffy, leaning toward what he hoped would be an answer that would help him live vicariously, but contentedly through the rest of the day.

Nigel handed the paper back to him. "Actually, I was hanging upside down off a building this morning."

Jiffy shook his head and made a *tsk*-ingsound that sounded more like a pigeon pooping.

"You kids today with your new fads, hanging off buildings upside down, I ask ya! In my day, there was none of that, we were respectable folk back then, hard working, too. I walked myself to school 'cause there were no buses, not like today. It was a long walk an'all, through the snow in winter, through the rain in summer, uphill, both ways. Don't know how good you've got it, you lot. Ungrateful little—"

"Jiffy?"

"What?"

"Do you really think the dead aren't dying?"

"Maybe. No one's dropped dead at the newsstand yet, but it's still early."

"Has any of the news shed light on any possibilities?"

Jiffy rubbed his chin as his sixty-nine-year-old brain quickly recounted all the news he'd read that morning.

"Seems all there is are possibilities, and theories, lots of theories. It's probably some big joke. Some bugger probably got drunk in a pub, argued with a lamppost, and started the whole thing." Jiffy chortled at his own reckoning, which also, for some odd reason, sounded more like a pigeon pooping.

As close to the truth as Jiffy was, Nigel felt none the wiser and decided he should get on with the day, and bid farewell to his old friend, who again advised him, in his own idiom, that hanging off buildings was just plain stupid. Nigel managed to leave before Jiffy launched into another rant bashing the teenagers of today to anyone who would listen.

Dead not dying. Things like this just didn't happen very often. Occasionally, strange things would happen in London's West End, but it often just turned out to be a bunch of theatre actors trying to express themselves and certainly never anything of this magnitude. There was, after all, still the case of Mrs. Jones' cat to take care of, and all this dead people not staying dead business wasn't going to disappear anytime soon.

Nigel's intelligent mind chose that point to spring to life, as it often did. He quickly worked over the possible reactions, reasons, and consequences of such events. But then he abruptly stopped himself as he decided it wasn't worth the effort quite yet. He might as well get this whole possessed cat thing out of the way first. Figuring out the world's problems was one thing, but a possessed cat was something else entirely.

First things first.

Celina sat on the kitchen counter and finished off another tub of low fat yogurt. She had grown bored of trying to get out and so she decided to break into the kitchen, something that proved a heck of a lot easier than trying to get through the security doors. Celina's anger flared when the kitchen door refused to open when she simply turned the knob, and it took a bit of encouragement and some light pummeling with a heavy chair to convince it otherwise. She persevered, much to the desecration of the kitchen door, and found herself rewarded with the yogurt that was her primary reason for coming to the lunchroom in the first place.

Her cell phone chirped to life as it sat in the garbage bin in the lunchroom. Celina ignored the incessant beep. Chances were the call was probably just the video store again and she wasn't of a mind to talk to them. Instead, Celina let her thoughts race back a couple of years, stumbling here and there over memories of a failed romance and several calls from her mother complaining about her lack of grandkids, before it ground to a halt at the memory she was looking for.

Artificial intelligence seemed so remarkable and so full of possibilities when the research began, but now it all seemed so confusing and dangerous. Artificial intelligence was exactly how it sounded, an artificial mind that wasn't actually alive. It was fake. False. Synthetic. Non-natural. Simulated. Not real.

The first attempt to create AI began with computers. Every household computer had its own AI to a point. It sensed when a virus was present and it could obey commands. But the command part was where the fatal flaw laid; it needed an action to produce a reaction. There was no way a computer would turn itself on just for the hell of it.

Majestic Technologies, in order for the Santa Claus Project to work, needed to go one step further. Celina and her team tried to produce a computerized brain that could operate independently and make its own decisions. The brain would need a host, so they built a host. A small host, just in case it got out of control. No point in creating a host that resembled a ten-foot gorilla and then have it go berserk, killing thousands. And so the world's first fully functional AI unit was born in the form of *Betsy the Hamster*.

Betsy the Hamster blinked to life at 7:30 a.m. on March 7, 2009. A remarkable success; Betsy instantly began to walk around. She looked up at her creators and blinked a few times. Then she awed the scientists as she began to talk. Simple stuff at first; she recited the alphabet, and then numbers. She identified colours. She went on to recite poetry; she hummed a few bars of Beethoven's Fifth. She delineated the uses of quantum mechanics in relation to light speed and navigational trigonometry. She moved on to define life on planet Earth and started to explain the reason that all the ducks in the near future would begin to suffer from severe nervousness.

At 7:33 a.m. on March 7, 2009 Betsy the Hamster exploded into several thousands of small pieces. About ten minutes later, the disappointed scientific team figured out why Betsy had blown herself to bits. There wasn't a computer on Earth that could hold all the information of the world and process new information at the same time. The several thousand small pieces of Betsy the Hamster agreed and proved the point.

The Majestic Technologies robotics team admitted that they might have been aiming a little too high for their first try. Unfortunately, eccentric billionaires demanded results of their highly paid research teams, and when Neville peered into the plastic container that once held mayonnaise and was now the new home of Betsy the Hamster's remains, he simply snorted and told everyone to do better. Except for Celina, whom he winked at on the way out.

Five minutes after Neville left, the research team decided that testing new units and computers would take way too long so they decided to skip the testing altogether and move straight on to the main phase.

Diagnostics drawings for the elves began the very next day.

Seven.

Nigel noted that the colour of Mrs. Jones' house, a sordid light green, made it stand out from the rest of the sickly, hospital-cream-coloured houses attached to it.

The street had recently fallen into chaos, as Mrs. Beatty from two doors down had woken up that morning after being dead for a full hour and a half. People had been lining up at her front door since the event to ask her questions about the afterlife and to see if she needed a cup of tea.

Tea had long been a highly favored drink of the British. They fought wars over it, attributed miracles to it, and once, a religious crusade, just a small one, had been launched over the lack of tea in a small Welsh village. With the world in chaos over no one dying, the logical thing for any British person to do was to sit down and have a nice cup of tea, offer tea to others who were not drinking tea, chat warmly about tea, and maybe have a scone, too.

Nigel inferred from the incessant laughter that Mrs. Beatty was having a whale of a time and, according to the handwritten sign hung on her garden wall, had even started charging five pounds a person for entrance into her house. Nigel fought the compulsion to join the lineup, continued up Mrs. Jones' steps, and gave her door a somber yet authoritative knock.

The somber yet authoritative knock received a response in the form of the ominous sound a shotgun makes when being cocked.

Nigel's suspicions about the sound proved true two seconds later, when there came a loud *bang* and the sordid light green door exploded out into many sordid light green bits of wood, leaving a gaping hole.

"Take that, you furry bastard!" came the screech from inside.

Somewhere in between the knock at the door and the explosion of said door, Nigel had stepped aside and stood pressed firmly up against the wall. Suddenly, the head of a four-foot-tall old lady stuck her head through the two-foot-wide hole in the door. She looked around wildly before looking at Nigel, who smiled back politely.

"Did you see him," she said, "did you see him?"

Nigel was surprised that such volume could come from such a small head encased in a knitted woolen bonnet. Nigel flashed his badge.

"Detective Reinhardt. You are Mrs. Jones, I presume?"

"Ms. Jones. Mizzzz! Did you see him? He's going to come back for me, you know? He told me he would," said Ms. Jones with a hint of alarm. Her eyes scanned the street like a weasel looking for dinner.

In his mind, Nigel rolled his eyes; physically he continued to fix his gaze on the deranged old woman.

"I don't suppose you'd like to hand me the shotgun?"

Ms. Jones thought about this for a while before answering a resolute *No*, then asked if he'd like to come in for a cup of tea, proclaimed that he seemed to be a nice young man, and then apologized for almost blowing his head off. She unlocked the door and let Nigel in.

The people standing lined up outside Mrs. Beatty's house had been busy staring disapprovingly at the hullabaloo. Comments like, "No respect for the dead," and, "Always trying to be the centre of attention," got thrown around.

On closer inspection, Nigel found that Ms. Jones was actually shorter than four feet. She was more like three and a half feet. The word *elf* wandered through his head but didn't feel right in relation to Ms. Jones, and so it left. Her small head encased in the woolen bonnet sat gingerly upon her shoulders, almost as if independent of the rest of her rather stumpy body. Her body moved and her head would reluctantly follow, as if resigned to the fact that it had no other choice.

Ms. Jones showed Nigel to the living room, a place that already had the smell of old lady poured into the very particles of every object in the room, right down to the hand-knitted doilies.

"So, Ms. Jones—"

"Mrs.!" she snapped. "Mrs. Jones! I was married for fifty-two years to our Arthur, God rest his soul."

"I'm sorry?" said Nigel completely perplexed.

"It's Mrs. Jones thank you very much," she replied. "It was the drink that did him in."

"Arthur?"

"Hit by a Guinness truck coming home from the pub one night. He didn't drink Guinness, mind you, reminded him of drinking motor oil, he always said."

Mrs. Jones stared at Nigel as if waiting for a reply.

With the sudden change in recent world events, Nigel decided that this wasn't a big issue and he might as well just ignore it. Plus, the old woman was still nursing her shotgun. She looked very much to Nigel like an unhinged English version of Granny Clampett. A slightly confused and uncomfortable silence ensued.

"Oh, tea!" She shrieked and ran off to the kitchen. She left the shotgun leaning against her easy chair. Nigel thought it best if he moved the shotgun for the time being, so he hid it under the couch cushion he was currently sitting on. With any luck, she'd never notice it was gone.

Nigel closed his eyes and proceeded to do some breathing exercises he'd learnt from an ex-roommate of his. *Beware the elf,* flashed across the inside of his eyelids as Mrs. Jones scuttled back into the room.

"Here you go, I'm sure you'll like it," she said, passing a tiny, china teacup to Nigel.

"I'm sure I will." Nigel placed the teacup on the coffee table, took out a pencil and pad, and proceeded with caution.

Mrs. Jones settled back into her easy chair and sipped her own tea. The lack of a shotgun at her side momentarily escaped her notice.

"The report that you filed with Scotland Yard was a bit on the sketchy side. Just for the record, I don't suppose you'd like to elaborate a bit?"

Mrs. Jones shuffled herself around in her chair.

"Well, it was all very strange," she began, "I've had that cat for six years and he's never said bugger all before. Then two nights ago, he wouldn't shut up."

Nigel shot Mrs. Jones a calm glance, which she returned instantly with a stubborn glare.

"Go on."

"Well, I was coming back from the Hare and Hound; we have a nice little darts competition going with the sewing circle girls from Notting Hill."

"That's the pub on Rhodes St.?" ventured Nigel.

Mrs. Jones snorted at the interruption.

"Yes. I came home earlyish because I had to feed Fuzzbucket."

Nigel wrote down the name *Fuzzbucket*, then began to wonder whether he'd heard her right.

"I'm sorry. The cat in question, the one you say is possessed by the devil, his name is Fuzzbucket?"

"Yes, Fuzzbucket. When I got home, the cheeky little bastard was sitting at the kitchen table eating a chicken I'd been defrosting for Sunday lunch. Said he'd got hungry and decided to cook himself some food. And then he told me to go out and buy him some cigarettes."

"This must all have come as quite a shock to you. What happened then?"

"I told him that it was most unnatural for him to be talking and smoking all of a sudden like that. And that he should stop doing it, and then I asked him who he thought he was."

Mrs. Jones suddenly began to look around the small living room. She was missing something and couldn't remember what.

Nigel caught the searching look and quickly urged her on.

"So what was his reply?"

"It was most peculiar. He looked me straight in the eye and proclaimed that he was the Prince of Darkness, the Devil himself, and that he'd come to wreak havoc on the Earth. And then he babbled something about small robots, and flocks of nervous Australian ducks, and then told me that he would be borrowing my cat for a while and that he'd come back for me one day so I'd better watch out."

"Humph," said Nigel uncomfortably. At his last testing, Nigel's IQ measured at over 200. And then, at another point it measured at 76, just because he felt like being stupid that day. He had always been smart, and he knew how to spot a liar. What disturbed him was that everything Mrs. Jones said, as far as he could tell, appeared to be completely true.

He decided to adjust his seating position. Whether it was Nigel's movements, or whether it was just meant to be, the shotgun under the couch chose that moment to fire off. The pellets ripped half the couch apart and destroyed some lovely little ceramic pots that had been sitting on the fireplace. They were souvenirs from a little seaside town in the south of Wales called Tenby.

"Bollocks," exclaimed Nigel as Mrs. Jones' heart gave out.

She clutched at her chest and died right there on the spot.

"Bloody hell! A castle!" exclaimed Jeremiah for the one-thousand-seven-hundred-and-eighty-second time as he swam around his bowl. But then it hit him, a tingling feeling somewhere behind his eyes. A feeling that he may or may not have had before, because he couldn't remember. It felt familiar, but uncomfortable. A phrase popped into his head. He tried to hold the thought; he swam to the bottom of his tank and pushed his coloured rocks around, trying to make a memory of what he saw.

Then he couldn't remember what he had been doing. He wondered why the rocks at the bottom of his tank formed funny letters.

"Most peculiar thing for rocks to do."

Jeremiah looked around the bowl, forgetting the rocks. "Well, well, well, look at that," he said, "there's a castle in here!"

There were some feelings that just couldn't be explained. No matter how hard he tried, he just couldn't make head nor tail of them. Nigel had one of those inexplicable feelings while he sat sipping his tea, a smoking shotgun on his left and a dead, yet, funnily enough, happy-looking old lady on his right.

He'd already checked her pulse. Nothing. He'd tried shaking her. No result. He'd even tried tickling her, thinking that maybe nobody had ever tried that with a dead person before. Not a titter. It was a most unfortunate situation.

For the first time since he'd set his mother's best wig on fire by accident when he was six, he had absolutely no idea what to do. Thoughts and ideas rushed at him at an astounding rate. He tried to duck and avoid them, but it was no good. He thought that maybe he should make a run for it, so he stood up. *No, that wouldn't even be close to rational.* He sat down again.

He tried to think outside of his own head; surely people heard the blast. But then again, this crazy old lady shot a hole through her front door in broad daylight, and all she'd drawn were a few glares of disapproval and some angry comments. They were all too preoccupied.

There was a stunned moment of complete silence as the realization smacked him in the face. The sensation felt like a cross between getting hit in the head by a startled gerbil that was just shot out of a cannon and that wonderful feeling which happened when people woke up and thought they were late for work but then realized it was actually their day off. That was the kind of feeling he got slapped with.

The dead not dying had everyone preoccupied. So really, Nigel only had to wait until Mrs. Jones got bored with the afterlife and then came back. Nigel relaxed a little and flipped on the TV, resolving to stay there until the old bat woke up.

Eight.

Celina dug through the garbage can trying to find her cell phone, which must have rung about seven times since she'd thrown it there. It finally occurred to her that maybe the people outside of the cafeteria might be trying to contact her, and she felt pretty stupid that she hadn't thought of it earlier. And then she realized that she could have made a call to the people outside at any time. She felt stupid for a second time in as many seconds.

Celina came from a proud Scottish clan that had built a reputation on not asking for help when it was so obviously required. As a result of that stone-headed, slightly drunken way of thinking, Celina was the last of her line. The last McMannis. Her father, the second to last McMannis, had been busy having a heart attack one day but refused to call the hospital for help, so in a stubborn attempt to prevent his heart from stopping he took a lovely, handcrafted, stainless steel fork and plugged himself into an electrical socket. The unfortunate result was his heart stopping.

Four hundred years ago, a large portion of the McMannis clan had been wiped out. One of the younger members had made an unmentionable, and possibly unpronounceable, rude comment to one of the young ladies attached to the McKale clan. The McKale clan numbered around fifteen thousand, whereas the McMannis clan at the time numbered fifteen, six of whom were women and one of whom was a beloved family sheep who had been adopted as a daughter. Flossy McMannis was her name, and many a minstrel wrote songs about her.

The two clans met at a spot in the Highlands especially designated for shedding blood. Many McMannises from previous centuries had already lost large amounts of their blood at that same spot, and the ghosts of those long-dead clan members stared up at their relatives as they strode above the spirits, closely followed by a worried-looking sheep.

The clan elder at that time was Morris McMannis, a barrel of a man with a red beard, small dark eyes, and a temper that could have a wild pig roasted over it. His options were simple. He could either march his fourteen family members over the battlefield and fight the fifteen thousand angry and slightly drunk McKale clansmen, or he could ask for help from the neighboring clans. His pride, as usual, held him firmly by the testicles and he said, "Not a chance."

The battle was short. The McMannis clan managed to take down seventy-three McKale clan members before being almost completely wiped out, thirty-nine of whom were killed by Flossy McMannis who at the last minute discovered her inner warrior and tore through McKale clansmen before they realized they were being slaughtered by a sheep.

The souls of the newly dead McMannises evaporated into the Highlands like the good fallen warriors they were and joined their long dead comrades who all agreed that Morris was an idiot for not asking for help and that it was a good lesson learnt. Tempers flared and the ghosts became grumpy and have remained so to this very day.

The clan was survived by a young McMannis boy who played dead very convincingly after nearly being run through by the sharp end of a sword after an unusually energized, angry, and slightly drunk sheep accidentally knocked him flying.

Celina found the phone buried within some leftover spaghetti. The phone was still chirping away. She answered it and was completely unprepared for what she heard.

"Hello?"

"They're free! They're free!" cried a desperate voice. "Save yourself, Celina!"

"Roger? Is that you?" said Celina looking around as if her co-worker, or worse, one of the imps, might be lurking under a table.

"They're stealing the Santa Claus unit! We tried to stop them but they're too strong, they've broken their program—oh no! There's one in here. Get away from me, get away. Get out, Celina! Get out!"

A struggle seemed to ensue on the other end of the phone.

"Roger? Roger?"

A creepy, nasal sounding voice lurked onto the other end of the phone.

"Hehehehehe we're free, we're free."

"Look, what are you trying to do? What do you want?" cried Celina.

"Hehehehe. Nighty-night."

There was a shrill scream, then the line beeped dead. Celina tried to gather her thoughts but she couldn't escape the feeling of terror creeping over her. The lights chose that precise moment to go out.

Mrs. Jones opened her eyes slowly, as if waking from a deep sleep. She blinked a few times to pull her world into perspective, but things weren't making complete sense just yet. A tall, not quite handsome man sat on the couch flicking through TV channels. She scanned the room quickly; it looked like her living room, but there were subtle differences. For starters, her trinkets that used to sit on top of the fireplace had vanished. And the couch had been moved on a slightly different angle and covered with a blanket; the shape seemed a bit off though. *That's odd.* The man on the couch noticed that Mrs. Jones had woken up, and he smiled a warm smile, an almost inviting *can I help you across the road* kind of smile.

"Glad to see you're awake, Mrs. Jones."

"What, what happened? Who are you?"

Nigel got up and offered his hand to her.

"Detective Reinhardt. Came about your devil-possessed cat. You just dropped off for a moment and you looked so peaceful I didn't want to disturb you."

Mrs. Jones looked around the room again as she shook Nigel's hand.

"Oh, I see. Well, sorry about that."

Nigel smiled and sat back down.

"It's quite all right, just didn't want to wake you. Now, back to your cat, have you seen him since?"

Mrs. Jones looked back at Nigel, her tired brain trying to put the pieces together as to what had happened. She felt like she'd just had the most curious dream. Something about a neon sign that didn't make much sense. Confusing.

"Uh, Mrs. Jones?"

"Sorry . . . umm, no, he hasn't come back. Said he was off to wreak havoc."

Nigel nodded.

"I don't suppose you know what kind of havoc he was looking at wreaking, do you?"

Mrs. Jones glanced around her room again; something was definitely not right here.

"Nope, didn't really elaborate too much."

Nigel watched as, like the sun dawning on fresh grass, Mrs. Jones' memory started to creep back. *Time to make a run for it.* All in one breath and a swift movement, Nigel stood, handed Mrs. Jones his card, and excused himself, adding, "If you remember anything else don't hesitate to give me a call and I'm sure it'll be all right."

By that time, he was at the front door and Mrs. Jones was shuffling after him.

"One moment, young man!"

Busted was the only word in Nigel's head. He turned to face the old woman, preparing for the onslaught and a possible death by shotgun, if she could find it. He had hidden it up the chimney.

"There was something else I remember."

"Oh," said Nigel, taken aback.

"Majestic Technologies."

Nigel leaned in a bit.

"I'm sorry, what was that?"

"Fuzzbucket," said the old woman, "he mentioned something about Majestic Technologies, don't know what it means, never been much for technology. I'm always getting that TV and that electronic cooking thing mixed up."

"You mean the microwave?"

"Yes, that's it. Sat in the kitchen for hours once watching a ham defrost, thought it was a very bad cooking show."

"Ah, I see. Well, thanks."

"Glad to help." And with that she slammed the door.

Nigel watched through the rather prominent hole as Mrs. Jones went off to search for something she was certain she was missing.

Nigel walked back down the street wondering what, exactly, Majestic Technologies was. Nigel held the firm belief that everything presented itself for a reason, and for whatever reason this information had come to him, he was sure it would all make sense sooner or later. He decided he should probably check in at work.

The word *elf* slipped through his mind, but only momentarily, as a loud shotgun blast blew out the top of Mrs. Jones' chimney, completely obliterating a poor bird that just happened to be sitting up there at the time.

Nine.

At around the same moment the obliterated bird had been making himself comfortable upon Mrs. Jones' chimney in London, several thousand miles away in the Bahamas, Dr. Ranja was looking at a most curious patient who had recently passed out at a local beach bar, possibly from the intense Bahamian heat. Dr. Ranja deduced additional causes to be the sheer abundance of margaritas the man had consumed, or maybe it was the realization that the entire Universe, all of it, even the little bits that no one ever saw, was about to unravel itself into an untidy heap of nothingness.

What he found curious about the patient was that he was a practically perfect human specimen, looked a bit long and drawn, and the dark robes were a most peculiar ensemble, especially in the heat of the Bahamas. No distinguishing marks, no scars, no blemishes, eyes that seemed to change colour, which fit right into the face that appeared different every time he looked at it. Perfect muscle structure, pale complexion. No wait, tanned complexion, nope, darkish, pink . . . .

Dr. Ranja's head began to throb, and he rubbed his temples as his frontal lobe laughed at him.

In Dr. Ranja's professional experience, neither he, nor anyone else he'd heard of, had ever come across such an individual. He'd been examining him for five straight hours. The doctor had to keep leaving on one such emergency or another, and upon leaving the room, he would forget all about the figure lying in the bed, so it came as a completely new shock to him every time he walked back.

He'd noticed something new on examination this time. There seemed to be a profound lack of pulse to the gentleman. And although it was obvious he was alive, because he kept moving and talking in his sleep, technically, he was dead. It wasn't long after the pulse discovery that the doctor found that the man was also lacking in another considerably important area. He had no genitals. Of any kind. There was just nothing there.

Well, this was obviously a discovery of woolly mammoth proportions; it needed documenting, it needed reporting. He could just picture accepting his Nobel Peace Prize for his contribution to society by discovering this new form of human. Aside from all this dead not dying business, this could be the new foundation upon which mankind would be built. A new independent being, maybe even extraterrestrial.

The question of how the creature planned to have sex crossed the doctor's mind, as obviously, it lacked the correct equipment for the job. But no, he was getting too far ahead of himself. He wandered around the bed a few times, seeing if he'd missed anything. No, he decided, first things first. This all hadto be written down.

Dr. Ranja left the examination room and walked down the hallway. *Oh what a magnificent day this was turning out to be.* It had seemed like such a bad day at first. He woke up to find his wife had not come home again; maybe he was overreacting but taking two weeks to fetch milk was a bit much. Dr. Ranja was currently in denial of the fact that his wife had left him for a Polynesian midget.

Everyone knew, including himself, he just chose not to acknowledge the fact. People would ask him how she was doing, and he'd smile and tell them she was doing great; he'd even begun regaling people with made up stories of things he and his wife hadn't done the night before. At first, the stories amused others, but his denial was quickly becoming disturbing. The doctor did not care; he had just discovered something big, something huge, something of mammoth proportions.

Only he couldn't remember what it was. He remembered going to fetch a pad and pen, he knew that much. And he planned on writing something down, but wasn't sure what. Maybe it was a grocery list? He was running low on milk, as he was still waiting for his wife to bring some back from the store. That must have been it. He strolled back down the hallway, passing an examination room with a tall man dressed in dark robes lying on the table.

Hmm, wonder what this is all about? Dr. Ranja decided to check out the interesting looking patient.

Thousands of miles away, the cat formerly known as Fuzzbucket, who was now an Earthly vessel for the Prince of Darkness, sat quietly on top of a garbage can and systematically licked himself.

"Urrgghhh," came the sound from the semi-conscious Animal Control agent.

Being a cat proved exhausting; the licking, the sleeping, the licking, the sleeping, the insistent feeling of having to bury his own fecal matter.

"Ermmffgg," said the Animal Control agent as he struggled to regain consciousness.

Lucifer the cat spent a good chunk of the morning interrogating would-be henchmen. The task at hand proved next to impossible for a mere furry feline. He needed some hands, and more than anything, a driver. The underground railway system in London was one of the great mysteries of the world and despite spending an eternity in the depths of Hell, the thought of descending those subway steps sent a shiver down his back, causing him to arch in that cute way that cats did.

He'd interviewed five henchmen so far. The first three were useless, the fourth was worse than useless, and the interview with the fifth suffered a rude interruption by the intervention of an ill-fated

Animal Control agent. The fifth candidate weighed close to three-hundred pounds and answered to the name Slim Jim.

Where the *slim* aspect of the moniker came from was lost on pretty much everyone else in the world. Their conversation went something like this.

"So you're the Devil," said Slim Jim, practically out of breath from the effort.

The Devil stared up over the belly of Slim Jim and nodded.

"But you're a cat?"

"Nothing escapes you does it, Slim?" hissed the cat. "In return for your services, I will reward you with an air-conditioned room when you arrive in Hell. It doesn't sound like much now, but believe me, you'll thank me when the time comes."

Slim Jim pondered the cat, pondered the flashing lights coming toward him, and turned and ran, believing the cops were after him. The lights belonged to that of an Animal Control vehicle whose driver was ill fated, only he didn't know it yet. Incidentally, after Slim Jim's encounter with the Devil, he renounced his current life of crime and within four years was appointed to be the High Bishop of York. He was upset to discover that he ended up in Hell anyway, as forging religious documentation passing him off as an appointed member of the Church was a big no-no. As he sat in a particularly hot part of Hell, Slim Jim really wished he had air conditioning.

The Animal Control agent, Cedric by name, had abandoned a promising career as an executive security analyst with Her Majesty's Secret Service to become an Animal Control agent based upon the self-realization that he loved kitties.

Cedric, haphazardly, moved toward the Devil. In one hand, Cedric held a lovely-looking net, in the other hand a bag of cat treats.

The Devil eyed the net and instinctively, at least for a cat, raised the hackles on his back.

"That's a nice kitty, who's a cutie wootie kitty witty," cooed Cedric.

The Devil tried to summon the powers of Hell. A spark of fire appeared in his glassy cat eyes. He felt the residents of Hell far beneath the earth writhing in agony, the torture, the pain, his legions of demons dancing to popular eighties disco music—the spark of fire went out and a small cloud of steam arose from the cat. The demons would end up paying for that one later.

Cedric advanced.

"Do you want a treat, my fuzzy wuzzy little buddy, a little treaty weaty?"

The Devil tried again. He fixed Cedric with the sort of stare that would make Jack the Ripper whimper like a little girl, give up killing, and open a dental practice.

Cedric, oblivious to such things, especially coming from a cat, made ready to swing the net.

"I really don't recommend you do that," said the Devil.

Cedric stopped advancing. This was the first time a cat had spoken to him, and he didn't really know how he felt about it.

The alleyway seemed to be getting darker as the Devil concentrated harder and harder. The outside world shrank away like watercolours flowing down a window as the Devil pushed his little cat-like brain to the very brink. In fact, he pushed it over the brink, so far over the brink he could look behind him and see the brink that he'd just come over. His voice momentarily lost the strained cat effect and contracted a more dark and sinister sort of presence.

Cedric began to feel hot and uncomfortable.

"Now listen to me, you insipid little creature, and listen good." Somewhere off in the distance, an orchestra began to play a tragic and ominous tune backed up by the Czech Republic's Gregorian Boys Choir. Fumes of sulfur arose from the ground; they always did that when the Czech Republic's Gregorian Boys Choir rehearsed.

"I fell from grace, plummeted through the ether, passed between the Earthly mortality and crashed into the Earth itself. I have dwelt in the fires of Hell next to the lake of fire, sentenced to writhe in agony for all eternity with my only solace being the large number of ignorant, foolish, and evil souls I can drag down to join me."

Cedric wet himself.

The chanting grew louder as the Devil swished his tail.

"If you think for a second that a mere net held by a tiny monkey-like creature, who in my eyes is comparable to the crusty things you have in the corner of your eyes when you wake up, will scare me, then you're dead wrong." The music reached a crescendo and the Czech Republic's Gregorian Boys Choir came close to screaming their chant.

Cedric passed out.

"Don't you pass out on me, I haven't finished with you yehaacckkoffghhjajajacooffghjjaackk!"

A hairy blob spewed forth from the cat's mouth. The world returned to its normal state, the orchestra stopped playing, and the choir went out for lunch.

"Hairballs," said the Devil, "I hate hairballs." The Devil decided to give himself a quick cleaning and then stalked off to take a nap. A cat's body just wasn't built for Hellish behavior and he was quite exhausted. Henchmen interviews would have to wait for an hour or two.

When Cedric awoke, he was alone in the alleyway wearing a wet pair of pants. He continued his career of animal control agent for another week before having to retire due to a nervous disposition, which caused him to wet himself every time he came across a cat. It was safe to say at this point that Cedric no longer loved kitties.

Ten.

A severe lack of happy faces greeted Nigel when he entered his police station to check in for the day and let people know that he was actually working. The faces themselves didn't strike him as being all that peculiar. He always thought that they usually looked a bit on the weird side anyway; the fact they looked away from him as he walked by, now, that was strange.

This was not a good sign. He'd seen this happen before, he just couldn't remember where; maybe it was in a movie? He waved to the receptionist as he walked by; she half smiled, glanced around to see if anyone had seen her, and then concentrated on her pen.

Strange.

He continued on through the station, saying *hello* to some, *good morning* to others and all he received in return was a quick *hmph* or a sharp *ehh* followed by a fake-looking smile. The kind of smile that happened because someone was about to act polite but then realized that this was neither the time nor the place so they instantly regretted it and consequently stopped smiling altogether. Everything suddenly hit Nigel all at once. Much like the feeling one experienced when slapped with a fresh herring.

He looked at his normally messy desk and found it to be empty, with everything packed neatly into a cardboard box. He noticed that there was a younger, better-looking-than-himself man sitting at his desk, unpacking his own cardboard box. The young man's name was

Colin Baskerville and new to the detective division. Nigel, his mind still in shock, strode up to Colin.

"Colin!" he squeaked. It was meant to come out a little more demanding than that but his voice wasn't quite prepared to speak yet.

Colin spun around and turned a squashy kind of mauve colour, as he always did when placed in a confrontational position.

"I, uhh . . . . Nigel," he stammered.

Nigel leaned in.

"What are you doing at my desk, Colin?"

"Well I uhh, you see . . . well, it's uhh." But words, as they often did, failed him.

"I'm hoping there's going to be some fabulous reason as to why, exactly, you're putting your own stuff into my desk while my stuff sits in this cardboard box. I'm expecting some amazing story involving giants and forgetful wizards, villagers, and toadstools, all topped off with a lovely, great big punch line!"

"Well, I, uhh." Colin's mauve colour turned pale.

Nigel leaned on his desk.

"Yes, that's what I thought you'd say."

Many African tribes believed there were creatures living in the Zambezi. Creatures that were ten feet tall, that had large jagged teeth, a voice like a volcano, and the worst bad breath known to man. What the African tribes didn't know was that a similar creature dwelt in the north end of London, got up of a morning, got dressed, put on his badge, and drove to the police station where he held the title *captain*.

"Reinhardt!"

This creature stood in his office doorway pointing a demeaning finger toward Nigel.

"Get in here!" said the captain most referred to as *Fluffy*, but whose real name was Captain Anthony Jameson Jeeves.

Nigel hopped up onto his desk and sat down.

"Forget it, you want to fire me, I'm not moving. This is my desk, I have every right to stay here."

There was a stunned silence. Nigel was famous for seemingly ridiculous theories and stunts, but they always had a purpose and always turned up results. This one seemed to have little purpose, and the results weren't going to be pretty.

Captain Jeeves made a *hmphing* sound. "Have it your way. Baskerville! Carter! Be so kind as to bring the detective and the desk he seems so attached to into my office."

Colin and another wet behind the ears detective picked up Nigel's desk, with Nigel on it, and carried it into Captain Jeeves' office. Nigel seemed unaffected by the move; he pulled out a notepad and started scribbling down a note.

Colin and Carter dumped the desk with a *thump* in the office and left quickly so as to avoid the oncoming unpleasantness.

Captain Jeeves sat down behind his desk, his large frame dominating the small chair that had no choice but to hold his sizeable bulk.

"So, what do you have to say for yourself?"

Nigel ripped a note off his pad and handed it to the captain, who read it aloud.

"I refuse to talk until you give me my job back." Jeeves screwed up the paper and threw it in the trashcan.

"Well, at least we're being mature about this. Not a chance. We've discovered strange anomalies regarding your spending, not only of your own money but of the department's money."

"What kind of anomalies?" said Nigel before he slapped his hands over his mouth realizing he'd just broken his short-lived silence.

"Trip to Vegas last February?"

"It was a vacation!"

"You took the Mayor's helicopter!"

"I needed a ride."

"And lost it in a game of poker!"

Nigel frowned.

"I did pay you back for that."

"With money, we have now discovered, taken from the evidence locker!"

Nigel couldn't be sure, but it appeared that the Captain's voice got increasingly loud.

"That's circumstantial."

"And then you replaced that money with the money from that drug bust we did in June!"

Nigel couldn't believe what was happening.

"A drug bust that I headed up, a case that I cracked almost single-handedly!"

Captain Jeeves let out a sigh that sounded like a thousand pigeons all taking off at the same time.

"You have a problem, Nigel. A gambling problem. We've overlooked a lot of questionable past events because of your excellent record. But you have to get help. We have enough on our plates at the moment with this whole living dead thing."

Nigel gripped his desk.

"So I'm fired, then?"

Jeeves got out of his chair, which was most relieved to have the large man off it, and leaned on his desk, leering at Nigel.

"Suspended! Pending psychiatric evaluation. Now, get out!"

"I'm not leaving my desk."

Jeeves let out another pigeon sound-filled sigh.

"Have it your way."

Outside the police station, a bird happily munched away at a discarded sandwich that a policeman had dropped. The bird had it solidly fixed in its mind that this was its lucky day. A bird didn't come across a full sandwich every day. He couldn't wait to tell his friends about this; they'd be green with envy. Birds, incidentally, didn't really go green with envy; they turned a light mauve colour but as they're covered with feathers no one ever saw it; however, they did still use the term *green with envy* as the saying was universal among all species.

The bird thought today was going to be a bad day after he saw that fellah hanging off a nearby building this morning. And from what he heard through the amazing bird communication system of the sky, otherwise known as *The Daily Feather*, his friend Martin had been shot up the ass by a deranged old lady.

Well, it just doesn't pay to get out of your nest some mornings. He looked at his sandwich hungrily. *And then again, sometimes it does.* At that very moment, while the bird gloated to himself about having fantastic luck, he was suddenly crushed by a recently suspended detective sitting on a desk which was flung from the station's main entrance.

"The South Pole is a damned cold place to live," said Gerald to no one in particular.

Why anyone wanted to live in such a climate was beyond him. Sometimes, when Gerald went swimming, he would often run into a sort of semi-warm current and imagined the water traveled a great distance from some lovely, hot, tropical place just so it could run into Gerald and remind him that where he lived at the South Pole was not warm in the slightest. It was bloody freezing. And this depressed him.

Lots of things depressed him; the cold, the ice, the angry walrus that wandered around when it was especially cold. Gerald always wanted to just look him straight in the eye and tell him once and for all to stop barging around all the time and to drag his sorry blubbery ass off to someone else's enormous chunk of ice. But he couldn't, and that depressed him too. The crowding was another thing.

People didn't think of the South Pole as all that crowded but, in actual fact, every time Gerald turned a corner, someone else was always standing there. Trying to get any privacy was next to impossible, and as much as Gerald tried, he couldn't find anywhere where he could just be alone. Or, that's what he told everyone.

That was not true. Gerald found his own little hiding place, deep in the water, just left of the iceberg they all liked to call *Snuggles*, although no one could remember why. An ice tunnel went deep into the iceberg itself. And if one swam far enough through the tunnel, one found an opening into a large ice cave, which was nice and dry, with lots of fish in the little pond that led to the tunnel. Gerald often went there to get away from it all. But not too often; otherwise, someone might follow him. Gerald shivered.

"Damn blasted cold!" he said.

He'd often thought about writing to someone and complaining about the cold. Maybe there was some kind of politician who held jurisdiction over the area? It would only take maybe a few hundred space heaters to make the place more livable. But no, Gerald would probably just live out his days in a state of constant coldness.

Gerald's condition of feeling constantly cold caused a great deal of amusement to most of his friends, who were rarely cold and thought that the South Pole was one of the best places on Earth to live. Not that any of them were all that aware of any other places, really. They were so content to be living in their own little bubble that they knew little of the outside world. And furthermore, they had no wish to find out anything about it. Gerald would have very much liked to tell all of them to piss off, hop on a passing cruise liner, and sail away to freedom and hopefully warmer climates.

Unfortunately, Gerald couldn't do any of these things, because Gerald was a penguin.

Eleven.

Celina couldn't see anything. The reason for her not being able to see anything was due to the fact that the lights were not on. The reason that the lights were not on was due to the fact that a group of hyper-artificially-intelligent-made-for-good-but-turned-evil elves had taken over the building. Or, that was what it seemed like, at least. And no one in the outside world had any idea what was going on.

Majestic Technologies wasn't exactly the most public of companies. The sensitive nature of its operations and the fact that, with a slight tweaking, a large amount of what was created within those hallowed walls could be turned to wreak the most unimaginable amount of destruction upon the world, were the main reasons for such privacy. The inventions would highly appeal to any number of armed services, as one of their favorite pastimes just happened to be wreaking unimaginable amounts of destruction upon the world. With this in mind, Celina took a good hour before deciding to call the local cop shop and trying to explain the situation to them. Needless to say, the call didn't go very well and there was a fair amount of giggling on the other end. The conversation began something like this.

"9-9-9 Emergency Services, how may I direct your call?" came the entirely too chirpy voice on the other end of the line.

The question stumped Celina. She wasn't entirely certain which department handled the apprehension of deranged robotic elves.

"Well, you see, the thing is," she said, "I'm trapped in the kitchen."

"One moment, please, I'll connect you with the fire department."

"No, no! I don't need the fire department!" But her plea came too late. A strange sort of punk version of elevator music signaled she'd been put on hold. Celina thought it both amusing and disturbing that the emergency departments even had a hold on their phone service. What if she'd been burning to death? She'd almost be crispy right about now.

A burly, pudgy-sounding voice that Celina highly suspected was emerging from somewhere behind a beard brought the disturbing elevator music to a standstill.

"Fire Department! How may I direct your call?"

"Well, I didn't really want the fire department. You see—"

"Is your house on fire, ma'am?"

"No, you see, I'm not in my house and—"

"Is someone else's house on fire?"

"No, I'm trapped in the cafeteria at work and—"

"Would you like us to send out a locksmith, ma'am?" interrupted the fireman.

"No, I don't want a bloody locksmith!"

"There's no need to raise your voice, ma'am," said the fireman calmly. "If nothing's on fire and you don't want to get out of wherever you're trapped, then why did you call the fire department?"

"I didn't call the damn fire department! Can you please transfer me back to 9-9-9?"

"Absolutely, ma'am, one moment, please." There was a click and then the distinct sound of the dial tone.

"Bastard!" said Celina.

Ring went the phone. Celina answered the phone with a sharp and in no way polite, "Yes?"

There was a brief pause while whoever was on the other line calmly and courteously explained their situation, during which a certain heated redness filled Celina's cheeks. This couldn't be seen due to the current darkness and the fact that there was no one else in the room to see it anyway. There was another brief pause while Celina chose the correct words to answer the question.

"No, I didn't bloody well rent *Good Loving in the Amazon!*"

There followed a pleasant *beep* as she hung up the phone and tried to breathe calmly. She punched 9-9-9 for the second time.

"9-9-9 Emergency Services, how may I direct your call?"

"Listen to me very carefully," began Celina. "I am trapped in the cafeteria at work—"

"There's a lot of that going around today, ma'am, one moment, I'll transfer you to the fire department."

The elevator music started playing once more but quickly got drowned out by Celina screaming something that sounded like it might rhyme with *clucking bell.*

The lawyers of Chatham, Chitham, and Chump sipped their tea calmly at the boardroom table and discussed the fact that they were filthy rich. They didn't address the point directly, but enjoyed alluding to their great wealth in such a roundabout way that someone who didn't follow conversations easily would almost think they were poor if they hadn't been smiling so smugly. They would say things like, "It's a shame, you see, because Dorothy wanted to invite the Dutch side of her family on the cruise but the yacht had only twenty bedrooms and we simply couldn't accommodate all of them," or, "The King of Spain wanted us to spend another night with him, but after living in the palace for three months, it felt as if we were imposing."

The lawyers were well off because the firm used its talents for one very rich client. The client was so very rich that they didn't need to have any other clients, and actually turned work down on a weekly basis. The client in question was none other than Neville Bartholomew Snell Jr III, eccentric billionaire extraordinaire.

The law firm of Chatham, Chitham, and Chump had been founded on Neville's first brush with the law, which happened not long after he'd made his first ten million pounds. Someone sideswiped Neville's brand new Mercedes while traveling along the M6. The large, beat-up sedan that did the swiping belonged to a thirty-something-year-old university dropout who lived a semi-comfortable life as a Shropshire restaurant owner. The restaurant specialized in serving cheap, pre-cooked, frozen for most of its life, food. The restaurant owner was of Greek descent and his name was Erastos.

Erastos liked hitting rich people's cars, as it gave him a sense that he was sticking it to *The Man*, which really wasn't the case and wasn't a good phrase to use on a regular basis anyway.

Erastos' act of stupidity made Neville realize that he had a severe love for eccentric forms of revenge.

After having his Mercedes repaired, he hired a group of men to hunt down Erastos' car and steal it. The car found itself shipped to Africa and dropped in the middle of a small, newly built arena. Around the same time that the car was sprayed inside and out with rhinoceros pheromones, a singing telegram showed up at Erastos' front door and indicated, rather musically, that he'd do well to turn to Channel 3. He did so, along with the rest of England who hoped to catch *Coronation Street. Coronation Street,* for possibly the first time ever in history, was not on. But there was a special documentary about African rhinoceros and the effects of pheromones. In the arena in Africa, Neville's camera crew transmitted live a group of enraged rhinos beating the living hell out of Erastos' car, and then proceeding to try and have sex with it.

The impending lawsuits from multiple animal rights groups, several avid watchers of *Coronation Street*, and one lawsuit from a Shropshire restaurant owner kept the lawyers of the newly formed Chatham, Chitham, and Chump busy for the following couple of years. They charged ridiculous amounts for their services but had a real knack for tying things up in the British legal system forever.

The lawyers called their respective secretaries and ordered more tea. A large red phone installed on the boardroom table was a direct line from Neville's personal assistant to the lawyers and it came as little surprise when the phone suddenly rang. Neville hadn't had any lawsuits for at least three months, so it was around that time again.

"Chatham, Chitham, and Chump, Charles Chitham speaking," said Charles as he answered the phone.

"Matthew here, Charles. Neville has asked that we move to a yellow alert. We have a possible situation in London," said Neville's assistant, Beatrice.

"Splendid," said Charles, "we will be at the ready," and hung up. He addressed the rest of the boardroom. "Good news, chaps, looks like we'll have a busy month, we're now on yellow alert."

There were several mutterings of approval and just as the great legal minds of Britain began to jump into action, more tea arrived and they all decided there was probably time for one more cup.

Twelve.

Jeremiah the goldfish was at this moment chasing his tail. He didn't remember seeing it behind him before, but had the distinct feeling that something had been following him for quite a while. When he finally worked up the courage to look back, he noticed his tail. The smug way it wiggled at him made Jeremiah feel it was making fun of him, so he decided to chase it. This had been going on for just over three minutes when he stopped, couldn't remember what he had been doing, looked around, and then got the distinct impression that something was following him.

Nigel wandered through the streets of London. Life had been so much simpler this morning, hanging off a building, and then all of a sudden, his once stable life had been taken to with a rather large sledgehammer, destroying reality as he knew it to be. He kicked an empty pop can out of anger and frustration, only to have it hit an unsuspecting seven-year-old boy in the head. The boy burst into tears as Nigel ducked into a nearby alley and continued moping.

He hadn't moped in such a long time that it all felt rather unfamiliar to him. The last time he moped was back in college. Things seemed fairly simple back then, as well.

The early morning sun flung rays that danced from drop to glistening drop of dew sitting atop the grass in front of St Mary's College, Birmingham. As anyone from Birmingham would understand, it was a complete rarity for anything to be dancing across the grass, especially sunlight, as England constantly loses sunlight to nicer, brighter countries like Australia. Ironically, Australia was the place where England sent its criminals. They were caught doing some illegal act in a dreary, dank, and gloomy country where drizzle was a common factor throughout the day, and then they got shipped off to a beautiful sandy beach, very close to the Great Barrier Reef. Punishment was obviously a skewed thought in everyone's mind, back in the olden days. Probably something to do with the rain falling and softening what were obviously already very soft heads.

Nigel had been attending St Mary's for the better part of a year already and learnt fast that college was a place to grow. A place where his talents and intelligence were unmatched. A place where he experienced a breakthrough. Everyone, at some point early in life, experienced those sorts of days when everything seemed perfect. Literally perfect. And everyone knew that perfection existed because they had that perfect feeling inside of them. It felt like their best and favorite emotions battled amongst each other, only they were not really battling, they were dancing. Nigel had one of those days when his breakthrough happened.

He woke up in the fourth-floor apartment in the student housing building, much as he always did. He rolled out of bed on the left side, just like any other day. He stepped over an unconscious roommate, just like normal, because there was often an unconscious roommate or two lying around the floor in the morning. Usually a product of a heavy night's drinking. The kind of heavy night that caused people to wake up to find someone had painted their feet blue and they had a traffic cone glued to their head. Nigel half staggered, half slid over to the full-length mirror that his roommates had bought so they could take naked pictures of themselves, a common practice among British college students. Nigel looked at his reflection and saw how horrible he looked.

He grimaced and wafted a hand dismissively toward the mirror, which subsequently and quite unexpectedly smashed into a million pieces which organized themselves not entirely so neatly on the floor. Nigel looked at his hand, looked at the smashed mirror, then continued on to the kitchen. He rubbed his head and wondered why there was a strange tingly feeling somewhere in his frontal lobe. Then he remembered the night before.

His friends had gone on a pub-crawl, which was traditional on any night of the week that wasn't a Thursday. Thursdays were special. On Thursdays, it was an ironclad tradition to play Hide the Kipper, *an altogether different kind of drinking game that involved several pints of beer and a few dead fish. The rules for* Hide the Kipper *were as follows:*

Preparation: All you needed were two pints of beer per person, per round, a stopwatch, a pen and paper to keep score, and a dead fish. Preferably, a kipper, as that was the name of the game. If a kipper was unavailable, then any dead fish could be used, but the name of the game must be altered accordingly, i.e., *hide the herring, hide the smelt, hide the cod,* etc.

The game takes place on the doorstep of someone's house or in front of a student apartment building, otherwise known as *home base.*

Rules:

The participant takes a pint of beer in his/her right hand and the dead fish in the left hand.

A moderator must stand to the participant's left to observe alcohol consumption and to operate the stopwatch.

A scorekeeper must stand to the participant's right to keep score as directed by the moderator.

At the moderator's command, and usually a whistle or a good solid *Go!* will suffice, the stopwatch is started and the participant must down the entire pint of beer.

If the participant downs the entire pint without stopping, then he/she is awarded one point. Upon finishing the beer, the participant must throw the glass up over his/her shoulder where the other participants await their turn. The participant who catches the glass is awarded one point.

The participant with the dead fish must then run out into the street, followed by the moderator, and find a passerby, otherwise known as the *victim.* Upon finding the *victim,* the participant must then shove the dead fish down the victim's trousers and then leg it back to the *home base.*

Upon reaching home base, the participant must then down the second pint of beer, where he/she will receive another point if he/she manages to drink without stopping. As soon as the second glass is empty, the stopwatch is stopped.

Points for time are awarded as follows: One minute and under, ten points. Between one and two minutes, eight points. Between two and three minutes, six points. Between three and four minutes, four points. Between four and five minutes, two points. Anything after five minutes is minus one point and the failing participant must drink another pint.

The next person steps up with his/her pint and dead fish and the game continues until everyone has a turn.

Then the second round begins.

Games normally last ten rounds, or until the beer runs out. The points really don't matter; it's mostly to do with shocking strangers by stuffing dead fish down their trousers.

Nigel grinned at the memory of last night's shenanigans. They must have hit about seven pubs in the space of three hours. Probably the reason for the fuzzy feeling in his head. Although, at the moment, the fuzzy feeling in his head was matched only by the gooey feeling in his heart. The reason for that feeling was Harriet.

Harriet was a fellow student, majoring in Biology, and had a love of riding expensive horses that her daddy dearest was all too happy to buy for her. Harriet and Nigel had been seeing each other for a month and Nigel was ecstatic about her, especially since, last night before the shenanigans began, he clearly remembered Harriet telling him that she loved him. What could be better than that, he thought? He'd had a fabulous night out, his girlfriend told him that she loved him, and he had no classes today. Things were going perfectly. To prove the point, he stood in the centre of the kitchen and stretched happily, throwing his arms out on either side. What he didn't expect was exactly what happened next.

The kitchen window exploded outward, the kitchen cupboards splintered into many small pieces, cutlery scattered everywhere, dishes and crockery exploded, and

Nigel grasped his forehead as huge lightning bolts of pain threw themselves around inside his head. Gradually, he passed out. First, the kitchen became kind of blurry. Then he saw the vague shape of one of his roommates, obviously one who wasn't unconscious, standing in the doorway of the kitchen with a kind of shocked expression on his face. Then Nigel's world turned to watercolour and everything kind of slipped off the page. And then everything went black.

A penguin. A flightless bird with rubbery skin and a penchant for black and white. And normally the kind of bird who was quite at home in the cold. As far back as Gerald could remember, he had always been a penguin, ever since he was born. But there had always been this nagging inkling at the back of his mind that kept telling him that he was meant for greater things and that this rubbery complexion and cold atmosphere comprised only a temporary setback. And one day, he might even have the distinct pleasure of stopping the world from destroying itself. But after all, that was only an inkling and Gerald was only a penguin, and so he never really put much more thought into things than that.

Yesterday had been no different than the day before, and today had been no different than yesterday. He had a sneaking suspicion that tomorrow was going to be very much the same, as well. He'd get up, eat some fish, find somewhere semi-private to do his morning business. Maybe he'd waddle around a bit and stare menacingly at other penguins who usually were not in the least bit intimidated and had long ago just taken to ignoring Gerald altogether. And then, just after lunch and a second helping of fish, he'd swim off to his cave and have a nice little nap without all this chatter going on in the background.

It was like a constant cocktail party going on and whether he wanted an invitation or not, it was mandatory to attend. But not Gerald; he had his cave.

"In fact, I think I'll pay it a bit of a visit." And with that, he dived into the water and headed straight for his tunnel, weaving a bit here and there so as to lose anyone who might think of following him.

The cave was exactly how he'd left it the previous day; he slid out of the water on his stomach and skidded happily across the ice. The ice in here was so clear that he could see into it, showing reflections and a blue swirly thing. That was what Gerald had been looking at for a while.

In the very centre of the cave there was an almost perfectly formed block of ice about twenty feet high, and each side measuring a width of about ten feet. But that wasn't what was amazing. Although it was quite amazing that there was an almost perfectly rectangular block of ice in the centre of an ice cave within an iceberg somewhere in the South Pole, what was more amazing was the blue swirly thing that seemed to be trapped within the oversize dice cube.

Of a clear, deep blue colour, it spiraled up in a swirly kind of formation within the ice. It looked very much like it should be moving but the ice seemed to prevent motion. Gerald had waddled around the cube many times. Today was the first day he'd noticed a flaw. The cube seemed to be melting, which was very unusual, as Gerald was definitely not feeling any warmer. He waddled around to another side, which also turned out to be melting.

A thought slowly crept into his head; it felt like it had traveled a great distance. In actual fact, the notion originated from within a fishbowl somewhere in London's East End. It simply said, *duck*. And Gerald did. Just in time. The ice block exploded, unleashing the blue swirly thing, which swirled in a hyper-hurricane type of way, with bits of electrical charges thrown in for good measure. Chunks of ice flew by Gerald, then all of a sudden stopped, as if frozen in time. For a moment, everything seemed to stop; even the blue swirly thing slowed down. Gerald experienced one of those rare times when his mind turned completely blank. This was a rare occurrence for anyone, but happened on a daily basis to someone, somewhere in the world. Usually, to someone presented with an impossibly impossible situation who didn't know what to do about it.

Gerald staggered forward a few steps as if he'd been pushed. *Nope, wait a minute.* He'd been pulled. Chunks of ice began flying back past him as the blue swirly thing shifted directions. Before, it had been spinning anti-clockwise. It appeared to have changed its mind and now spun clockwise, and in doing so, sucked anything not tied down into its blue swirlyness. Gerald turned and began to waddle as fast as he could but he didn't seem to be going anywhere. He waddled faster, but to no avail.

This is the end. I'm done for!

The blue swirly thing moved faster and faster and within a split second Gerald, the chunks of ice, and a rather shocked fish got sucked into the blue swirly thing and vanished.

Consequently, the blue swirly thing heaved a sigh of relief and blew itself out.

Thirteen.

Nigel woke up on the couch and looked into two very worried-looking faces. The faces, to the best of his recollection, belonged to his roommates, Giles and Herbert.

Giles, tall and skinny, could consume large amounts of food without gaining a pound but as a consequence, couldn't hold his liquor and often ended up passing out on his bed. Although, more often than not, he fell off his bed and ended up on the floor.

Herbert was a rich kid with a serious distaste for money, so in order to get rid of it, he tended to spend vast amounts of it at a time. Herbert paid for the apartment they rented. Herbert bought all the food and alcohol consumed within a mile of the apartment. And all the crockery that laid in many bits and pieces on the kitchen floor had been bought by, and belonged to, Herbert.

Nigel rubbed his head and tried to shake the fuzziness from his eyes. He had the strong sensation that something had happened, a breakthrough of mammoth proportions. He could feel everything in the room around him; even the stuff he couldn't see from his spot on the couch was firmly etched in his mind.

"You all right?" asked Giles. "You took a nasty fall."

"What the hell happened to my kitchen?" said Herbert with a smaller trace of concern in his voice than Giles had expressed.

Nigel still felt shooting pains in his forehead, but they seemed more organized. Not quite as chaotic as before. He sat up and looked around the room. Shards of crockery littered the doorway to the kitchen.

"Did . . . did I do that?" he asked.

90

"I heard the smash and came in just in time to see my kitchen destroyed, and then you passed out. What did you have to drink last night?" said Herbert.

"How did you do that, Nigel? The kitchen, I mean?" asked Giles.

"I, uh, I don't really know," was the only response that Nigel could think of. He stood up, then steadied himself. "I was thinking about what a good night we had and how well things were going with Harriet and how everything was going perfectly."

The buzzing in his head turned into a low hum.

"And that's why you destroyed my kitchen? I was hoping for something a bit more melodramatic," said Herbert disappointedly.

Nigel looked around the room. Everything seemed exactly like before, nothing had changed. And yet it all felt different. It was a strange sensation, but he felt like he had control over everything. He had the distinct feeling that if he waved his hands at the couch, he would be able to move it without even touching it. He decided to test the theory and in doing so, using only his mind and a simple wave of his hand, forced the couch up through the ceiling and off to God knew where. God did know; as it turned out, where was actually a nude beach in the south of France where, to this day, people still enjoy sitting on the couch that some claim fell from the sky.

Giles and Herbert, who had been standing next to the couch at the time of its ascension, dusted the plaster out of their hair and tried hard to glare at Nigel in anger. This proved too difficult, as they were both somewhat afraid that Nigel would fire them through the roof, too.

Nigel smiled. He'd read about this kind of thing. Telekinesis: the ability to move things with the mind. Usually some kind of trauma or episode would bring this form of talent and power to the surface of one's mind.

In Nigel's case, everything in his life had suddenly become perfect and, in doing so, a rare power that existed hardly anywhere else on Earth had been handed to him. He couldn't help but laugh; this was life changing. This was amazing. The things he could do! He picked up Giles and Herbert, suspending them both in mid-air, which caused both of them to panic simultaneously. Nigel floated them both toward him and gave them a big hug. This day really was perfect.

Unbeknownst to Nigel and his newfound powers, disaster was fast approaching. The disaster decided to wear a particularly nice mini-skirt today, with a lovely, fuzzy red sweater. The knee-high leather boots that most would consider looked better on a hooker, but which the disaster thought rather stylish, completed the outfit. The disaster was about to ruin Nigel's life for quite a long time.

The disaster walked up to Nigel's apartment building just in time to see a couch fly out of the roof and head off toward France. The disaster flicked her long blonde hair, as if to say, "That's not the first flying couch I've seen," and entered the building.

Nigel, Giles, and Herbert had lots of fun testing out Nigel's newfound abilities. The apartment got messier and messier, as Nigel hadn't quite figured out the strength of his mind, but none of them cared as a cardboard cutoutof Marilyn Monroe sauntered across to Giles and head-butted him. This in turn sent Nigel and Herbert into fits of laughter. The laughter encountered an interruption when disaster knocked at the door. Nigel swung the door open from ten feet away to reveal the disaster in its entirety.

"Harriet!" said Nigel. "I have the most amazing news."

Harriet quickly held up a finger and flashed a look that would silence any male, human or animal.

"May I talk to you for a moment, Nigel?" said the silky voice.

Nigel stepped over the mess of clothes, traffic cones, and various broken objects.

"Of course," he said in a highly enthusiastic voice.

He bounced out of the room after the blonde hair but not before raising Giles and Herbert off the ground and sticking them to the ceiling. In response to which they both burst into hysterical laughter.

"Nigel, dear," Harriet said somewhat sadly.

"Harriet is something the matter? You won't believe what happened today!" said Nigel, still humming with newfound energy.

Harriet yet again raised a finger, an annoying habit she picked up from her mother who was highly pompous and rich.

"I have something to tell you, and I don't want you take it the wrong way, but I've met someone else."

Nigel's enthusiasm suddenly dropped a few inches.

"His name is Troy and he's a Genetic Fruitarian and you ought to know that we love each other very much and are getting married."

Nigel's enthusiasm, if it still could be called that, dropped another few feet, along with his face.

"I know this must come as a bit of a shock but it all kind of happened last night after I went home and I know that I said I loved you but a girl can change her mind. And I think it'd show a lot of understanding and maturity on your part if you'd come to the wedding. It's this Saturday at St Ethel's." Harriet pursed her lips, signaling the end of the monologue.

Nigel's enthusiasm took a flying leap off an imaginary cliff. The humming in his brain stopped abruptly, followed by two loud thumps from the inside of his apartment that he could only presume meant his roommates fell from the ceiling. Perfection, it would appear, is fleeting.

After the fits of rage subsided. After his heart started beating again. After the realization that he'd suddenly lost his power of telekinesis as quickly as he'd got it. After realizing that his day had turned into the exact opposite of perfection, Nigel found himself moping along the River Thames. All because of a disaster in a mini-skirt.

Fourteen.

Celina found herself on hold again. After doing battle with the chirpy switchboard lady another four times, after she'd been transferred to homicide, auto theft, the special tactics unit, and the bakery on Melville Street, she'd finally been transferred to general enquiries.

The hold music for general enquiries was of the electric jazzy style that most British teenagers were so fond of. In fact, they would stand in large rooms for hours on end, wearing next to nothing, dancing to this music they could hardly hear over the sound of their own pulse while bright lights bounced off the walls.

Celina was in no mood for dancing. She was more in the mood for possibly maiming small animals. Her Scottish roots allowed her to go from not angry to absolutely raging furiously in under a minute. At one time, she had taken classes to learn to control her anger, and in the end, she had been thrown out of the group due to a negative and violent attitude. As a consequence, she had thrown a chair through a window to prove that she was well in control of her anger and that she could stop whenever she liked. The point was ill proven. The arresting officer was a nice gentleman who actually succeeded in calming her down. She remembered his name to be Nigel or something.

A strange, nasally, female voice that sounded like it had two pencils shoved up its nose popped onto the line just as the music reached a particularly low point.

"Hello, general enquiries, my name is Rhonda, do you need a squad car sent out to your house?"

Celina breathed and counted to ten quickly.

"I'm not at my house, I'm locked in the cafeteria at work, now listen carefully to me—"

"Would you like me to send a locksmith, madam?"

Celina counted from eleven to twenty.

"No, thank you. I don't need a locksmith. What I'm trying to tell you—"

"Let me transfer you to the fire department, this is more their area. One moment, please."

"Now wait a bloody second!"

Somewhere in the northern Highlands of Scotland, the chilling sound of bagpipes floated across the misty grass. The long dead and buried ancestral ghosts of Celina McMannis stirred, if only a little, to the battle cry. A few of the ghosts thought that *wait a bloody second* wasn't so much of a battle cry, more like a statement, but the anger and want for battle indicated in the voice was undeniable. The dead McMannis Clan smiled to themselves. Their warrior brood was alive and well and threatening war. Or, that's what it sounded like, at least. This was not entirely the case. Although Celina was definitely done with counting to ten.

"Now, listen to me! Or I swear the second I get out of here I'm going to hunt you down and rip out your nose hairs. I am trapped at Majestic Technologies Research and Development Lab; the address is in the phone book. I am locked in the cafeteria. This morning there was a security breach and—"

"Uhh, madam, I think that—"

"Let me finish!"

A round of applause rose from the Scottish Highlands.

"This morning there was a security breach; something climbed over the fence and triggered the security systems. The building is locked down."

"Umm, madam? I don't suppose you'd like a squad car to come round, would you?"

There was a long pause while Celina weighed up the consequences of possibly exposing her work to the world. And then, on the other hand, she didn't really want to be trapped in the cafeteria forever. But what would happen if the elves got out? What would Neville think about all of this? Surely he was aware of the situation.

The operator didn't want to prod but the pause became excessively long. "Madam?"

Celina shook her head dejectedly.

"No, it's fine, I'm sure it's nothing."

"Are you sure? You seem rather distraught."

"No, no I'm sure it was just a cat or something. No sense in worrying about it. I'm probably just overreacting."

The ghosts lying in the Highlands let out the same sound that spectators at a soccer match made when there was only one minute to go and someone missed what very well could have been the winning goal.

"Okay, madam. Have a nice day."

Click—beep.

Despite her red hair, her constant anger, and that sense she portrayed to everyone who talked to her that she was liable to kick them in the nuts even if they didn't have any, Celina sat down and began to sob quietly.

Somewhere across the city, a prophetically blessed goldfish received a string of numbers, which he proceeded to fling out of his mind, as they proved of no use to him. He had the profound sense that someone else somewhere could make use of those numbers, and he hoped that he'd flung them in the right direction. And then, upon the discovery of a rather nice castle in his bowl, the goldfish forgot all about the numbers.

Moments later, a string of numbers slammed into Celina's head, knocking her off the table where she had been sitting.

Fifteen.

Gerald groaned, blinked a few times, then bolted upright and screamed. Everything was dark. Gerald screamed again.

"I'm blind!" he said. No, wait a second; he could just make out the faint image of the ocean lapping up on the beach about twenty feet away from him.

The moon sent a silvery shimmer down across the water, and as Gerald's ears adjusted to being back in reality and not in a super-continental-semi-vortex, which is what the blue swirly thing consisted of, he could hear the waves breaking and feel the gentle warm night wind brush against his face.

Warm wind? This was not the South Pole. He distinctly remembered being in the South Pole with ice, cold water, ice, penguins, and more ice. He was certain about that, and then he faintly remembered the swirly blue thing, and then it would appear he had landed on a beach.

A warm beach. A warm beach with palm trees dotted here and there. Gerald smiled. Then he thought for a moment; something wasn't sitting right with him. He felt a bit woozy; he'd just been hurtled up into the cosmos, traveled a few thousand miles, and ended up on a rather nice beach. But there was something else; something just didn't fit, like a wool sweater after it's been washed at the wrong temperature.

Then it hit him. Penguins couldn't scream. They just made an odd kind of chattery, quacking noise. He reached his hand up to where his beak would normally be, but never touched it. The reason being, not only was it not there, but he was too busy staring at his hand. He had a hand. He was sure that when he'd woken up on his cold block of ice this morning, he had two shiny flippers. Now he had a hand. He held up his other hand. Two of them! He wiggled his fingers. And there were arms attached to both of them.

He touched his face with his newfound hands to find that it had more holes in it than normal and there was a strange kind of stringy fur on top of what was once a shiny-looking black head. This was all too much to handle; he had hands, with arms attached to them, and Gerald and his hands were all on a warm beach together.

Gerald had seen humans before; they often passed by his lump of ice in search of cute furry seals to kill. Or sometimes a cruise liner would pass by with a large amount of drunken humans on it. They would wave and shout and sometime flash bright lights at him. That never made much sense, really. For the longest time, Gerald believed that it was a boat full of crazy people and that was just what humans did with their crazy people; put them on a boat and floated them off into the sunset. In fact, he still believed it.

He was a human. He slowly took the time to examine the rest of his new body.

Funnily enough, he discovered that he knew what a lot of the parts were called and what their functions were. Whatever had turned him into a human had also given him rudimentary knowledge of himself and his surroundings. Everything in the world seemed vague to him, kind of like someone's name that he just couldn't remember but swore was on the tip of his tongue.

"I suppose," said Gerald, testing his voice, "that everything will make sense sooner or later. Listen to me, I'm speaking, lalalalalala."

His voice was quite deep and melodious.

"Hey!" he said, and then jumped. "That was loud, I should speak quietly, I should stop speaking to myself, the other humans may think

99

I'm crazy and put me on a boat. Look! I'm still talking to myself! Okay I'm going to stop now."

He stood up and brushed the sand off himself. The beach was empty and completely quiet, aside from the sound of the water. A rock pond nearby looked like a good place where Gerald could take a look at himself, so he wandered over.

Wandering over wasn't quite as easy as Gerald had expected. He just wasn't used to walking on human legs and so he looked very much like those newborn giraffes often seen on the nature channel.

He staggered over to the pool and almost went in head first before he realized that he had inherited something that he was fairly sure should be called reflexes. He peered over the edge of the pool and came face to face with himself. Although Gerald had very little in terms of a basis for comparison, he was quite impressed with the way he looked. *He looked good.* In actual fact, the body that had been specially chosen for him had previously belonged to a rather handsome swimmer turned reclusive billionaire playboy reported missing around the same time that all the dead people started to get up.

Despite his many downfalls in life, the handsome man in question had saved a young boy from getting hit by a bus by putting himself in harm's way. The impact killed him instantly, and his soul was the last one that Death guided to heaven before he quit. The body, moments after the impact, before anyone could get a good look at it, was sucked into an orange swirly thing and whisked up into the cosmos where it traveled around, been fully healed, swung once around the sun, and then collided with a blue swirly thing.

There was a quick trade made, and Gerald had inherited a rather nice body while his penguin body entered another dimension where humans worshipped penguins and would see the arrival of the penguin body as some kind of mystical sign from their Penguin God.

Gerald ran his hands through his thick black hair. Gerald looked very much like the underwear model pictures often displayed in high-class department store windows. Short, curly hair covered various parts of his body but aside from that, everything seemed to be in order. He walked around a little more, trying to get the hang of his legs, when a thought hit him so hard that it knocked him onto his back. The thought had originated within a goldfish bowl, flung out across the world, specifically looking for Gerald. The thought was *black robe*. And that was it.

Gerald committed it to memory and decided that this must be a human trait that he was just going to have to get used to. He jumped to his feet and rather nakedly walked off toward the group of bright lights at the far end of the beach. As he walked, he got the distinct impression that he should be covering his body up with something but as nothing sprang immediately to hand, he decided he'd just have to wing it.

He laughed to himself.

"Wing it," he said.

This morning he had wings, not that he could ever fly with them, but even so, for a moment there, everything seemed strangely and amusingly ironic. Oh, how he wished the other penguins could see him now. Gerald was getting closer to the lights, and he could make out some words in front of a large building that was the source of the lights, which funnily enough, he found he could read. The building was apparently something called a *hospital*. There seemed to be some kind of a ruckus at the front of the building, and Gerald's memory suddenly sprang into action as a man in a black robe came sprinting out of the front of the building, followed closely by three large orderlies dressed in white.

The Angel of Death skidded to a confused stop as he suddenly came face to face with a naked man who had once been a penguin and whose soul he was sure he had guided to heaven not too long ago. However, that was all he had time to think about as the orderlies tackled him, knocking him into the naked ex-penguin, who shrieked unhappily.

Everyone, not really knowing what to do for the best, lay in a sort of disorganized mess as other orderlies came running from the building.

The last thing the naked man yelled, probably a little too loudly was, "Please don't put me on a boat!"

Sixteen.

Jeremiah the goldfish remained very still. He had suddenly noticed there was a castle in the middle of his goldfish bowl and he was remaining very still in case there was something inside it, and he didn't want to disturb it in case it turned out to be an angry and violent something.

"Where had the castle come from in the first place?" he wondered. And then he began to wonder why he was staying very still. And then the castle slipped from his mind altogether as the large black squiggly object outside of his bowl began to ring.

A recorded male voice clicked on, accompanied by a vast amount of hissing.

"I'm obviously not here, otherwise I would have picked up. Just thought I'd leave a message telling you so. At this point I'd like to encourage you to leave me a message in return if you feel so inclined. If you don't, well, that's your decision, then, isn't it?"

There was a sharp beep, then a frantic female voice popped into the atmosphere. Jeremiah glided around his watery kingdom, quite content not to be hearing the voice due the sound-dampening power of liquid. The answering machine message went something like this.

"Uhh. Hi. I feel a bit stupid doing this, only I'm stuck in the lunchroom at work and, well, a group of deranged cyborg elves has taken over the building and I can't get out. And your number kinda just popped into my head out of nowhere, actually knocked me down on the floor. And since I can't get anyone else to help me I thought you might be able to. Anyway, I'm feeling more and more stupid the more I talk, so I'm going to shut up now. I'm at Majestic Technologies."

There was a click, followed by a sick kind of whirring sound as the antique answering machine attempted to rewind the equally antique cassette tape.

Completely oblivious and suddenly in a most gleeful mood, Jeremiah the goldfish swam in and out of the castle that he had just discovered right there in his bowl.

Seventeen.

Feeling completely dejected, Celina sat down in the chair. The phone number had seemed like a completely sane idea at first, but after making the call, she thought it all rather ridiculous. She should know better than to go with her instincts. Receiving strange thought-waves that were definitely not her own was a fairly new concept to her.

When she was younger, she was convinced that Prince was actually speaking to her, and only her, through his music. It was a theory that, in her younger years, quite often got her beaten up by the other girls.

The lights in the kitchen flickered for a moment and tried to come back on, but to no avail. A chill suddenly ran down her spine and then carried on right down to her feet. When it reached her feet, the chill decided that there was still something to be chilly about so it ran right back up her legs and raced up her spine.

There was always a part in horror movies where someone knew something bad was about to happen, everything else happened in the right order, the people were in the right places. The power went out, the phone lines were cut, and Sandra the blonde-haired, big-breasted co-star has been missing for over an hour in the creepy abandoned house that no one in their right mind would go into, not even a bunch of high school kids. If Celina had been in a movie, this would have been the point where she found herself at this particular moment. Although everything had been deadly quiet for the past six hours, suddenly everything seemed even quieter. And although the lights had been out for quite a while, everything seemed more chillingly dark. And then the click of the dining room door being unlocked made her heart pound loudly inside her chest.

Celina froze in place. The thought of moving was of great appeal but her legs had other ideas and wanted to stay firmly rooted. She heard the door creak open, then a set of quick footsteps entered the room. She had to hide, she had to hide, why the hell weren't her legs listening to her?

The dining room door swung all the way open; light spilled through the kitchen doorway. The short, quick footsteps of oncoming evil got closer and closer until, silhouetted in the doorway, a man appeared. A short man. Three feet tall, dressed in traditional elf clothing from the jingle bell on his hat right down to the pointy shoes that curled at the ends. A maniacal grin smeared across his mouth.

Celina, having hidden herself in the walk-in freezer, could see the elf through the crack she'd left in the doorway. The elf, a half-crazed look in his eyes, moved quickly around the work table that sat in the centre of the kitchen. He climbed up on the counter and started opening cupboards, spilling canned foods and all sorts of other packaged goods out on the floor. He then proceeded to go through the kitchen drawers, emptying them as he went. There was such a determined look on his face that anyone watching him would have said, "Well, I'm sure he knows what he's looking for and he's bound to find it, I mean look at the little fellah, he's so determined."

The determined elf seemed to be getting more frustrated as he came to the last of the cupboards and obviously did not find what he hoped to find. He swung open the fridge door and added its contents to all the other stuff that sat on the floor in a messy heap. The elf stopped and looked around the kitchen until finally settling a mean-looking and still quite crazed eye on the freezer door.

Inside, Celina had been watching the ransacking of the kitchen with complete horror and a touch of confusion. Why was the elf destroying the kitchen?

There was a scratching sound at the freezer door. Celina stepped back and looked around the freezer. Pieces of meat hung on a rack, sacks of frozen peas were stacked haphazardly into one corner, boxes were stacked in the other. The scratching continued. Celina could see the elf in the reflection of one of the metallic kitchen cabinets.

Outside the freezer in the kitchen, the elf was leaping at the handle to the freezer, completely oblivious to the fact that the door wasn't completely closed.

Due to having a bad case of being short, this task was proving difficult. The elf stopped and stared up at the door. His maniacal smile twisted into a half-smile and then dropped completely into a frown. The elf ran back into the dining room and returned quickly, carrying a chair. Hopping on the chair next to the freezer's edge, he opened the door and swung it wide.

A rush of cold air hit him in the face as he hopped down and walked into the freezer. His nasty, beady little eyes quickly took stock: frozen peas, frozen carcasses of dead animals, boxes of bad, frozen food often found in crappy cafeterias. The elf reached into his pocket and pulled out a two-way radio; he clicked the button once and spoke into the microphone.

"This is Cuddles calling Fluffy, come in Fluffy, over."

There was a mess of static and then a gruff voice came back. "Fluffy here, go ahead Cuddles, over."

"I'm in the kitchen, no lemons here, over."

"Did you try the cupboards? Over."

"Yes Fluffy, tried all the cupboards, no lemons, over."

"How about the freezer? Over."

"Nope, no lemons in the freezer, over."

"Are you sure you checked all the cupboards? Over?"

"Dammit, Fluffy, I checked everywhere, no lemons, none."

There was a momentary pause while Cuddles' eyebrows twitched spasmodically.

Static.

"You didn't say over. Over."

"Go to hell, Fluffy, over."

"Very well, proceed back to operations, over."

Cuddles the elf swore to himself, stuffed the radio back into his pocket and then left the freezer, shutting the door as he went.

The stack of frozen peas shifted slightly and a bag from the top raised itself off and threw itself to the ground. Celina's extremely cold-looking head managed to motivate the rest of her body to stand up and start moving again. She shook off the bags of peas and stood up, teeth chattering incessantly.

"L-l-lemons?"

Eighteen.

No one captured Death, *no one*! And if they did, they'd definitely never ever consider tying him to a hospital bed. That was, until recent events had taken place, causing Celina to hide in a freezer, Nigel to get fired, a penguin to turn into a man, a goldfish to predict the future, and all people in the world to stop dying. And where was God in all of this?

There was a very good chance that at this particular moment, God was serving wine at a small restaurant a stone's throw from Piccadilly Circus. Death was not too concerned with God's whereabouts at this point in time. He was more concerned that someone had him tied to a bed in a rundown-looking hospital in the Bahamas.

Gerald, tied to the bed next to Death's, was less concerned with anything and was happily busy watching his toes wiggle, an altogether new experience that he'd recently discovered after being manhandled by a group of large male nurses and then tied to a hospital bed. He was equally overjoyed that no one had mentioned anything about sending him away on a boat.

"I demand to see the doctor in charge!" shouted Death for the umpteenth time.

"Have you ever noticed how nicely my toes wiggle?" asked Gerald of the gentleman dressed in the black robe tied to the bed next to him.

Death was forthright with his answer. "Piss off!"

"Hmm," said Gerald. That altogether new phrase didn't seem to be in his vocabulary. He'd have to remember the words and try them out sometime.

Death got a bit perplexed at this point, and it had nothing to do with the naked, toe-wiggling gentleman to his left. In angelic form, Death was quite powerful. He had been in a few battles and had held his own each time. He'd even been in some nasty bar fights and had come through unscathed. He was an Angel. At least, he was, until he quit. It had never occurred to him that certain strengths would probably leave him after a while. As hard as he tried, he could not break the straps that tethered him to the bed. His ability to have people forget who he was appeared to be intact and was reinforced when moments later Barney the nurse walked in, followed closely by Dr. Ranja.

"We caught this man outside the hospital," said Barney, pointing to Gerald. "He was all naked and out running, seems a bit confused."

Barney then looked at Death.

"I don't know who that is, but he looks a bit pale."

Barney had been one of the nurses who had restrained Death to the bed, but the instant he had left the room and lost sight of Death, the memory had begun to fade until it no longer existed. No one should see Death until it was time for each of them to see Death.

Dr. Ranja looked at both patients, perched on a stool, took out a pen and notepad, and smiled comfortingly. It had taken him years to figure out how to smile comfortingly. The first three years as a doctor, he found his smile had inspired nothing but fear and a small sense of loathing; the following seven years, he'd tested out several different smiles, until he finally sat himself down in front of a mirror for sixteen days and figured it all out. It ended up being a simple matter of squinting his eyes slightly and raising the left corner of his mouth just a touch higher than the right. Voila, comforting smile.

"Now," he began with the utmost confidence, "let's start with your names. You in the black robe."

"Death incarnate. And you are?"

The doctor sounded out the words slowly as he wrote them down.

"De-a-th in-ca-rn-ate. Good, good. And the naked gentleman?"

Gerald stared at the doctor for a moment, trying to focus on what his name was when he was a penguin, as he presumed it still applied now.

"Gerald," he said, and then added quickly, "I used to be a penguin, you know."

Dr. Ranja nodded enthusiastically.

As a quick afterthought, Gerald added, "But I'm not crazy."

"Yes, yes, excellent, of course you're not crazy. Used to be a penguin, that's good." Dr. Ranja suddenly re-noticed Death and although he looked slightly familiar, the Doctor couldn't quite remember seeing him before.

"Ahh, and you in the robe, what's your name?"

"Does it matter? I mean, really? You have to let me out of here."

"Really?" said the doctor, "and why would that be?"

"Because it's all gone horribly wrong, people aren't dying, that's not the natural order of things, the world will be overrun with people, I have to stop it. I have to find God and set it straight."

The doctor nodding as if he knew exactly what Death was talking about.

"Yes, I understand completely. My dear beloved wife is very spiritual. I expect her home any day now. She just nipped out to get some milk."

"No, she hasn't!" snapped Gerald. The denial surprised both Death and the doctor and even Gerald himself, because he wasn't quite sure where the words had come from. He had spoken them, but the words were just something that had popped into his mind.

Several thousand miles away, a prophetic goldfish was having a bit of a fit, thoughts and words were flying at him fast, and he couldn't help but swim around in small circles quickly and fling them out of his head as fast as possible to the person who needed them. The person, in this particular case, was Gerald.

The doctor's smile dropped off his face and rolled somewhere under the bed. This was momentary, as he regained control of himself and grinned at Gerald while the thought of Death leaked from his memory. He began calmly.

"I'm sorry, what was that?"

Gerald shook his head but more words appeared and he couldn't help saying them. "She's run off with a one-legged Polynesian midget!"

The doctor let out a nervous titter.

"That's ridiculous," he said with a small amount of confidence. "She's just nipped out for some milk."

Death chuckled as only Death could.

Dr. Ranja's face began to turn a little red but his composure held firm.

"And you, whoever you are, what exactly are you finding so funny?"

Death stopped chuckling, and looked first at Gerald, and then to the doctor.

"Well, it's funny, isn't it," said Death, "your wife's run off with a one-legged Polynesian midget, and you're in denial about it."

The doctor maintained his composure for all of three more seconds before exploding like a large, angry volcano. "How dare you, how. . . I . . . it's . . no she didn't!"

This was all Death needed. He mustered what little supernatural strength he had left and ripped the restraints off his bed.

"Oh no you don't!" said Dr. Ranja.

But it was too late. Death sprinted out the door and ran down the hallway, quickly ducked into a nearby office, and closed the door. He counted to twenty, and then stepped calmly out into the hallway.

A livid looking Dr. Ranja ran past in search of someone who had just insulted him, he was sure of it, he just couldn't remember who had done the insulting.

Death walked back up the hallway and back into Gerald's room.

Gerald still had a big grin on his face as he found that experiencing everything for the first time was rather fun.

"You're back!" said Gerald.

Death ripped open Gerald's restraints and pulled him to his feet. "You, my friend," said Death, "are coming with me."

"Why?" said Gerald happily.

"Because throughout the duration of our fifteen-minute friendship you haven't forgotten who I am. And that is a rare trait indeed."

"Excellent!" said Gerald, "where we going?"

Death threw Gerald a nurse's uniform that sat on a nearby shelf.

"To London, to find the Creator of the Universe."

"Splendid!" said Gerald.

Funnily enough, London was exactly the place where Nigel was currently trudging. After trudging along the Thames for a while, it occurred to Nigel that he had yet to eat. After being hung upside down off a building, and then all those people not dying, and that unfortunate business with the bird, Nigel realized that he was extremely hungry and so he proceeded to his favorite restaurant, not a stone's throw from Piccadilly Circus.

It was a quaint little bistro that had no name because the sign had fallen off years before in a thunderstorm, and some local kids nicked it to use as a coffee table in their new apartment. Since then, the owners never deemed it necessary to replace the sign, as all the people who entered the bistro were regulars. In fact, there hadn't been a new customer for years.

The exterior of the bistro looked run down, the paint was chipping, and the door made an ugly squeaking sound, and it didn't really look like they ever cleaned the windows at all because the glass looked kind of murky in a semi-classy sort of way. This shabby appearance could have been the very reason why there were never any new customers. Or another possible reason, however implausible it seemed, could be that this was the part-time getaway hangout of the divine Creator of the universe. But the thought never really entered into anyone's mind, let alone their imagination.

The interior of the restaurant was completely the opposite of the outside, as it was, in fact, the inside. And it was quite a nice inside, very classy. The whole place was two floors, well-decorated, warm colours, and the sort of lighting that made it feel like it was night time no matter what time of day it actually was. A spiral staircase led up to the second floor, which was smaller than the first but quite quaint, with little windows looking out at the bustling London street life; which could quite often be interpreted as a homeless gentleman peeing on a lamp post. Such sights were not rare in London.

The bistro owners, Marge and Bernard, remained absent from sight, as they were always in the back kitchen cooking away. The front staff included one waitress, one waiter, and a wine waiter named Heinrich who, despite his name, was not German.

Nigel wandered in and headed straight up the stairs to his usual table in the corner next to a small window that allowed the patron a bird's eye view of the massage parlor across the street, which was actually not a massage parlor but a bordello. Interesting people, mostly businessmen trying to look nonchalant by hiding behind their papers when ducking into the establishment, could often be seen.

On a normal day, this amused Nigel to no end, but business appeared to be slow today.

The waitress, a sultry-looking girl who looked to be between eighteen and forty-seven depending on what day it was, popped up next to Nigel's table.

"What can I get ya, m'dear?"

"I'll have the usual and a large bottle of wine to go with my large headache caused by my large boss who it's come to be my opinion is nothing more than a large ass!"

"I'll send Heinrich right over, love."

The waitress vanished and left Nigel alone with his thoughts. He was the only patron on the second floor, which, in Nigel's opinion, was a good thing as he really didn't feel like talking to anyone at the moment. Until Heinrich showed up.

Heinrich was an unusual person. No matter what mood Nigel was in, Heinrich could always calm Nigel down, cheer him up, straighten out his thoughts, or even inspire him. Heinrich's face had a calming effect that felt very much the same way that people did when they were three-years-old and sick but everything was fine the second their mum came in with a warm blanket and said to stay in bed and watch cartoons all day. Nigel had been coming here for years and had found Heinrich to be the best person to unload problems onto as, at least it always seemed, all he had to do was wave his hand, pat Nigel on the back, and everything would be fine again.

Heinrich always looked to be young, in an ageless sort of way. His face seemed impervious to the effects of the years or stress and always shone with a child-like gaiety that most people left behind when they graduated from elementary school. Along with all these remarkable abilities, Heinrich could also pour a glass of wine with such accuracy that he never once spilt a drop. Nigel, lost in his recollections, never even noticed Heinrich until he stood right next to him holding a bottle of the restaurant's finest red wine.

"Oh, Heinrich, how are you?"

Heinrich eased into a friendly smile and raised an eyebrow.

"The day's shaping up quite nicely. By the look on your face, I'd say you're not doing too well."

Nigel gave a sort of *plagh* sound and pushed his wine glass toward Heinrich, who proceeded to flawlessly fill it. Heinrich nodded knowingly and pulled up a chair.

"Why don't you tell me about it, then?"

Nigel savored the smell of the wine for a moment before taking a gulp. He wiped his mouth on his sleeve and let out a sigh.

"I've been walking around trying to figure it all out, the dead people not dying, the nervous ducks, me getting fired, the elf warnings, the powers that I once had, we've been over that before, the first time we met, I think?" He let out another sigh. "I can't help thinking that there are too many strange, random events, that maybe they're all connected. I think I'm supposed to be the one figuring it out. Things always happen for a reason but I don't know where to start."

Heinrich shrugged.

"The most random things can often be connected, even at a very remote level. The best place to start is always at the beginning. Which really is just common sense; if we started things like this at the end, there'd be nothing to figure out. I'm sure everything will turn out okay in the end." Heinrich stood, patted Nigel on the head, dropped a napkin on the table, and vanished.

This wasn't quite the advice or response he had hoped for. In the past, Heinrich sat and they spoke for hours; this time, he hadn't even had chance to get to the part about his gambling problem.

Well, this is turning out to be a rather disheartening da—Nigel stopped in mid-thought. He had picked up the napkin Heinrich had dropped with the full intention of wiping his brow when all of a sudden he noticed the writing on the back. Heinrich had left him a note.

My dearest Nigel,

I apologize for the inability to talk with you openly but unwanted eyes and ears are observing us. There are many things happening which you will soon understand to be important. However, in order to discover them, you are going to have to stop prattling around, forget the gambling, forget your lack of employment, and get back on the right path. In order to accomplish this I can offer you two pieces of advice. 1) Go home and check your messages. 2) If you see any black cats, kick them as hard as possible. This last one is extremely important and must be followed to the letter.

Kindest regards,

Heinrich.

Under the circumstances, the note didn't come as a complete surprise as it had hardly been a normal day to start with. Heinrich had never led him wrong in the past, and although at first glance it would appear that his favorite wine waiter had gone off the deep end, there was still a good possibility that his note had some sense to it. Taking all this into consideration, Nigel stuffed the note in his pocket, ordered his food to go, and headed off home to check his messages. The drive home took longer than usual as traffic had to be diverted due to rioting morticians and funeral workers who were angry that they had suddenly found themselves out of work.

Nineteen.

The cat formerly known as Fuzzbucket, the unholy vessel for Satan himself, was at that very moment standing in a telephone box on the outskirts of London. He experienced extreme difficulty using the phone as, firstly, he didn't appear to be tall enough to reach the receiver, and secondly, he had no money. The former he finally solved by jumping up and balancing on top of the telephone itself. His perch, however, was not very large and although he'd managed to hold the receiver between his two front paws while dialing the operator with one of his free back paws he had developed a bad habit of losing balance and slipping off.

"Bloody typical," said the Devil. "Of all the cats in the entire world I get the one with no sense of balance."

After several attempts, the Prince of Darkness finally managed to place a call and get the operator on the line, a free call which resolved his second difficulty. The operator sounded a little like a seagull that had been punched in the nose, or rather, the beak: squeaky, with a sort of nasal quality.

"This is the operator, how may I help you?"

The essence of all evil in the world pondered the best way to go about answering the question.

"Hello, my name is Marcus and I work in the kitchens at Majestic Technologies. I'd like to know where I can purchase around two thousand, three hundred and seventy-two lemons and have them shipped here immediately?"

The operator's brain clicked over the request a couple of times before realizing that the asker of the question was being completely serious.

"I'm sorry, sir, I don't think anyone provides that sort of service in the local vicinity."

The Devil didn't miss a beat.

"Ohh, really? That's too bad, because I have to make a rather large lemon meringue pie and that just won't work unless I get these lemons."

"Well, I'm sorry, sir, but I can't even imagine where you'd—oh, that's strange."

"What's stra—hacckkaffagchhchh!" said Satan.

"Are you all right, sir?" said the concerned nasal reply.

"I'm fine, just a hairball. You were saying?"

"Well, I was just glancing over the morning news and noticed that there's an advertisement for Bahama Lemons. Apparently there's a big lemon sale this weekend, they're going to be flying in tons of them all week."

"Ahh, I see," said the Devil, "and when you say flying in, where exactly will they be landing?"

"Well, I suppose the airport."

"You're sure about that?"

"Well, yes."

"The airport."

"Yes, the airport."

"Ahh, I see."

The Devil pondered this while the operator nursed a pregnant silence.

"Excuse me, sir, is there anything else I can do for you?" said the operator.

"No, you ridiculous mortal," said Satan. And with that, he hung up. "This is perfect, a plane loaded with lemons. Now all I need are some idiotic underlings to do my bidding."

The thought provoked a warm, fuzzy feeling in the pit of his stomach, the kind he always got when he considered reducing mortals to being his henchmen. This kind of job would take brains and brawn, two qualities rarely found in a single individual, much less a minion.

Fuzzbucket the unholy possessed cat grinned from ear to ear. Laughter engulfed him, a soft giggle growing into a terrifying and heart-chilling cackle that could split rocks and turn the hardest murderer into a crying little girl, which was promptly interrupted by a *hacckkaaffaagchhchh*as the Ruler of Hell spat up another hairball.

"Lemons," repeated Celina to herself.

She'd been sitting on the kitchen table for a good half hour, considering the many reasons why deranged mechanical elves might be looking for lemons. She considered, then discarded, the possibility of the creatures wanting to eat as impossible; it wasn't even in their basic programming.

When the catastrophe that was Betsy the Hamster occurred, the programmers realized that no AI unit could hold the vast information of the universe, so when they built the elves, their brains were given limited capabilities and only functional reasoning so they would be obedient servants. Their knowledge consisted of Christmas traditions and basic knowledge of math, science, English, and physics. There didn't seem any need for anything else. Their function was to be a Christmas elf, give out gifts, look cute, that was it.

Lemons. Since her close encounter with the evil elf, which proved exactly what she suspected had happened, she understood that the artificially intelligent elves were running around of their own free will.

This defined the problem with artificial intelligence; if it wanted to do something, it would do it. Such technical errors had hounded The

Santa Claus Project since the first elf blinked to life. The thought process of the elves, and the main unit itself, utilized a series of mathematical algorithms that weighed up the possibility, reasons, and choices of any thought or action. These algorithms then produced an answer that then compared to a statistical database that in turn produced the final decision.

For example: the elf would be switched on. It would realize that it was very dark. The algorithms would kick in and come up with the two answers: that it was either nighttime or the elf's eyes were closed. Both answers would be drawn up in a pros and cons list and compared to a simple statistical database that would hold the percentages of a number of tests to do with the level of light at nighttime and the percentage of people who cannot see through their own eyelids. Being that the light level was low, the elf's artificial brain would determine that its eyes were in fact closed and would then open them. The entire process took a quarter of a millisecond. The algorithms were written by Celina and other experts considered the system flawless. However, the statistical databases were written by a French scientist who had worked on The Santa Claus Project for the first four years before getting fired for constant acts of indecent exposure, raging flatulence, and licking people when they weren't looking. Such acts were common in the southern regions of France, but they proved to be a little distracting for those working around him. The company had to let him go. After his departure, flaws began to show up in the statistical data; some of them seemed downright fictitious.

Despite the team's best efforts, they were unable to iron out all the flaws and had been trying to fix the mistakes for almost a year. In the meantime, the team build the rest of the elves but kept them switched off, as the elves' thought processes, although intelligent, were somewhat deranged. An unfortunate incident occurred involving a flock of sheep on a farm just outside of London when one of the elf units powered up by accident. The marketing team covered over the event and had it written up in the local newspaper as a possible alien attack. The general public figured it was just a bunch of kids fooling around. The farmer was probably the angriest of everyone, as he couldn't figure out for the life of him why anyone would want to paint all his sheep fluorescent orange and then glue them to the nearest trees. Although such events were not entirely unheard of in certain parts of Yorkshire, things like that just didn't happen near London. It was uncalled for.

"Lemons," said Celina. Maybe she had looked too far into the problem. She put down the rolling pin that she'd been nursing ever since the evil elf left, and paced back and forth, trying to clear her mind. The lights had been switching on and off for the past fifteen minutes and chose this moment to shut off. Celina sprang for her rolling pin as if expecting elves to come charging through the door at any moment. When none came, she eased up a little and continued pacing.

Lemons? And then it hit her.

Neville watched the Ukrainian mountain goat stalk around in its cage. He had special plans for this creature. He'd had it flown in from Ukraine two months ago for a very specific purpose.

"Mr. Snell?"

"Yes, Beatrice," said Neville, still watching the goat.

"Thought you'd like an update on the Majestic Technologies situation, sir."

The goat noticed Neville and threw itself at the bars with so much force that the bars bent outward ever so slightly. The thing about this particular Ukrainian mountain goat was that it was absolutely deranged. Neville had specifically ordered a deranged one. A Ukrainian goat expert needed several weeks of searching to find one.

"Meh-eh-eh-eh-eh," said the goat. It was important to note at this point that the goat did not actually say *meh-eh-eh-eh* but if the sound of a goat was taken and written on paper, that was exactly what it would look like.

"Feisty, isn't she?"

"Sir?"

"The goat, man, the goat!"

"Oh, yes, sir, very feisty. Lord Cherrytick will be most surprised," boomed Beatrice.

Lord Cherrytick was a third-generation rich kid who wasn't really a Lord but insisted that people refer to him as one because it made him sound important. He despised Neville and just for good measure, Neville despised him back. The incident occurred four months ago at Dingo's, an exclusive gentleman's club that required a great deal of money to get into. Men generally went there to escape their wives, have a drink with other rich men, play cards to win other rich men's money, or enjoy a fantastic meal prepared by the hands of Chef Generalloux.

Lord Cherrytick fancied himself a bit of a card shark and took great pride in beating most opponents when it came to the game of poker. Four months ago, he and Neville were the last two standing in a game of poker at Dingo's. After finally deciding to sit down, Neville and Lord Cherrytick continued to play.

The pot was up to three million, far past the usual club limits. The two men displayed their hands. Neville believed he had won, but due to a lot of alcohol and the misconception that the three of hearts actually was the queen of spades, he lost to Lord Cherrytick. Neville didn't care, three million was nothing.

As Neville left the table, Lord Cherryticks sneered, "Next time I'll write the winning combinations on a sticky note, might help you with your game."

The other rich gentlemen laughed as only rich gentlemen can and Neville felt a feeling that he did not like: embarrassment. Unfortunately for Lord Cherrytick, Neville was famous for quite inventive revenges.

"Meh-eh-eh," said the goat and charged the cage again.

Neville laughed. "Beatrice, have the goat delivered to Lord Cherrytick's bathroom this evening at around 2:00 a.m. I'm sure when he takes his 3:00 a.m. constitutional, the appearance of a half-deranged Ukrainian mountain goat in his bathroom will come as a bit of a shock."

"I dare say it will, sir."

"You had some news for me?"

"Yes, Mr. Snell, we've been unable to contact anyone inside Majestic Technologies all morning. We fear there may be some sort of situation."

"Meh-eh-eh-eh," said the goat.

"All right, better to be proactive about these things. After lunch, get the car ready, and we'll head to the lawyers. Call them and let them know we're coming."

"Very good, sir."

"Meh-eh-eh-eh," agreed the goat.

Twenty.

Death incarnate and his newfound friend sat aboard a cushy Boeing 747 waiting for the plane to take off. Apparently, there had been some delay, as a lemon shipment had yet to be loaded into the cargo bay. The delay was a nuisance, but Death could deal with it. He could even handle Gerald's constant questions. He could not, however, deal with the flight attendant who continued to offer him peanuts and then return ten minutes later and repeat herself, believing she hadn't seen him before and should therefore offer him some peanuts.

This repetitive scenario drove Death crazy until he took to drinking the small bottles of free wine that Nexus airlines provided for all international flights. The flight attendant was completely oblivious to the amount of wine she gave out, as she could not remember Death, or ever seeing him before, or ever giving him any wine or peanuts.

After a two-hour delay and seven small bottles of wine, Death started to warm up to the flight attendant and had taken to calling her Peanut Lady whenever he had the chance. Instead of refusing the peanuts, he accepted them and then would gleefully fling them backward over his head.

An elderly man named Stanton Waring, who was partially blind in his right eye, partially deaf in his left ear, and had no sense of smell, was in constant confusion, as every ten minutes a packet of peanuts would hit him in the head. He had come to the conclusion that one of the flight attendants was angry at him, but being the old war horse that he was, and seeing no reason for the constant throwing of peanuts, he had taken the relentless assault as an act of war. He watched the flight attendants closely as they walked by, eyeing them up and down for any kind of malice, sizing up the precise moment when he would exact his revenge.

Gerald, on the other hand, had a fabulous time. Not only had he ceased to be a penguin and become a human, not only had he been assaulted and tied to a bed, but he'd also managed to make a friend, and discovered the joy of small bottles of wine that Death happily shared with him. Gerald had pelted Death with questions since their escape from the hospital, and Death had done his best to answer them even though he didn't really understand the whole penguin business himself.

"So what is this we're sitting in?" asked Gerald.

"S'plane, big metal thing with wings, allows humans to fly all over the place," answered Death.

Gerald pointed to a woman wearing a large pink hat and asked, "Who's that?"

"S'woman."

"And that?"

"That's a child."

"And that thing up there?"

"That's a bag."

"Hmm, a bag. This is all very interesting. All this stuff is floating around in my head but it doesn't all connect."

"Yes, well, let's take it slow. I mean, you were a penguin this morning and now look at you. More wine?"

Several minutes later and under the influence of the cheap booze, Gerald found himself glued to the window staring at the men who were trying to load crate loads of lemons into the cargo hold.

An older, taller man who looked to be the superior of the bunch waved his arms and shouted at the other men. The situation was such that there just wasn't enough room for all the lemons in the cargo hold unless they wanted to offload some of the passengers' luggage. The workers took the superior's comment as being literal and offloaded half of the luggage. This made the superior furious, hence all the arm waving and shouting.

Gerald, of course, didn't know this but found the whole event rather entertaining as he thought the man looked like he was trying to fly by flapping his arms and getting himself nowhere.

The flight attendant approached and offered a sickly sweet smile through a pair of dark red lips and heavy eyeliner.

"I'm sorry for the delay, gentlemen, we will be ready to leave in a matter of minutes. Could I get you some peanuts? Or some wine, perhaps?"

Gerald was too busy looking out the window but Death happily took the offer on both counts.

"I'd absholutely love shum peanuts my lovely peanut lady," said Death. "And my friend here, he wash a penguin ya know, he'll take two," proclaimed Death and held up four fingers to enforce the point.

The flight attendant cheerily handed over three packs of peanuts and refilled the wine.

Death flung all three back over his head in rapid succession.

Gerald giggled to himself as the situation outside drew to a close with the rest of the lemons successfully being crammed in with the luggage, and the workers moved off the runway while throwing lemons at each other.

The *fasten seat belts* sign flicked on and a voice boomed over the PA system.

"Passengers of flight 34x-19457EKL, this is your captain speaking."

"Wassat?" asked Gerald.

"That, my lil pegwin, ish the bloke whosh flying the plan."

The captain continued. "We'll be taking off in a matter of moments and apologize for the extensive delay. The flight attendants will now explain the safety procedures. I hope you enjoy the flight and please feel free to try our excellent Lemon Meringue Pie." There was a loud *bing* and the plane began to move.

Jeremiah the goldfish was completely astonished to find that someone had placed him in a glass bowl, filled it with water, and dropped a castle into it. This exact same surprise had occurred one-million-thirty-three-thousand-two-hundred-thirty-three times in his life. And this would not be the last time, either.

Jeremiah's premonitions and constant prophetic abilities appeared to be getting more severe as the day progressed, although he didn't actually know this because he couldn't remember. Words, letters, and numbers continued to fly into his head on a seemingly regular basis. He continued to try and record what he saw by moving his little coloured rocks around, but what he created made no sense to him at all and made him frustrated. However, moments later, he completely forgot what he was frustrated about and instead decided to swim in and out of the castle that he'd just found in his bowl.

Jeremiah was quite happy doing this, right up until he heard a muffled sound outside the bowl. Jeremiah swam up to the edge to see what made the sound but he couldn't really make out any distinct shapes. A tall sort of blur looked to be moving around, but Jeremiah failed to see any details. Then he forgot all about the sound and the blur and instead began to wonder why he was staring out of his fish bowl. He shrugged, as well as a fish can shrug, and turned around, only to have a creepy feeling run right up his spine. It would appear that someone had placed a castle in his bowl.

Nigel lived in a respectable, uptown, London apartment that overlooked a quaint greengrocer, a video rental store owned by two generally happy East Indian fellows known as the Raja brothers, and a small pottery shop that no one ever entered. The apartment building itself had been built well over a hundred years ago, but due to fire damage had been renovated several times.

Nigel lived on the third, and best, floor. The ground floor was the lowest, and anyone walking by the ground floor apartments never fought the urge to look through the windows. Thankfully, the ground floor was occupied nearly entirely by exhibitionists and they loved the attention.

The first floor had been the residence of a very cunning and talented arsonist responsible for the fires in the building and several more around London until he was finally arrested and sent to a prison in the northern regions of England where he was re-named Snugglyboo by his large, yet well-mannered, cellmate.

It was rumoured that the second floor was haunted by a marauding band of sheep poachers who had holed up in one of the rooms back in the late eighteen hundreds in order to avoid the authorities. One of the sheep they had recently stolen from a nearby farm became violent and ferocious due to eating some bad fruit and ended up killing the poachers. The story related that their ghosts haunted the second floor looking for the one sheep that turned bad. And so not only was the third floor the highest, it was also considered the best, as there was no lack of privacy, no ghosts, and no prior history with Snugglyboo the arsonist.

Following Heinrich's orders, Nigel entered his apartment and checked his messages. He found three. The first was a telephone salesman offering fantastic rates on the latest and greatest edition of an encyclopedia that would no doubt transform even the dullest, dimwitted person into someone of magnificent intellect. Nigel deleted the message without giving it a second thought, or a first one for that matter.

The second was a message from his mother asking him to call and talk to his father who had, apparently out of boredom and old age, decided to start a *Save the Ducks Foundation*, after he read a report about how ducks were being used for nerve gas testing in Australia.

129

His newfound passion for the feathered, quacking birds drove his wife up the wall, as there were regular shipments of nervous ducks coming in from Australia. Being that the Reinhardts lived in a one-story bungalow somewhere south of Essex, there just wasn't enough room for all the ducks and Nigel's mother was highly concerned about the state of her fake Persian rugs.

Nigel made a mental note to call his parents sometime in the near future and continued to the last message, which appeared to be a woman in some form of hysteria ranting about out-of-control cyborg elves at Majestic Technologies.

A thought at the back of Nigel's brain shifted slightly and peered around many other thoughts. The memory of Mrs. Jones mentioning that her cat Fuzzbucket, that had been possessed by the devil, had mentioned Majestic Technologies shifted nervously. It felt it was about to be disturbed.

Nigel had once read an article about the advancements in modern technology allowing robots to learn and solve problems. Japan was definitely a forerunner in the advancements, as they already had robots walking up walls, bringing the morning coffee, and completing simple household tasks. The leading American artificial intelligence research lab had the misfortune of being located in Texas. The most impressive thing the crack group of scientists at the Texas Institute for Technology, rather unfortunately abbreviated TIT., had accomplished was making a small robot dog belch the alphabet.

The Irish had managed to form a committee to undertake the research and development of artificial intelligence, they'd purchased the necessary equipment, built a laboratory, and then all gone down to the pub to celebrate and had been there ever since. All this Nigel knew to be true, as he'd read it in a popular and renowned magazine.

Cyborg elves sounded like something straight out of a bad science fiction movie. After all the goings-on of the day, this was the last thing that Nigel hoped for. Things had been entirely too weird, with people not dying anymore, getting fired, the disturbing flashback, not to mention the whole hanging upside down off a building incident.

Although it went against every natural urge in his body, he decided that enough was quite enough, even more than enough, in some people's opinions. He would not respond to the crazed woman who had left him a message.

Probably just a prank, anyway.

For a while, Nigel had been receiving phone calls from a left-wing communist religious cult that had become convinced that Nigel's goldfish represented the missing link to the saviour of the universe. Nigel had received a total of three-thousand-two-hundred-sixty-three phone calls from the insane cult members before finally deciding that they were in fact a bunch of complete nutters and changing his phone number. What Nigel really wanted was some food, as he hadn't eaten since breakfast and—

"Food!" said Nigel.

Two thoughts crisscrossed his mind and then collided somewhere in the middle. He'd forgotten to feed his pet fish. Nigel was immensely obsessed with his pet fish, Jeremiah, for reasons of which he himself was completely oblivious. He never really had any pets growing up and, as a consequence, was no great lover of animals, although he did feel a small twang of grief about the bird that had been crushed inadvertently by his falling desk earlier in the day. Nigel could never understand the human fascination with keeping animals in their house, the comfort that they allegedly provided, and the amount of waste that they excreted in a one-week period: it none of that balanced correctly in his mind. It all seemed rather bizarre to him, and so he had never really ever thought about getting a pet until one day, while visiting his Great-Aunt Margo in Birmingham, he came across a small pond located somewhere in an obscure piece of countryside where Nigel got himself completely lost. Every time Nigel tried to recount, even to himself, the events that brought about the consequence of him owning a pet goldfish, everything seemed to blur and he often blacked out. He remembered leaving London in a rented car, he remembered getting lost somewhere after Essex, he remembered the pond, and Jeremiah staring innocently up out of the green goo, and then he was back in his London apartment looking for something to put his new fish in. As far as he remembered, he never made it to a visit with his aged relative. What was even stranger was that he later discovered that he'd never had a Great-Aunt Margo in the first place. The whole trip seemed like some sort of deranged dream.

Life continued as it normally did and Nigel ceased to dwell on the subject. Day in and day out, he came home, and happily cooed at the fish, tapped on the bowl, and sprinkled tiny flakes of food into the water. However, this time Nigel did not make it to the sprinkling part, as a wave of shock passed over his face, spread right across his head, and proceeded down the length of his body. The words *beware the elf*, nicely arranged out of colourful rocks in the bottom of Jeremiah's bowl, stared right back up at the shocked Nigel.

Jeremiah happily blew some bubbles, as the dark shape outside his bowl seemed to fall over and vanish from sight.

Once Nigel regained consciousness, he fed Jeremiah and ten minutes later was in a taxi on his way to Majestic Technologies.

Twenty-One.

A taxi driver named Rupert manned the cab that Nigel had the misfortune of climbing into. It took him twenty-three minutes to convince Rupert that Nigel wasn't even slightly interested in Rupert's collection of hotel soaps from around the world. Disgruntled, confused, and slightly pissed off was the state of Nigel's mood by the time he managed to tell Rupert where exactly he wanted to go. It took an additional hour and a half, including two stops, one to pick up cigarettes and another for Rupert to write his name on a wall in an alleyway, which apparently was something he liked to do all over London, to finally reach Majestic Technologies.

A light drizzle began to drop itself toward the ground as the almost non-visible sun dipped toward the horizon and Nigel, very much relieved, exited the confines of Rupert's cab. The two dark grey towers of Majestic Technologies rose up behind a tall security fence, looking angry and lacking in light against the dimming backdrop. The drizzle suddenly changed temperament, decided to quit with the light rain, and resolved to throw itself down instead.

Instantly soaked to the skin, Nigel made his way toward the entrance.

Celina sat in the corner of the dining room and rocked back and forth like a little girl lost. To her left lay a very shiny and obviously sharp kitchen knife; to her right was a mess of empty yogurt cartons.

In the space of a day, her world had been tipped upside down. She had woken up, the same as any other morning, hair a mess, breath that would stun a donkey, and the distinctly optimistic view that this would be the day she would come up with a solution that would make the whole Santa Claus Project fall into place. As it turned out, this was actually the day when the elves would revolt, take over the building, force Celina to hide out in the company dining room all day, and live in a perpetual fear for her life, as she really had no idea what the elves were capable of.

A creak off to the corner made her lunge for the knife and roll sideways, ending in a poised crouch that she'd seen action heroes and heroines do in movies all the time. At this point, she felt something tap her on the back, making Celina jump, let out a small yelp, and turn to come face to face with an extremely short, pudgy elf with a round and very red face.

"Hullo," said the elf and grinned.

Celina made a sort of *hulmph* sound and passed out.

The plane taxied to a stop at Heathrow Airport's Terminal 3, Gate 25. A small contingent of frustrated airport security guards waited to meet the plane. Close to the end of their shift, they had received a message from an incoming flight from the Bahamas. Apparently an elderly gentleman who didn't listen very well, and couldn't really see much, had attacked one of the flight attendants under the misapprehension that she had been pelting him with packets of peanuts for the duration of the flight. Several passengers had to pry the gentleman off the stewardess but not before he sank his false teeth into her upper arm. The airport security guards escorted the subdued gentleman off the plane despite his protests and claims that he was provoked into the attack.

The plane slowly emptied until the final two heavily inebriated passengers who had no luggage staggered out of the gate, completely oblivious to the fact that they had both completely lost all feeling in their legs. The passenger wearing the black robe and pale complexion headed for the nearest airport pub while the other passenger who had previously been a penguin relieved himself into a fake potted plant, much to the distress of the Skipton Women's Sewing Group who sat waiting for their plane to Paris.

Big Ernie sat at the round poker table in the basement suite of his employer's apartment concentrating hard. In order to concentrate hard, Big Ernie had to screw up his face; it looked like he had tried to ingest several sour candies all at once. For ultimate concentration purposes, Ernie would also stick the tip of his tongue out of the left side of his mouth. The whole scene of Big Ernie trying to concentrate would very likely have scared any small child and caused nervous glances from any adult, young or old.

The door behind Big Ernie began to rattle, followed by some *clicks,* before finally swinging open to reveal Itch, standing in all his smallness with an angry smirk on his face and several boxes of cereal in his arms.

"This isn't good at all, Ernie, not good at all!"

"Uhh, Itch?" said Ernie.

"Not only did you almost drop one of my customers today while holding him over the edge of a building."

"Umm, Itch?" said Big Ernie again.

"Not only did you eat all my cereal for lunch."

"Well," began Ernie, to which Itch held up a hand.

"Not only did you put a nice scratch down the side of my car, but you also locked me out of my own house while I was out buying more cereal. Now, my large, none-too-bright associate, care to explain?"

Itch moved out of the doorway and dropped the cereal boxes onto the couch. He swung around, planning full well to fix a mean and frightening glare straight on Big Ernie, but his facial expression never made it. Instead, he half smirked, raised an eyebrow, frowned, and then creased his forehead.

"Ernie?" said Itch.

"Yes, Itch?" said Ernie.

"Ernie, why is there a cat sitting at my table?" asked Itch, somewhat bewildered.

Sure enough, the black cat formerly known as Fuzzbucket sat in the chair opposite Big Ernie, his yellowish green eyes fixed upon Itch.

"He'd like to talk to us," said Big Ernie, "about some lemons."

Jeremiah swam around his bowl as fast as possible; the sheer exhilaration of the water rushing past his gills felt most satisfying to him. He stopped for a moment, struggling to remember what it was he was doing and why he was doing it, when all of a sudden, a rush of energy surged through his tiny brain, causing electrical sparks to flash around his bowl. Jeremiah mustered all his strength and flung the unknown force out of his bowl, out of the apartment, and away from London at an astonishing speed.

The unknown energy slowly began to take physical form as it raced across the sky before finally crash-landing and skidding some thirty miles to a halt somewhere to the south of the Himalayas. A light breeze floated through the air as an Entity which had not been seen on Earth in over two hundred thousand years stood up, dusted itself off, and proceeded to walk in the direction of London.

Twenty-Two.

Model#2984739 clicked to life and looked around before realizing that its eyes had yet to come online, which would explain the blindness he currently experienced. He, if he was in fact a *he*, ran a diagnostic check. A series of ones and zeroes ran instantly through Model#2984739's computer processor mind and formulated the result—*yes*, his body seemed to be in working order; he wiggled his fingers to prove it. His personality files suddenly sprang to life and began to feed personal information into his memory banks, which, for space-saving reasons, were located in his left thigh.

A minor ache formed behind his left eye, then just as quickly disappeared. Model#2984739's onboard scanning software dismissed the ache as non-threatening and he flicked on his eyeballs to prove it. Model#2984739 blinked a few times and zoomed his vision in and out before finally bringing his surroundings into focus. A sharp *ding* signaled the completion of the upload of his personality files; he could proceed with mission parameters. This time, an excruciatingly sharp pain slapped him across the back of his head, causing his circuit boards to jump and the little bells on the end of his shoes to dingle.

His onboard scanning software tried once again to load the mission parameters. The pain was so extreme that Model#2984739 gave out a slight yelp. And then, without any provocation whatsoever, Model#2984739 started to dance; it started as a slight wiggle of the hips, and then an occasional head jiggle, before blowing up into a full-out groove.

There was no music, no band or DJ, just a half-empty warehouse and a robotic elf dancing to the sweet rhythmic tunes of silence. As Model#2984739 executed a lovely sideways shimmy, a string of letters ran through his mind, formed words, and promptly spelled out:

Model#2984739: aka: Eggnog

Mission Parameter Files not loaded.

Error! Error! Error! Error!

The dancing came to a stop as quickly as it had begun. Model#2984739 stared inwardly at his name until it faded away.

Obviously, there is something wrong here.

His system administration software immediately recognized Eggnog's self-awareness of the problem and advised him to seek technical help from the nearest technician. Eggnog examined his surroundings and decided that there were no technicians in the immediate vicinity and that he should go and look for one. He straightened his little elf hat, which had become dislodged while he danced, and wandered off across the warehouse floor toward a red exit sign that emitted an annoying sort of electronic buzzing sound.

After exploring several hallways, visiting more than one bathroom, and climbing up several flights of stairs and through a rather nice ventilation shaft, Eggnog found himself in some sort of cafeteria. He walked around the perimeter of the dining room before noticing a woman sitting by herself in the far corner; she seemed to be rocking back and forth in a distressed fashion.

The memory banks in Eggnog's upper left thigh told him that she was indeed a technician. He walked under several of the tables and brushed against one of the cheap plastic chairs that creaked slightly, causing the technician to grab a nearby knife, leap to her feet, and awkwardly roll sideways. Eggnog hurried over to her and tapped her on the shoulder. She spun around with a terrified look on her face.

"Hullo," said Eggnog.

The technician made a *hulmph* sound and passed out.

Eggnog hopped back, obviously startled, and looked around, trying to think of what to do next. A computerized feeling, very comparable to confusion, washed over him. At this point, his onboard computer came up with several error signals and his body broke into a sort of Funky Chicken dance.

The cat formerly known as Fuzzbucket sat at one side of the table, a dark glint in his eyes, tail swishing ominously.

Itch and Big Ernie sat at the other side of the table, looking confused. Itch couldn't figure out why a cat would want two tons of lemons, or why they should steal them for the cat, or even why this cat was talking in the first place.

"I'll explain it again," said the cat coolly. "This body I am in is that of a cat, as I'm sure two smart gentlemen such as yourselves have already realized. My intention was to fall into a much nicer body, a body I had picked out myself. He was once a swimmer, actually, but for some strange reason the opportunity was stolen from me, and I ended up inside this ridiculous feline."

"My head hurts," said Big Ernie.

"Easy does it," said Itch to the cat, "You'll have to use smaller words, you're just confusing him."

The cat fixed Big Ernie with a glare and raised his hackles a little.

"I am in fact the Prince of Darkness." He paused for dramatic effect, letting the full impact of his words soak in. Unfortunately, it appeared, to the Devil at least, that some minds are less sponge-like than others.

Both Itch and Big Ernie stared blankly.

The cat rolled his eyes.

"I am Beelzebub!"

Big Ernie scratched his head.

"Lucifer!"

Big Ernie let out a short laugh.

"Lucy's a girl name."

"Not Lucy, Lucifer, *Lucifer!* The Devil, I'm the Devil."

Itch shrugged. "But you look like a cat."

"I'm inside the cat!"

Big Ernie leaned closer and stared into the cat's eyes. A smile spread across his face and he scratched the Devil's head lovingly.

"He's cute," said Big Ernie, "can we keep him?"

"Stop that, you imbecile!"

Itch got to his feet and began pacing, because his thoughts often held more clarity while he paced.

"Let's just presume for a moment that what you say is true. And that you are in fact the Devil trapped in a cat's body. Why exactly do you want us to steal two tons of lemons from the airport and deliver them to some factory on the other side of the city?"

The Devil moved off the table as Big Ernie kept attempting to scratch behind his ears, and leapt up onto a nearby shelf so he was eye level with Itch.

"I have put some plans in motion that will cause utter chaos around the world. However, as with all masterfully thought out plans, there are always unforeseen snags."

"Snags," said Itch thoughtfully.

"Yes, snags," said the cat.

"And in order to bypass these snags, as it were, you need us to steal two tons of lemons from Heathrow Airport and deliver them to this factory?"

"It's a laboratory," said the cat.

"What do they do there?" asked Itch.

"It doesn't matter. I'm not paying you to know things," hissed the cat.

"You're going to pay us?"

"No, not really."

Itch stopped pacing and looked at the cat.

"I don't know, stealing isn't really our cup of tea, we're more into threatening and collecting money."

"And hanging people off the side of buildings," said Big Ernie.

"Yes, thank you, Ernie," said Itch, "we do that, too."

"We're very good at it," said Big Ernie.

"Very," said Itch.

The Devil's hackles sprung up, his eyes narrowed, and he fixed a cruel stare on Itch. "Allow me to put it this way for you, just so we understand each other. Either you do my bidding, or I set your house on fire, your choice."

With a flick of the cat's tail, the couch was on fire.

Big Ernie leaped to his feet in a panic. Itch stood motionless in shock.

The cat blinked and the flames died down and vanished.

"Now," said the Devil, "do we have an understanding?"

The airport lounge at Heathrow bustled with people heading here and there, trying to find their gate, their luggage, and their children or, as in most cases, the nearest duty-free store. It was customary for people with a lengthy stopover to take a nap on one of the most amazingly uncomfortable chairs lining the centre of the elongated lounge. And so the sight of a pale gentleman dressed in a black robe and a rather good-looking man dressed in a nurse's outfit snoozing together, Gerald's head resting on Death's lap, was not entirely unusual. Especially since few people gave Death even a second glance.

A polite British voice came over the PA system.

"Could Stanton Waring please return to the security station, Stanton Waring to the security station." At this point, a group of confused-looking security guards ran past the seats where Death and Gerald were sleeping. A rather sluggish security guard with odd-sized feet and an out-of-control beard stopped to catch his breath and barked into a radio.

"Have you seen him yet?"

A static-filled voice came back at him.

"Not yet, sir."

"Keep looking, a half-naked old man shouldn't be able to get too far in these crowds!"

"Affirmative, sir, out," said the radio voice.

The guard moved to chase after the other guards and accidentally kicked Death's leg. "Sorry," he offered as he vanished into the crowds.

Death woke up with a start and looked around, trying to grasp his location. A random haze of events seeped through his mind, something to do with Ireland, a beach, a hospital, no one dying, a Polynesian midget, some nonsense about a penguin, flying on a plane and then, rather unfortunately, it all clicked into place.

"Oh," he said glumly, "now I remember." He tapped Gerald on the head.

Gerald opened his eyes, stretched, and gazed up at Death. A gleeful smile spread across his face as he realized that he was still no longer a penguin. He sat up, far too quickly, and all the pains in the world suddenly congregated inside his head and started slapping each other.

"Ahrg," said Gerald.

"Yes, quite true," said Death.

"Ahh," said Gerald, "don't shout."

"I'm not shouting."

"It certainly sounds like you are. What's wrong with me? Is this what it normally feels like to wake up as a human?"

"I don't know, I'm not human, either."

Gerald clutched his head and moaned softly.

"It's called a hangover," said Death as he got up, "and it's one of the most painful feelings you're ever likely to experience. I suffered from them for the first couple of decades of my existence but it's been a good few thousand years so I'm pretty much used to them by now."

Death helped Gerald to his feet.

"Gaa," said Gerald.

"I know what you need," said Death and looked around the lounge.

A large man with tattoos on both arms, a shaved head, and dressed entirely in denim sat nursing a duty-free bag that clearly contained cans of beer.

"Stay here," said Death.

Gerald complied and promptly sat back down in the fond hope that the world would spin a lot less if he was closer to ground level. He was wrong.

Death walked over to the man with the beers, who observed him with a sort of disinterest right up until Death reached down and took a can of beer out of his bag. The man shot up like a rocket and poked a pudgy and vicious tattooed finger at Death.

"Here! What yer think yer doin?"

"I'm sorry," said Death, looking confused, "what's the matter?"

The man's face turned a pretty purplish-pink.

"I'll tell yer what's th'matta, matey!"

Death folded his arms.

"Yes, go on."

The colour of the man's faced turned back to normal and he lowered his pointing finger. He tried his hardest to think what he was about to say but the words seemed to be lost.

"I, uhh, well—"

Death tapped his foot impatiently.

"Come on, I don't have all day, is there something you want?"

The man sat back down, still trying to remember what happened.

"No no, uhh, sorry 'bout tha, dint mean t' be a nuisance."

"Quite all right," said Death and walked back toward Gerald. The large man felt very confused until he realized he was missing a beer.

Death handed the beer to Gerald.

"Down this, you'll feel tons better. It's time we got out of here."

Twenty-Three.

The Entity, after wrapping itself in a dark blue cloak and hood, trekked through the foothills of Tibet with no difficulty. The snow was little bother to it, and the cold had no effect whatsoever. Occasionally, a stray mountain goat would wander into the Entity's path, resulting in a swift kick that sent the animal hurtling through the air.

The sight of random goats flying through the air remained quite unnoticed until one of them crashed through the roof of an elderly Tibetan man's hut, landing on his wife. A few residents of the widespread Tibetan village got together to find out why the goats, after all these years, had suddenly begun flying.

One highly regarded member of the village, whose unfortunate given name was Bollux, given to him by his half German, half Tibetan, and the tiniest bit of Irish, parents, was among the group of flying goat hunters. Bollux was highly regarded for the simple reason that he was the only person within miles who owned a camera. Among the small villages of the Tibetan foothills, a camera, considered an extreme luxury item, was a rare thing. Lesser luxury items include blankets without holes in them and cheap toothbrushes donated by some far-off religious groups. Bollux had received the camera as a gift from his uncle in Germany who had as little to do with his nephew in Tibet as humanly possible, but never failed to send him a gift every Christmas. The gift was usually something his uncle had received and didn't want.

Bollux and the others headed in the direction that the goats seemed to be flying from, and before long they came upon a sight that none of them had ever seen before.

The Entity regarded them with little interest except for the fact they stood directly in its way. One of the beings raised a small square box, which flashed at the Entity.

Bollux managed to snap one photo before finding himself well over twenty feet away ina pile of half-frozen hay.

The rest of the flying goat hunting party fled, leaving the Entity to itself. The Entity pulled its cloak tightly around itself and looked up to the sun. The Entity resolved to move faster and broke into a run, beginning at a steady pace and quickly accelerating to the speed of a mature gazelle.

Once Bollux regained consciousness, he resolved to write to his uncle in Germany and send him a picture of what he had just seen.

Six months later, that very same picture appeared out of a fax machine in a small village called Lees located just to the East of Manchester in the northwest of England.

Twenty-Four.

Beatrice held open the door for Neville as he stepped onto the damp pavement and looked up at the twisted concrete and glass structure that was the law firm of Chatham, Chitham, and Chump. Neville loved lawyers;never before had there been such a scrupulous, underhanded, deceiving creature as the lawyer. And just to be on the safe side, Neville employed every lawyer in the entire building.

"Beatrice?"

"Sir?"

"This whole Majestic thing. You don't suppose Celina's in any kind of trouble, do you?"

Neville had tried several times to woo Celina McMannis and had failed miserably every time. Beatrice thought that Celina was cute, nice red hair, kind of skinny, but had a temper that could burn through lead. He understood completely what Neville saw in her; she was unattainable, and Neville liked the challenge.

"I'm sure she's fine, sir."

"I surely hope so," said Neville as he walked toward the law firm.

The last time Neville made a play for Celina's heart, it resulted in many injured flamingos, and Beatrice had a soft spot for pink birds and consequently didn't entirely approve of Neville's continuing pursuit. As a gesture of his love, Neville ordered fifty flamingos placed in Celina's apartment. The flamingos had been genetically manipulated to sing a famous Neil Diamond love song.

Unfortunately, the flamingos didn't have a chance. Celina walked in the door and saw that her apartment was full of loud, pink birds. She panicked, grabbed the nearest golf club, and the rest was a sad history with pink feathers floating everywhere.

A French interior designer named Germain LeFranques decorated the law firm of Chatham, Chitham, and Chump; LeFranques believed everything should be dark or metallic blue, triangular, and have pointy edges. And so the law offices reluctantly drowned in a sea of dark blue metallics with lots of triangles and many a flesh wound. It did, however, look very sharp and impressive, which was exactly what the lawyers wanted.

Neville took the elevator to the eleventh floor, stalked down the hallway with Beatrice and entered the boardroom with a flourish that made the lawyers jump ever so slightly. One knocked over his flower-imprinted teacup.

"Ahh, Mr. Snell," said Charles Chitham, "please have a seat."

Neville was already sitting but Charles continued regardless. "Have you heard anything from the Majestic Technologies labs?"

"No, we've been unable to make contact."

"You must admit, Mr. Snell, this is a little different than the usual legal proceedings. So far, there aren't any wild animals involved."

A few of the lawyers, knowing Neville's colourful legal past, tittered as only old rich gentlemen can. Even Neville couldn't help but smile.

"Very true, Charles," said Neville, "no wild animals this time." He paused for dramatic effect. "This time, there may be some trouble with a bunch of elves."

Twenty pairs of surprised beady eyes stared back at him.

"Elves?" said Charles.

Nigel found entering Majestic Technologies rather easy, as the entire place had been deserted. No security guards lolled at the security station, no lab technicians messed about in the labs, in fact, no one anywhere did anything. All was quiet. Although, after consulting a map of the place he found in the lobby, he thought it entirely possible that there could be people in one of the other buildings, as it seemed that Majestic Technologies spanned three different buildings and one warehouse in the same compound.

The woman on the phone had said something about being locked in the staff dining room, so that seemed to be the best place to start. Nigel found himself thinking about the day's events and how this day seemed not to relate to any other day he had experienced in the last several years.

There must be some sort of significance to all this.

While pondering his past earlier, as he had walked along the River Thames, Nigel couldn't help feeling that he was meant for so much more than the lot he had been dealt in life, and that somewhere out there was some lucky bugger living the life he was meant to have.

In comparison to most humans, Nigel wasn't bad looking, he had his health, lacked wealth but was super-intelligent, and had once possessed great telekinetic power. Surely, something in there should have brought some sort of good karma into his life. But instead, he found himself wandering around a deserted building following a weak lead that turned up on his answering machine. He tried calling out a few times, and then decided that attracting attention to himself might not be the best idea, so he apologized out loud for shouting out loud in the first place, and shut up.

What had the message said? Something about deranged cyborg elves. Firstly, he couldn't figure out why anyone would even create a group of cyborg elves, and secondly, how dangerous could elves be?

On top of everything else, he couldn't shake the fact that the words *beware the elf* had popped into his head on more than one occasion throughout the day, and finally, had appeared at the bottom of his goldfish's bowl. Something that had shocked and scared him, as he no longer had the slightest idea of what the hell was going on.

He ascended a staircase placed below a sign claiming that the stairs in question would lead to the fourth floor. As it turned out, the sign was completely correct and Nigel found himself in a long hallway that stretched out in both directions. Being that the only light source was coming through windows dotted here and there, and a weak light source at that, because the sun had begun to set, Nigel couldn't really see much, anyway. He wished he'd grabbed a flashlight from the security station. His map made less sense than a Chinese menu written in Italian, and so he decided to head down toward the right, for no other reason than it looked less dark and therefore less ominous.

Ominous things were something Nigel wanted very much to avoid, especially if there were elves sneaking around. He didn't want to underestimate a deranged cyborg elf, as he'd never met one and thus couldn't properly assess their capabilities.

While Nigel pondered the possible capabilities of a cyborg elf, a strange sort of giggling sound floated down the hallway straight at him. The sound took him by surprise, and his first inclination was to hide. His second inclination was not really an inclination, more of a question: where to hide? An open closet containing janitor's cleaning equipment proved to be the perfect answer and Nigel hopped in, leaving the door open just a crack, as he couldn't deny his curiosity.

The giggling grew louder and was accompanied by the sound of jingling, of something being dragged over carpet, and was backed up by a worried sort of muffled screaming, and every so often there was a small *pop*. Nigel's mind, smart as it was, had trouble comprehending what he saw next. First, the elf came into view. He was short, cute little nose, rosy cheeks, nice little green elf uniform, and bells on the curled end of his little shoes which dingled merrily with every step.

Aside from the fact that Nigel was staring at an elf, a fact that flew in the face of logic entirely, there was one aspect of the little creature that seemed un-elf like: his face, although cute, had a deranged sort of look to it. His lips curled into a sneer; his eyes, or rather, eye, as Nigel could only see him from the side, had a maniacal quality to it ordinarily found in mime artists. His forehead creased in such a way that he appeared to be angry, although this would seem to contradict the soft, gleeful giggling.

Nigel couldn't decide whether to laugh at the creature or fear for his life. This decision was made almost immediately. The elf dragged a rope that was obviously attached to something heavy, as the elf had to lean forward while he walked in order to haul the weight behind him. Nigel's eyes grew wide and then shrank down as he realized what he was looking at. A spine-tingling coldness ran the length of his back.

Attached to the end of the rope was a pair of legs, which in turn were attached to a man's body, the entire package wrapped up in bubble wrap packaging tied together with more rope. The man's eyes stared wildly through the plastic wrap as he shouted for help but to no avail; the plastic wrap muffled any sound aside from the occasional *pop* of a plastic bubble.

The man squinted as he noticed Nigel and fixed pleading eyes on him. Nigel could only stare back in horror. The man tried to struggle ineffectively against the bonds that held him so tightly he could barely move.

The elf stopped giggling for a second as he dragged the man past Nigel's hiding place and out of sight down the hallway.

"Don't worry," said the elf in a cheery, chipmunk sort of voice, "it won't be long now, the Master will be here soon." This was followed by more maniacal giggling and more muffled screaming.

Nigel closed the closet door and stood in the dark for what seemed like an eternity. He breathed heavily and tried to sort out in his mind what he had just seen, but he just couldn't. It was all too much. Resolutely, he decided that he should find the lunchroom, which meant leaving the safety of the janitor's closet. The most basic animal instinct rose to the surface of Nigel's mind and he started fumbling around in the dark for some sort of weapon. He emerged two minutes later, in one hand a heavy-duty flashlight, in the other, a mop.

Twenty-Five.

As anyone who has tried to get out of Heathrow Airport alive knew from experience, that was not an easy task. Death and Gerald, having never been through Heathrow, mainly because Gerald was once a penguin and Death was once a semi-omnipotent being, had a bit of trouble finding the exit.

Many experts believed that Heathrow Airport may very well have contained some sort of nexus of the universe, a sort of Bermuda Triangle without all the sun and sandy beaches, and may possibly lead to another dimension entirely if one only located the right door. In 1993, an elderly, severely malnourished gentleman wearing grubby clothes and a serious amount of facial growth emerged from the south exit doors of Terminal 3 at Heathrow and screamed at the top of his lungs, "Frreeddoomm!"

The gentleman's screaming attracted the attention of security personnel who dragged him, kicking and screaming, back into the airport. Fingerprints were taken, files were filed, and a lot of coffee was drunk until finally the gentleman was identified as one Alfred McEvoy of Shropshire, reported missing in the mid-seventies.

He claimed to have flown into Heathrow from Greece and tried to navigate his way through Customs in order to proceed to his connecting flight to Manchester. It turned out that the Customs Department of Heathrow had swallowed him up and slowly began to suck his life and good sense right out of his body. Anyone who's ever had to claim anything at Customs before can surely testify that the feelings and emotional state described by Alfred McEvoy are completely accurate.

Every door he tried led him to another room or another section of the airport, or, in some cases, he found himself in a deep and lush jungle; upon discovering this, he would close the door immediately and try another one, as the thought of trekking through a dense jungle was slightly less desirable than trekking through Heathrow Airport. He tried following people around, as anyone would logically expect sooner or later they'd have to leave the airport, but just when it seemed he'd found the exit, he'd get caught up in a rush of people and lose the original person he had been following.

He finally resigned himself to wandering around aimlessly as a non-entity, never acknowledged by anyone, feeding on whatever scraps he could find. Seemingly, this had gone on for almost twenty years before he accidentally tripped backward over a suitcase and fell out into the open air. The only detailed record of this event and Alfred McEvoy's testimony remained locked in a dusty filing cabinet in the basement area of the Heathrow security station at Terminal 3. The key for the filing cabinet was lost when the then head of security took a day trip to the south of France. On the return trip, his plane exploded and the key was lost somewhere over La Rochelle, a small winemaking village that suffered greatly when a plane exploded over it.

Upon his release, Alfred McEvoy, shortly after giving his testimony, stepped out of the terminal and breathed fresh air for the first time in twenty years. He looked around at the people, at the alien world around him, at a dog peeing on a fire hydrant, the birds in the air, and behind the birds, the wide open space most people referred to as the sky.

At that moment, Alfred McEvoy felt the grip of fear tighten around him and he quickly turned and ran, screaming and deranged, back into the airport. Security searched the terminal from top to bottom but there was no trace of Alfred anywhere.

One expert in particular, a charming yet disgraced professor with a penchant for ancient theology living in a small village called Lees in the northwest of England, formed a theory that Heathrow Airport had been built right in the middle of an inter-dimensional vortex, a sort of semi-black hole where, if someone was to get caught inside, it would begin to remove them from time and history altogether until, by sheer accident, they fell out of the vortex.

The once-renowned professor believed that such a thing had happened to Alfred McEvoy and may very well have happened to many others still trapped inside, people removed from reality, walking hither and thither, unable to escape, and completely oblivious of why they were stuck there. The professor concluded that being inside a vortex may not have been an entirely bad thing, as it provided a gateway to other dimensions if they could find the right door.

Of course, this was all just a theory from a man whom no one believed anymore as he'd been disgraced and the only person to back him up was a rambling testimony locked in the basement of Heathrow's security station at Terminal 3 from a man who appeared to have disappeared off the face of the Earth.

Thankfully, Death and Gerald did not get caught up in any sort of interdimensional vortex; they simply followed the signs and eventually found the exit. As they drove away in a shiny black taxicab driven by a man named Rupert who appeared to be obsessed with the little bars of hotel soap, a large truck and trailer pulled up to the airport terminal.

Two men exited the truck, followed by an angry-looking cat.

Nigel, armed with his mop, had finally fallen upon the cafeteria only to find an unconscious lab technician whose nametag identified her to be the woman who left the message on his machine and an elf who appeared to be tap dancing.

"Get back!" said Nigel to the dancing elf. "I'm armed," he said, tightening his grip on the mop, and then, with very little confidence, "and quite, quite dangerous!"

The elf stopped dancing and grinned at Nigel. The smile was not the same evil maniacal grin that Nigel had seen on the other elf; it seemed more innocent than anything else. Not knowing what a first conversation with a cybernetic elf would entail, Nigel was at somewhat of a loss. But being that Celina still lay unconscious, he decided to give it a go. The conversation went something like this.

"So, err, you're an elf then?" said Nigel.

"Yes," said Eggnog.

"Oh good, good. Do you have a name?"

"Umm, Eggnog," said Eggnog.

"Eggnog?"

"Yes, I'm fairly certain it's Eggnog," said Eggnog, nodding enthusiastically.

"Right then," said Nigel.

There followed a lengthy pause. Eggnog stared at Nigel, all the while grinning, and Nigel stared back, trying to think of something productive to say.

"So," said Nigel, "You wouldn't happen to be deranged, would you?"

Eggnog seemed to ponder this question while his mainframe onboard dictionary looked up the word *deranged*, then reported that he definitely was not.

"No," said Eggnog and began to dance a little jig.

Whatever Nigel's definition of a deranged elf would be, a short, grinning elf, doing the jig did not strike him as deranged so much as just plain weird, but in a delightfully amusing way.

He decided to leave the elf to his dancing and try and wake up Celina instead, who would probably prove more helpful, or at least, he hoped.

It'd been a while since Celina had passed out. The last time was two years ago at the Majestic Technologies New Year's party where Celina had managed to consume, to the great pleasure of her dead Scottish ancestors, almost two kegs of beer over the course of seven hours. The result of that evening's festivities involved Celina waking up in the monkey cage at The London Zoo wearing nothing but a lab coat and the words *I love bananas* tattooed on her rear end. The monkeys were not impressed.

When Celina woke up this time, she did not find herself in a cage, monkeys were not staring angrily at her, and to the best of her knowledge, no new tattoos had appeared anywhere on her body. However, through the bright haze of a flashlight, two figures stared intently at her. One was a rather rugged and intelligent-looking gentleman; the other was a round, chubby-faced elf, grinning broadly.

She first looked to Nigel and then to the elf, who had stopped dancing. Horror spread across her face and she began scrambling backward like a spider monkey who had just come to terms with the fact that he was face to face with a large, hungry lion, while a sort of primal shriek emerged from her vocal chords.

Eggnog looked at Nigel, and then back at Celina, and then, with a little more confusion in his features, he looked at Nigel again.

Celina backed herself into a corner and resembled a human raised away from society by llamas recently discovered by an international explorer researching llamas. She stopped shrieking, and Nigel approached her carefully and summoned his calmest possible voice.

"Celina McMannis? Hi. My name's Nigel, you left a message on my answering machine and—"

But Nigel got no further as a look of relief flew across Celina's face and she dived straight at him and gave him a big hug. Celina's fear suddenly returned as she noticed Eggnog perched on a chair smiling broadly; she gripped Nigel by the neck tightly.

"Don't let him hurt me!" She spun Nigel around and pointed repeatedly at Eggnog ferociously.

Nigel eased out of Celina's grip and smoothed himself off.

"I don't actually think he's dangerous. I've seen one of the other elves, and this one seems a little different."

Celina's eyebrows arose suspiciously, and she crinkled her nose, as if a bad smell had just entered the room.

"Why do you think he's so different?"

"Well," said Nigel carefully, "for one thing he doesn't look quite as dangerous, and he, err, well, he keeps dancing."

Celina swept her red hair away from her face and fixed Eggnog with a fierce stare.

"What do you want, elf?"

"Eggnog, actually," said Nigel helpfully.

"What?" said Celina.

"Apparently, his name is Eggnog."

"I know what his name is!" said Celina a little too loudly, "I named half of them."

Eggnog, happy to finally be given some attention, gurgled cheerfully.

"I was told to find the nearest technician," he said.

Celina moved closer to Eggnog with a little less hesitation. "What are your mission parameters?"

Eggnog gave a sort of shrug. "Don't know, they won't load."

"Try," said Celina.

Eggnog closed his eyes. He tried once again to load his mission parameters, and yet again the error message flashed behind his eyes and the overwhelming urge to tango took over his body.

"Strange," said Celina.

Nigel watched the whole spectacle before him with a certain unease. This moody, yet quite beautiful technician was talking to a very real-looking elf who was actually a robot, but not one of the dangerous ones, today Nigel had been held upside down off a building, fired from his job, had horrible flashbacks to happier times, and the constant *beware the elf* was just getting frustrating. He then remembered that he had completely forgotten to turn off the coffee pot that morning and this unnerved him further. Then there was the whole dead not dying fiasco, the possessed cat, and the rather unfortunate death of a bird, possibly two.

"Nigel," said Celina and snapped him back to reality. "You look perplexed."

"Yes, I often do," said Nigel. "How did you get my phone number?"

"Oh, well, I . . .it just came into my mind, as clear as day. It's a strange feeling," said Celina, "I don't think you could really understand it unless it happened to you."

Nigel pulled up a chair and sat down as Eggnog foxtrotted past him.

"Actually, a similar thing has been happening to me all day. These messages keep pouring into my head. All in all, it's been a rather unusual day."

"You're telling me. I've been trapped in here all bloody day."

"What happened here? How did you end up trapped in here? Where's everyone else, and"—pointing a questioning finger at Eggnog as he executed a tricky-looking break-dance maneuver— "what exactly is that thing?"

Celina let out a sigh and perched herself on the edge of a table.

"I don't even know how to explain it. The day began normally, everyone showed up a little late as usual, and then security alarms started to get tripped all over the place. The last thing we saw on the security cameras was a fuzzy black shape climbing over one of our fences and then everything went haywire."

Nigel processed all the information as quickly as his brain would allow under the circumstances, but something clicked when Celina said *fuzzy black shape*. He let out a sort of half laugh.

"I don't suppose the black shape could have been a cat?"

"I really don't know," said Celina, "we'd have to check the video feed."

"And where is that located, exactly?"

"The security centre, one floor up. But what about everyone else? I don't even know if they're still alive."

Nigel stood and picked up his mop. "Oh, I wouldn't worry about that."

"And why not?" said Celina, a little hurt that this seemingly nice gentleman didn't seem to care about her colleagues.

"Because no one's dying today," he said matter-of-factly. "We need to get to this security room, and on the way I think it'd be a good idea if we kept very quiet."

"What about him?" asked Celina. Both of them looked at Eggnog, who was doing the Funky Chicken with remarkable grace.

"Bring him," said Nigel.

Twenty-Six.

Chester Kronkel sat lazily in his favorite chair for two simple reasons: firstly, he had absolutely nothing better to do, and secondly, he was in mourning. Incidentally, Chester's chair was located in a lovely little cottage in Upper Ramsbottom. When caught in civilized conversation, which Chester made a habit of avoiding, people often asked where he lived, and he would automatically reply, "Upper Ramsbottom."

After forty-three years of life, the joke had worn thin, to the point where he'd begun ignoring the whole thing. Chester Kronkel was the manager of a prominent bank that had international ties and political endorsements that would make the Prime Minister of England blush. Chester had not gone into work today, as he was still mourning, much like the previous week and a half. The reason he was mourning was because Chester had gone and lost his biggest and most important client somewhere, who so far showed no signs of being found.

Chester flicked the channels and stopped on a channel that featured a wolverine taking apart some sort of water rat. For a brief moment, Chester wished he was a rat, then decided he'd rather be the wolverine, and then did a complete turnaround and tried to decide what he should have for dinner.

The client in question was none other than Raymond Miller; once an Olympic swimmer, inherited lots of money from his drug-dealing grandmother, hit by a bus in Portugal and whisked away in an orange swirly thing before trading bodies with an unhappy penguin.

Chester did not know this.

Mr. Miller had made a it a sacred tradition to check in with Chester every couple of days or so and in turn, Chester would cater to whatever needs Mr. Miller had with regard to his vast fortune that was carefully scattered all over the world, and to which, together, Chester and Raymond were the key.

Raymond trusted only Chester to move his money and Chester could not access Raymond's money without one of his voice-activated passwords, which could be delivered over the phone from anywhere in the world. Chester was mourning because the last he had heard from Raymond was a week and a half ago when he had checked in and then, later that day, a report faxed to Chester stated that Raymond Miller met the nasty end of a bus and vanished into thin air.

Over the past four years, Chester made it his life's mission to ensure that Mr. Miller's accounts ran like clockwork; in fact, the mission had become more of an obsession.

Chester changed channels and settled on the national news; he let out a depressed sigh and wondered where in the world his most important client could be. The name Ian Grubman appeared at the bottom of the television screen and the camera came to focus on a slightly balding man with sharp, little eyes and a crooked nose.

"You're watching the National News, I'm Ian Grubman," said Ian Grubman importantly.

He shuffled the pile of papers that all newscasters keep in front of them, although no one really understood why. Ian Grubman first did a recap of the day's big news of the dead not dying and the new theories proposed, which included some sort of claim of responsibility from the IRA. Funnily enough, at that exact moment, the IRA was planning a bomb attack and had claimed responsibility for the dead not dying in order to distract the world away from their impending attack.

Ian Grubman finished talking, shuffled his papers again, took the top sheet, quickly folded it into a swan and threw it off camera somewhere.

"In other news today," he said, "two fugitives are being sought after their escape from a hospital in the Bahamas. The two men were being held for questioning before overpowering guards and escaping onto a plane to London's Heathrow Airport."

Chester's leg began to itch so he scratched it accordingly. He fumbled around for the remote control and was about to change channels when his entire body froze solid. A hand-drawn sketch which looked unmistakably like Raymond Miller filled the television screen while Ian Grubman droned on.

"The two fugitives, one pictured here, are believed to be in London somewhere. If anyone has any information, please contact your local police department. A picture of the second fugitive will be made available as soon as someone can clearly remember what he looked like."

Chester missed the last part of the news program, which mentioned something about a woman complaining about her neighbors who had recently adopted a large amount of ducks, because Chester had already grabbed his keys and headed out the front door. Four hours later, he arrived in London.

At that particular moment, the former body of Raymond Miller was having the time of his life. All the people whizzing by provided such fabulous entertainment for Gerald that he almost completely forgot about his hangover. Rupert the cab driver had been going on and on about the different kinds of soaps he'd collected from hotels around the world, but neither passenger listened, which didn't seem to impair his enthusiasm for speaking in the slightest.

Death, on the other hand, was pondering as only an Angel of Death can. Something about this whole situation wasn't really making too much sense. God was always in the mood for a practical joke;

Death fondly remembered when He had created the platypus: half duck, half beaver, laid eggs. God thought that was hilarious. But this seemed a little farfetched, as the world had been tossed into chaos. The human mind wasn't equipped to deal with things like angels and dead people getting up and walking around.

"There was this one place in Las Vegas," went on Rupert, "all the soaps were in these little heart shapes, very classy, I thought."

The question that was really nagging away at Death was, why had God let him quit if he'd known it would cause all this craziness? If there was one thing Death knew, it was that God didn't do anything without good reason. There was always something behind it all, some underlying theme, or question, or reasoning. But Death couldn't put his finger on it, and then there was the man sitting next to him who used to be a penguin. Aside from all the other strangeness about Gerald, he always remembered who Death was, and that was not a human trait, as holding any memory of Death in a human's mind was like trying to collect a beach full of sand using a pair of tweezers. It was too much work for the mind, so it always ended up giving up, which was why no one ever remembered seeing angels.

"The thing about soap, ya see, is that it never depreciates," said Rupert.

Death looked over at Gerald.

"Gerald?" said Death.

"Yes, Death," said Gerald, still glued to the window.

"Did you really used to be a penguin?"

"Yup."

"A real penguin, black and white, flippers, little waddle, the whole bit?"

"Yes," said Gerald and nodded enthusiastically.

"Hmm," said Death, and carried on pondering.

"The last hotel I went to was a right disappointment," said Rupert, "no bars of soap, just liquid soap, didn't stay there for very long."

"Death, why don't people remember you?" asked Gerald.

The question caught Death by surprise, as so far, Gerald's questions had been all Earthly-based: Why is the sky blue, what's this for, why is it doing that, how come that woman is sticking her middle finger up at me?

"Well, it'd be very hard for us to move around and complete our tasks if people could see us all the time. So instead, we just fade from people's memories."

"What kind of tasks?"

"Well, it varies depending on the Angel's function. My job was to guide dead souls to the afterlife. Some help people, a little nudge here, word of encouragement there. Other Angels simply watch and document human lives."

"Even when they're in the bathroom?"

"Yes."

"Hmm. And no one gets to see you guys?" asked Gerald.

"They see us, but they forget quickly."

"Hmm," said Gerald, turning back to the window, "must get pretty lonely."

"Yes," said Death solemnly.

"Then again I suppose if you didn't complete your tasks, the world wouldn't really work anymore, would it?" suggested Gerald. "How come I can see you anyway?"

Death smiled.

"I think it's because you used to be a penguin."

"Ahh," said Gerald, "so, who's this God fellah we're off to see?"

Death leaned over the front seat.

"Here! Stop here!" Death turned back to Gerald and pointed across the street, "He's the creator of the universe and sometimes he works as a wine waiter at that restaurant. Let's hope he's working today."

Jeremiah floated upside down in his bowl; he didn't know why, he just enjoyed the sensation of everything being the wrong way up. He giggled, as only a fish can giggle, at his castle that leaned a little to the left while hanging from the ceiling.

The feeling that suddenly reached out and gripped him was like nothing that he had ever felt before, although it did feel familiar in a distant kind of way.

A blurry knowledge of foreboding and impending doom settled itself around Jeremiah's bowl, causing him to hide in his castle. The messages, premonitions, and feelings that Jeremiah normally experienced always had a purpose for someone else and the little fish sensed this, which was why he always flung them out of his head instantly.

The deep dark sensation surrounding him felt different; Jeremiah knew that this sense of fear wasn't for someone else. It was for him. He shivered a little bit and looked out from the castle window as if something could jump out of nowhere at any second and take him away. The moment passed, and the feeling slid from his mind, leaving him wondering why he was floating in a castle and shaking like a leaf as only a fish can.

Twenty-Seven.

"No, no, no, you insipid ape-descended creature!"

The cat formerly known as Fuzzbucket, who was the fluffy vessel for a currently irate Prince of Darkness, shouted at Big Ernie with as much anger and indignation as his body would allow.

"Pick up the shovel, the *shovel!* It's the flat scooping device right there!"

Big Ernie was no rocket scientist. His brain had never been equipped to deal with anything unusual, and an angry cat shouting at him was a bit much for him to handle.

"Err, Satan, umm, your grace, master," said Itch while offering a sort of bow, "I don't want to, uhh, question your judgment but couldn't we just pick up a couple of generators or something?"

The Devil turned his attention from Big Ernie, who was scooping lemons into the large box trailer, and fixed his eyes on Itch. It had already occurred to the Devil that Itch had a better grasp on the situation than Big Ernie and was obviously the smarter of the two. Fuzzbucket had explained his master plan to both of them. Big Ernie just stared blankly, as if someone had slapped him with a wet salamander. But the Devil could see the wheels turning behind Itch's beady little eyes and had no doubt that Itch was probably thinking how to turn the situation to his advantage. He was obviously underhanded and devious, and the Devil couldn't help but admire the ugly little man.

"If that was even remotely possible," said the Devil, "don't you think I would have done something about it already?"

He swished his tail for effect, and then began cleaning behind his ears. He had found the constant preening to be a severe hindrance at first, but the more time he spent inside the cat, the more he enjoyed it.

"Well, uhh," said Itch, "I just thought it might save us some time, um, your majesty."

"Indeed it would, my fiendish-minded little servant, but unfortunately it is not an option. Lemons are the only way! "The Devil turned back to Big Ernie. "Shovel faster, you giant ape!"

"But, umm, your magnificence, there must be easier ways to make e—"

"Look here," yelled the Devil, "this is my plan. I know exactly what's what and you will do as I say or I will reduce you to nothing more than a small amount of dust. And furthermore—"

The Devil looked past Itch across the runway. The three of them were currently outside an old hangar. A hand-drawn sign taped to the door read *Temporary Lemon Storage*. A hundred feet away from the hanger, a construction crew worked on a new section of runway. What caught the Devil's eye was the bright yellow front-end loader busily moving dirt from one spot and placing it in another.

"Hmmm," said the Devil slyly, "I have an idea. Come with me."

It took the Devil only four and a half minutes to convince the driver of the front-end loader that he'd gone completely mad, as he was talking to a cat and the cat was matter-of-factly talking right back to him, so obviously he couldn't be sane.

The construction worker then solemnly decided, at the Devil's urging, that this type of work really wasn't his cup of tea and that he should pursue his original career choice of being an astronaut.

Five minutes later, Itch wrestled with the controls of the machine as he loaded the remaining lemons into the truck's trailer. The Devil looked on with mild satisfaction and fought the urge to take a quick nap. "The time has come," he decided, "to get out of this damn body!"

The bistro was void of all patrons when Death and Gerald entered; the quaint chairs were the only things sitting around the equally quaint tables. The kitchen door at the back of the restaurant swung open, and the waitress walked out carrying a tray of appetizers. She walked right up to Death and Gerald, handed Death the tray, then pointed upstairs.

"Hello, dears, he's waiting for you just upstairs. Give me a shout if you want anything to drink" And with that, she vanished.

Death felt stupid for thinking that their visit would come as a surprise; of course He anticipated it, probably saw it a mile away.

Gerald helped himself to some food from the tray and munched away, happy to have something other than airline peanuts.

Death and Gerald proceeded upstairs. Heinrich sat in the same spot Nigel had sat and was staring out the window, a whimsical smile playing on his face. He stood up and turned to greet the two visitors. He swept Death up in a big hug, almost causing him to lose his tray of food. Death felt a colossal surge of warmth run through his body, and, for a brief moment, everything seemed right with the world.

Heinrich released him and waved to a seat at the table.

Gerald still had a mouth full of food when Heinrich shook his hand.

"Lovely to finally meet you, Gerald," said Heinrich. "Won't you please have a seat?"

Gerald sat down and looked at the hand Heinrich just shook; an oddly pleasing sensation crept over him.

Heinrich sat down across from the pair and poured all three of them a glass of wine.

"So," said Heinrich, "How's things?"

"Fabulous," said Gerald, feeling immediately at ease with the man who sat across from him.

"Not going all that well, actually," said Death, almost sheepishly.

"What's on your mind?" asked Heinrich.

"Absolutely nothing," said Gerald enthusiastically, not realizing that the question wasn't meant for him. He picked up the wine in front of him, drained half the glass, and felt extremely pleased for the thousandth time today that he was no longer a penguin.

Death looked Heinrich right in the eye.

"I'm sorry about all this, I really am."

Heinrich waved off the obvious concern in Death's voice.

"Think nothing of it, not your problem anymore; I'm sure it'll sort itself out. You need not feel any responsibility for it."

"That's just it though," said Death, "I do, I totally feel responsible. I quit and now look what's happening!"

"Death, my old friend," said Heinrich, "why do you feel responsible? You quit to get away from this job, didn't you? The loneliness, the repetition, yadayada."

"Yes, but it's who I am. I'm the Angel of Death, it's what I do."

"Did," said Heinrich, "past tense."

"You're playing with me, aren't you? You know it drives me crazy when you do this," said Death.

"Not at all," laughed Heinrich. "Just out of curiosity, though, what made you quit?"

"Well, I have to admit I'd had a bit to drink."

"I'd noticed," said Heinrich.

"What gave it away?"

"You kept calling me Nancy."

"Ahh. Well, everything was getting a bit much for me, I suppose I felt underappreciated, and then I got thrown out of a pub because no one believed who I was."

"Naturally," agreed Heinrich.

"And then a cat talked . . . me . . . into . . . quitting."

The words he spoke were like a kick in the crotch to Death's mind. How in the world had he not thought about the cat? Cats can't talk!

"Ahh yes, a talking cat," said Heinrich, "Are you sure it wasn't just the beer?"

"That's impossible," said Death, amazed at his own blindness, "cats can't talk."

"That's not entirely true. I mean, this fine fellow sitting next to you was once a penguin."

Death looked at Gerald and then back at Heinrich. "What's going on? I know you know, and you know that I know that you know. You should really just tell me what you know. You're always doing this to me," said Death.

Heinrich laughed and took a sip of wine.

"Of course I know what's going on. It's actually all quite simple, in a confusing sort of way." Heinrich topped up Gerald's glass, as it was now empty.

"Well, what is it?" demanded Death.

Heinrich leaned across the table, a twinkle in his eye.

"Let's open another bottle and I'll explain everything."

Twenty-Eight.

Somewhere across the city, in the powerless buildings of Majestic Technologies, a man, a woman, and an elf ran through the hamster-maze-like corridors in search of the security centre. They moved as quietly as possible in order to avoid any marauding elves they might come across.

So far, the entire place seemed deserted.

After ascending one floor and then turning so many corners that Nigel fully believed they couldn't even be in the same building anymore, they came to a room with large double doors with friendly letters above them that read *Security Centre*.

They entered the room and blocked the door from the inside.

The Security Centre was nothing more than a small room with a bank of television screens and some complicated buttons that might or might not light up. Everything was currently dead, as there was no power.

"Ah," said Celina.

"What?" said Nigel.

"No power. Oh, wait a sec."

Celina reached under the control panel with the fancy buttons and started pulling out wires.

"Hey you, Eggnog, can you come over here, please?"

Eggnog, who had been standing idly in a corner, was happy to have something to do and skipped over to Celina.

She turned the elf around and lifted up his shirt to reveal what looked to Nigel like a plug socket in the centre of Eggnog's back.

"The elves have a super-charged lithium ion battery that can recharge itself when they're on down time," said Celina. "Eggnog here should be able to power the security system and cameras for up to a good couple of hours if I can hotwire this thing."

There was a crackling sound as Celina pulled out two wires and inserted them into Eggnog's back. The control centre monitors flickered and came to life.

"It'll take a while for all the cameras to switch on, but we can look at what happened before the power went out." Celina pressed a few buttons, turned a couple of knobs, and sneezed.

"Bless you," said Nigel.

"Thank you," said Celina.

The monitor in the centre of the console flicked on and displayed the front security gate of Majestic Technologies. It looked to be early morning, as the sun was still low in the sky.

"Okay, this is it," said Celina and hit the *slow* button.

A black shape moving fast enough to blur slightly on the screen climbed up the fence and jumped over the razor wire, landing effortlessly on the other side.

"Pause it!" said Nigel and leaned closer to the screen. "I know exactly what that is."

"What?" said Celina, squinting at the screen.

"I'll bet you anything that's Fuzzbucket," said Nigel.

Celina looked at Nigel, and an expression, as if she suddenly realized that she knew absolutely nothing about this man and that he could very well be an escaped mental patient, crossed her face.

"I think you should explain yourself," said Celina.

Nigel considered how crazy what he was about to say would sound to this rather beautiful woman who probably thought he had lost all his marbles already. He never had any luck with women, so there was obviously no harm in telling the truth. He took a deep breath.

"This will all sound crazy but earlier this morning I visited an elderly woman who claimed that her cat had been possessed by the devil and had ran off to take over the world. Then, as a result of a bad gambling habit, I was also fired from my job. Then I got your phone call and my goldfish may have been telling me all day that I should beware of elves, not to mention that I used to be telekinetically gifted and I think it all ties in together somehow but I honestly can't figure it out."

Clearly, Celina wasn't sure whether to be terrified, confused, or just plain happy that someone was having as weird a day as she was.

"You're right," she said, "that does sound crazy."

At that moment, the cameras flicked on and displayed various locations around the factory. Several things caught Nigel's attention. Firstly, in a large warehouse sort of area, he saw a lot of people, technicians, and various other workers, all wrapped in duct tape or bubble wrap. Secondly, he noticed a large laboratory area cluttered with different mechanical equipment, but what was strange, aside from the amount of deranged-looking elves all over the place and the large sleigh with what looked like reindeer attached to it, there was also a large table.

The table was not unusual. It was the large man dressed as Santa Claus who lay on the table that was unusual.

The third thing that Nigel noticed was on the screen that showed the front security gate: a large truck and trailer crashed through the fence and hurtled on through the complex.

"Okay," said Nigel, "if we're going to deal with this I think we should start at the beginning."

Heinrich leaned back in his chair and stared thoughtfully at his glass of wine, which quickly turned into water and then rapidly became wine again.

"Showoff," said Death, with a grin.

"Oldest tricks are always the best," said Heinrich.

"So who's this Devil fellah again?" asked Gerald.

Heinrich took a sip and put the glass down.

"The Devil," said Heinrich, "is a sad creature. We used to be good friends. He got some pretty wild ideas about human kind."

"How wild?" asked Gerald.

"He wanted to kill them all," said Death.

"That's quite mean," said Gerald.

"Quite," agreed Heinrich. "So he was banished from Heaven and sent down to Hell, which became his domain. He tries his hardest to collect as many evil souls as possible and cause as much chaos as he can. I suppose in many ways I feel sorry for him, and it's probably why I decided to let him have a go at this contract of his."

"Contract," said Death matter-of-factly.

Heinrich smiled a broad smile. "Well, you see, he wanted to walk on Earth again, and I thought that wasn't such a horrible idea, he could probably use the fresh air, so I agreed as long as we put the terms in writing. He gets seven days up top, he can pick the body, yadayadayada. Of course, I added my own clause at the end that in the unfortunate event that the chosen body was suddenly unavailable, he'd have to go into a body of my choosing. He chose the body of a rather athletic ex-swimmer millionaire who is sitting across the table from me right now. Sadly, the millionaire got hit by a bus while performing an act of human kindness."

"That was me!" said Gerald. "I can remember something about that, there was a ball, a bus, and a swirly thing!"

"So the Devil had nowhere to go?" asked Death.

"Right, so I picked him a new body."

"The cat," said Death.

"Funny, eh?" said Heinrich.

The three of them sat in silence for a few moments and then burst into laughter, partially because of the wine, partially because the thought of the Devil trapped in a cat was quite amusing. Mostly, it was the wine.

Celina stared at Nigel with only the slightest bit of disbelief; she was actually warming to this guy and his crazy theories. "So you think that this cat, Fuzzbucket, has been possessed by the Devil and he's the one that tripped the security alarms and is . . . what?"

"I'm not sure yet," said Nigel. "Maybe you should explain these elves to me."

"Oh, well, that's all quite simple, really."

"Didn't you do the same thing to the Devil in the garden of Eden? Got him trapped in a snake or something."

Heinrich wiped the tears from his eyes, as the three of them finished another wine-induced laughing fit. "Yes, and much like that particular situation, he's making the best of it."

"Wait a minute," said Death, "why did you agree to the contract in the first place? You always have a plan of some sort. You never leave things open-ended."

"I needed a reason to bring some people together. You see, there's something else happening here, something bigger on its way, and this group of people, who our once black-and-white friend here is a part of, needed a good reason to come together. So that when this other thing happens, they'll be able to deal with it, because at that particular time, I'll be unavailable. Make sense now?"

"Clear as mud," agreed Death.

"Hiccup!" said Gerald.

"So what's Lucifer up to, then?" asked Death.

"Oh, you'll love this. He's hijacking something called the Santa Claus Project."

"And what is the Santa Claus Project?" asked Death.

"Elves?" repeated Charles Chitham with an air of disbelief.

174

Beatrice poured Neville a glass of water.

Neville examined the glass, looked deeply into the water, then threw it in the face of the lawyer sitting closest to him. He offered no explanation, and the lawyer was too polite and ever so slightly afraid to do anything about it.

"Yes," said Neville. "You see, a few years ago, I hit upon this stroke of genius. Due to the nature of this genius, I've had to keep it locked down, completely secure, but there's a possibility that the security has been breached and there could be legal ramifications."

"I'm extremely confused, Mr. Snell," stated Marcus Chump.

"Harumph," said Perciville Chatham. Funnily enough, *harumph* was all Perciville said these days. He was the elder of the three partners, at the ripe age of 73, and sustained a body mass to match a mature walrus. In his day, he had been one of the sharpest legal minds of Britain, his specialty being the legal argument. No one ever beat him in a debate at court, and other lawyers feared him. He was a ferocious wordsmith who thrust and parried better than anyone. He reduced hardened lawyers to tears and ripped expert witnesses to shreds. After making a lot of money, consuming hundreds of cases of red wine, and almost-raw steaks, his entire vocabulary boiled down to one word. "Harumph."

"The nature of the project is neither here nor there, and at this point I don't want to go into details, but I thought it best we be prepared for the worse," said Neville, with such simplicity that he might as well have been discussing the weather.

"That's all well and good," said Marcus Chump, "but if we are to form any sort of legal strategy, we need to know exactly what we are preparing for."

"Harumph," said Perciville Chatham.

"Well," said Neville, who was well aware of the possible flaws with the elves, "if I came to you and told you that there was a possibility that a certain scientific project may have gone horribly wrong, with the potential injury or death of employees working on the project, and a national threat to everyone's well-being projected as an unlikely, but latent, result of said project, how would you *legally* proceed?"

The lawyers murmured among themselves, a *harumph* was heard somewhere in the middle, and then Charles Chitham spoke. "As your legal advisory team, we recommend that you remain here at the law offices for the time being, and we will begin arranging the most deviously ingenious legal argument ever concocted."

The sound of cash flow rang through the partners' heads.

"Excellent," said Neville. He leaned over to Beatrice who listened obediently. "Keep calling Majestic, I want to know what's going on in there. And call the mansion; tell them to get the Ukrainian Mountain Goat ready for delivery."

"Hmmm," said Death, "that's actually an impressive plan, much better than his last one involving those circus performers and the bowl of porridge."

"He's getting cunning in his old age. I didn't really expect him to be able to pull it all together, but he is the Prince of Darkness, after all."

"So he's trapped in that cat for an entire week?" asked Death.

"For at least another five days, according to the contract. Although you know the rules of possession still apply."

"Hang on a minish," said Gerald, who was trying to get his head around the red wine, "if his plan is to do this Shanta Clawsh thingy, how come Death here had to quit his job, wash that all 'bout?"

"Simple distraction," said Heinrich. "The Devil knew what would happen if there was no longer an Angel of Death. If everyone suddenly stopped dying, it would throw the world into an uproar, which it has, and no one would notice the Devil quietly entering into the world, which they haven't."

"Wait, there has to be—"said Death.

"I know you have lots of questions, and I promise I'll answer them in due time, but for now, the minutes pass us by, and you two really need to get going. There's a cab waiting for you both outside."

"Can I have my job back?" asked Death, pleading ever so slightly.

Heinrich's eyes twinkled like an ageless star.

"Not just yet," he smiled.

Twenty-Nine.

Itch had a severely bad time controlling the large truck, as his feet barely touched the pedals, which made shifting gears a lot more difficult than necessary. The cat who claimed to be the Devil was not helping in the slightest, as every time Itch ground gears, the cat hissed in Itch's ear, which rather tickled at first, but now it was just starting to unnerve him.

Itch swung the steering wheel around, veering the truck into the shipping and receiving yard. The truck drifted sideways on the wet concrete and Itch shifted gears frantically to try and regain control.

The Devil hissed.

"Will you please stop that!" said Itch and then added, "uhh, Your Majesty."

The Devil observed Itch with a look of ill contempt that came easily to almost all cats. The plain and simple fact that this cat was also the Devil backed up the look of ill contempt, as it was one of the Devil's favorite looks.

While torturing souls in the very pits of Hell, he often sneered at them with a look of ill contempt right before he sentenced them to another six-hundred-sixty-six lashes with an oversized wooden spoon. A brand new and very stupid demon on his first day in the pits of Hell rather foolishly asked the Devil why he used a wooden spoon and not a whip or something more painful. The Devil rolled his eyes right around in his dark leathery head before turning to the demon, and fixing him with one of his best looks of ill contempt, proceeded to pummel the new demon with a large wooden spoon.

While the truck lurched from side to side as Itch tried to recover control, and Big Ernie looked like he was about to deliver his morning cereal all over the cab, the Devil wished that he had a large wooden spoon somewhere close at hand.

"Over there, you fool, there!"

Itch heaved a sigh and cranked the steering, causing the truck to swing in a wide arc, throwing Big Ernie flat up against the passenger side window. The Devil also inadvertently ended up plastered to the same window and looked like a cuddly soft toy with suction cups on its paws.

The truck screeched to a halt with the back of the trailer up against a set of large cargo bay doors leading into the main warehouse building.

The Devil slid slowly down the window as gravity took effect. Big Ernie rubbed his nose, which felt a lot more bent than normal. The three unlikely individuals climbed out of the truck. Itch was happy the Devil was no longer hissing in his ear, the Devil was happy to be out of such a hot, small space, and Big Ernie was happy to be back on solid ground.

Somewhere nearby, a large electronic motor whirred to life and the cargo bay doors drifted apart. The sight that met the three individuals on the other side of the door caused a plethora of shock from Itch, confusion from Big Ernie, and sheer delight in its darkest possible shade from the Devil.

At the peak of the four-hundred-seventy-third highest mountain in the world, the Entity satin front of a small fire it had built. Its journey so far had been an easy one, and it wasn't expecting to experience any other difficulties until it reached its destination.

The Entity wrapped the cloak around itself and pulled the hood over its head. Despite the cold conditions having little or no effect on the Entity, it still required rest and sleep if it was to maintain its pace. Sitting completely upright in front of the fire on top of the four-hundred-seventy-third highest mountain in the world, the Entity closed its eyes, fell asleep and dreamt of home.

Rupert the cab driver had found a nice alley where he could relieve himself in peace, then write his name on the wall. This was always good, as finding an empty alleyway in London was like trying to find Swiss cheese without the holes. He ventured back to his cab and to his surprise found the gentleman he'd dropped off not fifteen minutes earlier standing next to his cab, waving at him cheerily. There was a second man dressed in a dark robe and sporting a pale complexion, but Rupert had no idea who he was.

Ten minutes later, Rupert drove across town with his two new fares and tried his best to be interesting and informative by regaling them with stories about hotel soap. Death and Gerald sat in silence, ignoring Rupert and considering what they'd just been told. Everything being new to Gerald anyway, he took it all quite well and was just happy that he had a job to do. The three glasses of wine he'd consumed were also an important factor in his complete and utter calmness.

Death had gone through a series of emotions, including confusion, surprise, happiness, and then a slight disappointment when he was told that he couldn't have his job back right away. Since passing out on the beach in the Bahamas and then meeting this man who, although he'd been suspicious at first, he was completely certain had once been a penguin, he'd come to realize just how essential his job was.

Maybe it was a lonely job, and he was probably very underappreciated, but looking at the state of world as it sat at this very moment, Death certainly felt that the world would probably see him in a different light from here on out. It'd taken Death a while to understand why the Devil was allowed to come back in the first place, but after Heinrich's explanation, the whole thing made perfect sense.

Sometimes things couldn't be done directly; one thing had to happen before another could take effect, and so on. Both Gerald and Death had been given their missions, they knew exactly what they had to do, and as darkness fell over London, Rupert's cab sped on through the rain-filled streets toward Majestic Technologies where, at that very moment, two criminals and a group of elves were unloading a truck full of lemons, all under the watchful eye of a Devil-possessed cat.

Thirty.

The BBC network was one of the most prestigious and well-known broadcasting companies in the entire world. If the producers and executives at the BBC knew anything about the events happening right under their noses on the outskirts of London, they would have been the happiest people on the Earth, as the events would no doubt make television history.

The producers and executives were already in their element, due to the dead not dying, and were currently attempting to purchase a license allowing them to shoot one of their news anchors on live air, just so they could be the first to do it. They figured there was no harm in the event, as the anchorman could obviously not die. Several Middle Eastern countries had been broadcasting people getting shot on live television for years, but that was never on the news. Such things never happened in London, and so the BBC was jockeying to be the first to shoot someone on live air. At that very moment, the news anchorman scheduled to be shot once the license was obtained was interviewing a large gentleman on a news-related program.

The large gentleman, whose name was Terrence Macklesfield, sweated profusely, partly due to his whale-like frame and mass and partly due to the high-powered studio lights trained on him. The anchorman had been asking questions about Terrence's background, which included philosophy, religion, and highly speculative theories.

Terrence had worked for several high class institutions before presenting a theory about aliens not only building the pyramids but also inventing the mango chutney-curried chicken-mayo-dried cranberry sandwich.

After a highly prestigious career, the scholarly gentleman, who once weighed no more than one hundred fifty pounds, ballooned to well over three hundred pounds within a matter of weeks of being fired and discredited for introducing ridiculous theories. His eating disorder was attributed to his sudden downfall, and also to his sudden fondness for mango chutney-curried chicken-mayo-dried-cranberry-sandwiches.

Three years had passed since he'd broken his bathroom scale for the fifth time and now here he sat, back in the spotlight. When the media started reporting the dead not dying phenomenon, Terrence had been the first to draw up a theory, seeing the worldwide catastrophe as a chance to redeem himself. Although he had to pull many strings and call in every favor owed to him, he was certain that after he presented his theory, which through deduction, slight speculation, and hardened facts was actually absolutely correct, he would be thrust back into the academic community that had exiled him.

The anchorman, on the other hand, was a young gentleman with slicked-back hair and a strong desire to prove himself. Which was why, when the producers of the BBC had asked all the anchormen and women who would like to be the first to be shot on live air, the young man had leaped forward, probably a little too dramatically in hindsight, and was the first to volunteer. The young anchorman truly believed that the best way to become well known was to be hard-hitting and controversial.

Terrence wiped his forehead with an already damp handkerchief and shifted his weight from his right butt cheek to his left before deciding the right was far more comfortable but didn't want to go through the effort of switching back.

The anchorman shuffled his papers meaningfully, as all anchormen do, and smiled at the camera before turning his attention back to Terrence.

"So, Terrence," said the anchorman in a sickly sweet voice that would make cows throw up, "before we get to your theory on the current events, I was wondering if I could ask a question that I'm sure is on all our minds?" The anchorman smiled a toothy grin at the camera, as if the entire world was backing behind him and thinking exactly what he was thinking.

Terrence mopped his forehead again and realized he was getting quite hungry.

"Of course, of course," said Terrence, eager to please.

"Well, Terrence, I was wondering if you'd care to enlighten us with regards to the creation of the mango chutney-curried chicken-mayo-dried cranberry sandwich."

Terrence had learnt a long time ago that if a theory didn't work, he needed to drop it as fast as possible. If a theory ruined a career and inadvertently caused a severe eating disorder, then denial was the best cure. He was ready for this question.

"Hmm," said Terrence thoughtfully, "I don't seem to recall that one. Sounds rather ridiculous."

The anchorman was ready with a scathing response but the answer was unexpected; however, he wasn't about to be outdone by an overweight has-been.

"I believe it was a theory you presented at Oxford just over three years ago?"

Terrence shrugged his wildebeest-like shoulders.

"I don't seem to recall that at all. In fact, I don't believe I've been to Oxford within the last seven years, at the least. Sounds like a ridiculous theory, though. I wouldn't give it any thought if I were you."

Someone behind the camera snickered, and the anchorman bristled while holding onto a sparkling smile. His plan had gone awry and he started to feel stupid, but he was certain he could nail this guy to the wall if he tried, so he took one last stab.

"So you're saying that you absolutely did not, without a doubt, present a theory at Oxford explaining how aliens built the pyramids and then went on to invent the mango chutney-curried chicken-mayo-dried cranberry sandwich?"

Terrence looked at the anchorman as if he'd just said the most ridiculous thing in the world and spoke to him with the same calmness that teachers use to talk to five-year-olds.

"Are you okay? You seem a little overly obsessed with this theory, and you're starting to look flushed. Do you want some water?"

He motioned for someone behind the camera to bring some water while the young anchorman's mind began to recognize defeat at the hands of the large man opposite him. Nailing him to the wall was obviously going to be a little more difficult than he'd expected. The anchorman smiled at Terrence, smiled at the camera and shuffled his papers.

"No thank you, I'm quite all right, let's move on, shall we?"

"I think that'd be for the best," said Terrence calmly.

He'd been avoiding and deflecting questions about his career-ruining theory for three years and had become exceedingly good at it.

"Very well," said the anchorman, "so I believe you have a new theory to share with us about the dead not dying event that has swept the world. We've been receiving thousands of miraculous reports all day, reports of people being shot in the head, dying, and then coming back without a scratch."

"Yes. I believe the wounds heals up once the soul returns to the body, as no one could survive a gunshot wound to the head under ordinary circumstances," offered Terrence.

"We have had some reports about animals. A young boy saw a bird get shot this morning by an old woman trying to dislodge her shotgun from the chimney. In this case, the bird didn't come back. In fact, we haven't had any reports of animals returning from the dead, just humans. Would you care to speculate?"

Terrence gave into gravity and shifted himself back to his right butt cheek.

"Well, now, we're getting into the subject of souls. It's widely believed that humans have a soul, and animals do not. When a human dies, his soul leaves the body. In today's cases, the soul is returning to the body. Animals have no soul to lose and so they do not return."

Terrence smiled through an increasingly red face and took a sip of water.

"I see," said the anchorman, nodding slowly as if he was truly interested. "And you have a theory that explains this highly unusual phenomenon?"

"I do," said Terrence.

The anchorman perched himself on the edge of his chair to indicate his deep desire and interest in the oncoming information.

"And so how did you come by your theory? On what do you base your findings?"

"Well, it is after all just a theory, but through past research and data, philosophical standards, and many unsubstantiated rumors, I do believe that I know exactly what's going on."

The anchorman quickly shuffled his papers.

"Well, I'm certainly on the edge of my seat," he said and offered a fake laugh at his own sad joke. "Won't you please go on?"

This was what Terrence had been waiting for: his chance to redeem himself in the eyes of academia everywhere, to move himself back onto the A-list of high-class, intellectually stimulating parties. Terrence took a deep breath that almost burst the buttons on his shirt.

"I believe that the Angel of Death has quit his job in order to facilitate the arrival of the Devil on Earth who is using a large conglomerate media-hyped creation to re-enter the world as we know it and start the Apocalypse. Although I also believe God, who I think may reside in the Piccadilly Circus area, has his own plans and is using the oncoming events as a means to better a certain group of people and bring them together so they can learn from each other and prevent the crisis which may or may not happen, though it could all rest in the hands of a prophetic goldfish, but I'm not sure about that last part of it all."

The silence that washed over the studio was one of dumbstruck confusion, surprise, and pity for this poor, obviously completely off his rocker gentleman who had just made a complete fool of himself on national television.

The anchorman, who was slowly coming to the realization that Terrence had just nailed himself to the wall and flushed his career farther down the toilet than anyone would have thought possible, tried to compose himself and say something constructive. Unfortunately, he didn't get the chance.

"Oh, there's another thing," said Terrence. "There's something to do with a penguin as well, but I haven't got that bit completely figured out just yet, though I believe he is involved in the master plan and quite possibly a tool of divine intervention."

Including the anchorman, sound person, lighting people, camera crew, producers, director, and assistants, there were around twenty-three people other than Terrence who were in the studio watching the live broadcast feed. With the exception of a lighting technician named Lawrence, who was born without a sense of humor, the entire room burst into a roar of laughter.

Terrence, who up until that point truly believed he'd made a valid theory, suddenly had horrible flashbacks to seven years ago when he'd first introduced the mango chutney-curried chicken-mayo-dried cranberry sandwich theory. The laughing, coupled with the personal embarrassment, all held a vaguely familiar feeling. He struggled out of his chair, heaved himself to his feet, and bolted for the door.

The young anchorman, who was still laughing and holding onto his stomach as if it might try to escape his body, was ecstatic with glee, having just discredited and embarrassed a once-prominent figure in his field with hardly any effort at all.

Thirty-One.

Celina stared at the video feed of the truck that rolled to a stop in one of the shipping yards.

"Celina!" Nigel snapped his fingers.

"They're offloading lemons," she said. "I don't believe it, they're actually going to use lemons, and there's that cat again."

The Devil sat on top of a crate observing the unloading process.

"Use lemons for what? And why is there a Santa Claus lying on that table? I suppose it makes sense with all the elves running around here, but still. You were explaining?"

Celina looked at Nigel, the man who just moments ago she'd suspected of being crazy. But everything sort of made sense. If elves could take over the building and figure out a way to jumpstart the Santa Claus Project, then why couldn't a cat be possessed by the Devil?

"Okay, Nigel, I'll level with you."

"Glad to hear it," said Nigel and sat down, occasionally glancing at the monitors.

He hadn't told Celina that, aside from his suspicions about the cat, he also recognized the two individuals helping the elves unload the lemons. Big Ernie and Itch were not people who were forgotten easily, especially since it had only been this morning when he'd been hung upside down off the side of a building by the two criminals. Things like that tended to stick in a person's mind.

188

"It happened just over six years ago," began Celina. "Do you know who Neville Bartholomew Snell Jr III is?"

Nigel remembered the name, as for a while he'd been all over the news for one reason or another, but mostly he was known for his extravagant spending and equally extravagant purchases.

"Isn't he the guy who bought a herd of African rhinos, shipped them to his Australian mansion, and had them stampede through his neighbor's property because his neighbor's dog wouldn't stop barking?"

Celina also remembered that particular event. The neighbor had tried to hire a solicitor to sue Neville Bartholomew Snell Jr III, but not one dared take the case, as there were rumours that Neville had suddenly purchased a large family of ravenous leopards.

"That's the guy. Six years ago, he decided that buying large amounts of ridiculous things was no way to make his mark on the Earth, and like all ridiculously rich people he wanted to be remembered for something more profound after he died than stampeding a herd of rhinos through his neighbor's property. As far as I remember, once, when he travelled from one country to another, he read an article in an in-flight magazine, which he rarely did, as he believed that, much like the rest of the world, in-flight magazines are one of the most boring pieces of reading material the world has ever seen. Anyway, there was an article in there about artificial intelligence and the recent advances in the field."

Nigel's mind was working at hyper speed, and he had already guessed what was coming.

Celina continued." Neville always said that the happiest time of his life was when he was a child on Christmas morning and he would run downstairs early to see the piles of gifts waiting for him under the tree. His biggest disappointment in life was when he found out that Santa Claus didn't exist. That made the magic of the moment completely vanish, and ever since that moment, he'd lost interest in Christmas altogether."

Nigel read between the lines.

"So he decided to use AI to simulate that magic. To make the myth real, in a sense?"

"In a way, yes," said Celina. "The scheme wasn't without any sort of financial gain. Anyone with an average income or below would never be able to afford the services of the Santa Claus Project. Neville's plan was to sell this service to rich people for their children who wanted to keep the magic alive in their lives for as long as they wanted. He'd even envisioned people purchasing the service for an entire lifetime, so that essentially one person could go through their entire life believing that Santa Claus really existed because they had seen him on several occasions, and not just Santa, but his sleigh, reindeers, and elves, too."

"It's rather sick, really, isn't it?" said Nigel.

Celina pondered the whole thing for a moment.

"I could never decide if it was a horrific money-making scheme or an actual good-hearted attempt at preserving a warm fuzzy feeling, you know, a perfect feeling forever."

Nigel flashed back to his perfect moment, his apparent telekinetic power, and the disaster in a mini-skirt who destroyed it all.

"I don't think that perfect moments are meant to last forever," said Nigel sadly.

Celina looked at Nigel with a hint of compassion.

"Someone really did a number on you, didn't they?"

Nigel was a little surprised at how transparent he had been and shook it off for the moment.

"So the elves are all robots?"

"Yes."

"And the Santa Claus lying on the table is also a robot?"

"Yes, but we haven't charged his power cells yet, which is why they're using lemons."

"Because lemons can be used to create electricity?" asked Nigel.

"You paid attention in school! You get a gold star," said Celina. "Yes, a single lemon can generate just under one volt of electricity."

"Okay, but why not just plug Santa into a wall socket? And why are the elves rebelling? And what's the Devil, presuming there really is a Devil and that he has in fact possessed that cat, doing here?"

At that moment, there was a knock at the door that made both Celina and Nigel jump like a little girl who had just discovered a spider crawling over her leg. Nigel made a low shushing sound to indicate they should all remain quiet.

Eggnog, who had been tapping his foot happily to the music playing in his head, had no idea what a shushing sound meant and shouted out, "Who is it?"

The voice behind the door was a little muffled, as it was coming from behind a door, but the words were unmistakable and made Nigel wish that he'd never got out of bed this morning.

"It's the Angel of Death, open up!"

Down on the warehouse floor, Big Ernie unloaded the last of the lemons out of the truck. He wiped the sweat from his forehead and glanced a fearful glance at the cat who was still staring at him.

Big Ernie had definitely decided that he didn't like this cat in the slightest, Devil or not. Big Ernie, despite his size and natural strength, had always had a childhood fear of the boogeyman. That was the same irrational fear that all children had, the feeling that there was a creature hiding under the bed, but this fear had stuck with Big Ernie for a long time, and even now he would still sometimes check under the bed and in the closet. The cat, who would occasionally lick his paw and clean behind his ears, inspired the exact same childhood fear in Big Ernie. And he didn't like it.

The elves cleared the area around the table where the Frankenstein Santa Claus lay. Following the cat's orders, which is exactly what their programming told them to do, they began lining up the lemons around the table in a perfect spiral that stretched farther and farther outward. The array was actually quite pretty. The elves worked in a sort of production line, as was customary for all ordinary toy-making elves, passing the lemons along.

Another group of elves entered the warehouse, each carrying a large box.

"We found them!" shouted one of the elves with a box.

The Devil hopped off his box and walked up to the elves.

"Excellent, you found both?"

The elf nodded enthusiastically, the telltale maniacal grin spreading across itsface.

"Lots of copper in the labs and every office had paperclips."

"Perrfect," the Devil purred, "now get to work!"

The elves shuffled off with their boxes and started unpacking.

The Entity was currently waste deep in snow. Jeremiah was blowing bubbles. Celina and Nigel were currently preoccupied with the knock at the door. The elves were busy with their lemons. Itch was trying to figure out how to get out of his current situation. Big Ernie was shaking like a leaf. The Devil swished his tail.

No one was monitoring the front gate at Majestic Technologies.

No one noticed the figure dressed almost head to toe in black. Black boots, black pants, black hooded sweater, the hood covering a black ski mask with two black eyes peering out. Green socks. A large rectangular-shaped black box strapped securely to the figure's back. The figure had only a hint of Guinness on his breath as he entered through the broken security gate, happy that his entry was so easy and completely unnoticed.

Death and Gerald had been happy to get out of Rupert's cab. They both agreed that that they'd spent far too much time in that particular cab and had learnt more about international hotel soaps than they ever really wanted to know in the first place.

Death was happy to find that a certain amount of his angelic strength and powers had begun to return. He couldn't exactly travel at the speed of nothingness just yet, and he hadn't regained any sort of omnipotent strength, but he found that he could see quite clearly in the dark again, which proved quite helpful while trying to navigate the deserted corridors of Majestic Technologies.

The map they'd obtained at the reception desk had proved completely useless and more complicated than Hungarian algebra that had already been translated from Chinese. They'd finally resolved to walk around looking for any signs of life, or at least, Death looked; Gerald just held on to the back of his robe and tried not to stumble, as he couldn't see a thing.

After hearing muffled voices behind the door of the security centre, they assumed they had found what they were looking for. However, getting the individuals inside to open the door wasn't quite as easy as expected.

"Just open the door," shouted Death from outside the door.

Celina shook her head. Obviously, she wasn't in any hurry to meet the Angel of Death, if that's who it really was behind the door.

"How do we know you're not an elf?" shouted Nigel.

Eggnog began to shake his hips. There was a deep sigh from behind the door.

"Because I'm not. How many elves would claim to be the Angel of Death to make someone open a door?"

Nigel looked at Celina, who half shrugged with uncertainty.

"That kind of makes sense."

"You're damn right," said Death from behind the door, "now open the door."

Nigel pondered the possibility of there really being an Angel of Death and decided that under the current circumstances the chances were extremely good.

"What do you want?"

"I'm here to help."

"If you are the Angel of Death, what kind of help are you offering?"

"Actually, I'm a little foggy on that myself. Heinrich sent me."

Nigel moved toward the door.

"What did you say?"

"Heinrich, the wine waiter. He sent us to help."

"Us?" said Celina.

"Who else you got out there, Death?" asked Nigel, then added under his breath, "Easter Bunny, Tooth Fairy?"

"He's a friend."

"I'm Gerald!" said Gerald.

"Are you an angel too, Gerald?" asked Nigel.

"No I'm a human being at the moment."

Nigel looked back at Celina, who had started to look a little tired; the day was clearly getting to her. Nigel unlocked the door and swung it open.

Standing outside the door was, in fact, the Angel of Death, black robe, pale complexion, the wisdom of a million years sparkling in his dark eyes, and almost as quickly as he'd noticed him, Nigel slowly began to forget about him. In fact, it proved difficult to hold any part of this person anywhere in his memory. The other, well-tanned gentleman looked to be of a similar age as Nigel. He had a very faraway look in his eyes, as if he was seeing everything for the first time.

"I'm the Angel of Death," said Death and offered Nigel his hand, which Nigel took and shook while still trying to hold Death's facial features in his memory but it was like trying to carry a gallon of water without a bucket.

"This is Gerald," continued Death.

Gerald grabbed Nigel's hand and shook it vigorously.

"Very happy to meet you, Nigel, I used to be a penguin."

The man dressed almost completely in black, with green socks, peered around the corner of a parked truck and looked into the open warehouse. He'd had a couple of pints before embarking on his task, but he was sure he hadn't consumed nearly enough alcohol to warrant the spectacle he was observing: a large warehouse, in the centre of which was a large table where Santa Claus was lying, lemons lined up all around the table, a sleigh complete with reindeers off to the side, and a mean-looking black cat snapping orders at a group of leprechauns sticking bits of metal into the lemons and connecting them together with wires.

The man in black was, in fact, a part-time member of the IRA, which was a group of Irish people famed for blowing up parts of England and large chunks of Ireland in the name of peace whenever they felt the urge.

At his other job, he was a baker who was quite famous for making extremely good petitesfours, small balls of baked pastry containing whipped cream and covered with chocolate. For the IRA, he picked up and delivered bombs. He had been in Ireland just last night to pick up such a bomb.

The bomb had been lovingly crafted by an irate wife whose husband was always off at the local pub getting drunk, and as a result of his neglect, she had taken up bomb making and become exceptionally good at it.

The Baker, the appropriate nickname bestowed by his superiors at the IRA, decided that maybe this was God's way of telling him to quit drinking. He swung the bomb off his back, set the timer, activated the device, and very quietly and slowly slid the large black box just inside the warehouse. He ran for the exit and was back in his bakery making a batch of petites fours before the sun came up the very next day, completely sober and with a vow never to drink again.

195

Next to the door of the warehouse, the digital readout on the bomb began to tick away.

29m59s

Thirty-Two.

Jeremiah swam around in his bowl. He'd napped for a while but couldn't remember why, and seconds later, he couldn't remember napping at all. And so he swam. The castle in his bowl was beginning to turn a bit greenish, so Jeremiah was staying away from it for the time being, hoping that it would turn back to its normal colour, although he couldn't remember what its normal colour was.

The familiar feeling, although it played no part in the little fish's memory, returned to him. Information began to mount up in his tiny little head, but he didn't know where to throw it. Usually, he knew right away. The information just kept mounting up and mounting up, pictures, words, things Jeremiah didn't understand, but the feeling overwhelmed him. He started to swim in little circles, and then decided to hide in his little green castle just to be on the safe side.

Pleasantries had been exchanged; Nigel had finally found that if he kept glancing at Death, then he wouldn't slip from memory quite so easily. Celina wasn't having as much luck and had to keep asking who he was. Gerald was just happy to meet new people. Eggnog, who was still plugged into the monitors, hummed a little tune.

"All right," said Nigel assertively.

"Yes," agreed Death.

"Quite," said Gerald.

"Who are you again?" Celina asked Death for the seventh time.

They had all examined the monitors to see what the elves and the cat were up to. It had now been established that Death was in fact the Angel of Death; he'd explained his whole situation, and apologized for all the dead not dying. Gerald had explained, as best he could, his own situation, and they had all concluded that they were brought together by a divine power working as a wine waiter not a stone's throw from Piccadilly Circus.

"So why are they using lemons?" asked Death.

Celina gave Death a surprised glance as if she hadn't noticed him. Her head began to hurt.

"The first artificial intelligence we created was a hamster, and we loaded it with so much knowledge that it couldn't handle it all and blew itself up. When we created the elves, we gave them a more basic knowledge of things. Their programming, outside of anything to do with Christmas, is of a more simplistic nature. They wouldn't know how to restore power to this place, they wouldn't know how to jumpstart the Santa Claus unit, they wouldn't even understand the concept of a plug socket."

"But they understand lemons," said Nigel.

"They're all programmed with basic knowledge of chemistry, math, biology, and physics. For example, if they need electricity, they know how to build a battery from lemons."

"How do you think they broke their programming?" asked Nigel.

Celina began to pace, as she thought better while pacing.

"I've been considering that all day, and it never really hit me until you mentioned that you were once telekinetically gifted and that the Devil may have possessed that cat down there."

"Actually," said Death, "there's no may about it, he's definitely in that cat. That's the cat that talked me into quitting."

"And he's the same cat that was reported possessed by its owner this morning," added Nigel.

"Okay," said Celina, "the cat is the Devil. Could the Devil possibly be telekinetic?"

Death had the answer.

"Yes, absolutely. In the form of a cat, I expect the Devil's powers would be severely diminished; he'd probably even have trouble talking at first, but he would still carry a certain amount of telekinetic energy."

"And who are you again?" Celina asked Death.

"Angel of Death," said Death and offered his hand, which she stared at with disdain.

"Okay, so what about telekinesis?" said Nigel.

"Well, it's kind of confusing but I'll try and keep it simple. Recent studies have shown that people even with a small amount of telekinetic energy can affect matter on a micro-level."

"Sounds simple enough," said Nigel.

Celina held up a finger.

"By influencing micro-PK levels using the mind, researchers discovered that such things as random number generators, in which the subject tries to influence the random outcome of the machine in a way that is much greater than chance, are movable within the parameters of the tests."

Three blank faces looked back at her.

Nigel's mind finally caught up and blinked to life.

"So you're saying because the Devil's probably telekinetic, he was able to change the elves' programming by moving around all the 1's and 0'sand making them deranged?"

"Oh no, they were already deranged, A French scientist who used to work for us completely buggered up their database. Since then, they've been switched off. What I'm saying is that the Devil turned them on and then altered their programming so they would obey him."

"Ahh," said the three in unison. Gerald said *ahh* simply because everyone else said *ahh*; he really had no idea what was going on but he was quite happy to just try and fit in.

"What's the Santa Claus for?" asked Nigel.

"We know the answer to that," said Death.

"And who are you again?" Celina asked Death.

22m32s

The Devil watched his plan slowly unfold in all its magnificence. Being forced into a cat was not part of his plan, but it had all worked out rather nicely in the end. His two new underlings were perfect, the short one sickeningly devious and the large one sickeningly scared. Two traits that made the Devil practically drool.

The elves worked out exactly as he expected.

These will be the first.

The Devil had taken a serious liking to the deranged elves, and visions of an entire army of deranged elves now danced in his head.

Maybe I could use one of the technicians to develop more elves?

The best thing about this whole situation was that no one knew what he was doing. No one could stop him. His chance at world domination was finally here! The Devil hopped from his perch on top of a crate and weaved his way through the hundreds and hundreds of lemons, each with a piece of copper and a paperclip inserted into it, each connected to another by a wire. He jumped up to the table and sat himself on top of the large Santa Claus. This was a body that he could literally not wait to possess.

17m49s

Chester Kronkel, the bank manager from Upper Ramsbottom, struggled his way out of Heathrow Airport and realized that he had absolutely no idea how to find his missing client. On top of it all, Chester had absolutely no clue whatsoever that his client was no longer his client, as his client had been hit by a bus. The man who was his client was merely a penguin inside his deceasedclient's body. But Chester didn't know that. He was about to climb into one of London's famous black taxicabs when a construction worker who had recently been convinced by a black cat that he was far better suited to be an astronaut pushed Chester out of the way and climbed into the cab himself.

"Take me to NASA," said the construction worker to the cab driver. The driver eyed the large man suspiciously.

"That's in America, innit?" asked the driver.

"Yes, yes," said the construction worker, "now step on it."

The cab driver thought about this for a second.

"Right you are, then," he said and decided to drive the man around for a while and then dump him off back at the airport, tell him that Terminal 4 was actually the NASA Space Centreand collect his fare, which by that point should be quite substantial.

Chester picked himself up off the ground as the cab sped away. A second cab pulled up. Chester looked around carefully before getting into the cab, just in case there were anymore construction workers waiting to bowl him over on their way to space. The coast being clear, Chester hopped into the cab, which had a strange, soapy kind of smell to it.

Rupert looked back at Chester from the driver's seat.

"My, my, you do look a bit worked up, mate. Where can I take ya?" asked Rupert.

Chester tried to ignore the smell of soap as he closed the door and thought about his answer.

"I'm not completely sure, you see, I was sitting at home—"

"Well, well," said Rupert, "I knew it was going to be one of those days when I got up this morning. I tell ya, I've had a policeman in here, an escaped mental patient, some fellah in a dark robe that I can't rightly remember—"

Chester immediately perked up.

"An escaped mental patient?"

"Oh yeah, didn't know it at the time, just caught the news on my break. Thought it was funny he was dressed like a nurse."

"You're talking about the guy who escaped from the hospital in the Bahamas?"

"That's the one, nice fellah, really, didn't seem crazy or anything. Left me a good tip."

Chester took out a hundred pounds and waved it at Rupert.

"I don't suppose you remember where you took him, do you?"

"Remember?" said Rupert. "I don't think I've driven anywhere else today. Big industrial area, other end of town."

Chester pulled out another hundred pounds.

"I'll make it worth your while if you can get me there in ten minutes."

"Sorry mate, traffic at this time of night's a bit rough. Make it fifteen minutes and you've got a deal."

"Deal," said Chester, and with that, the taxicab squealed out into the flow of traffic.

15m22s

Thirty-Three.

The direness of the situation became apparent as Death finished his explanation. Nigel still suspected that this whole thing was nothing more than an enormous practical joke and that sooner or later, some guy with a video camera was going to pop up and explain that the Devil wasn't trying to bring about Hell on Earth by inhabiting the body of Santa Claus.

"Now wait a minute," said Nigel, "if what you're saying is all true, then the Santa Claus on the table down there isn't human, he's just a robot, like the elves. And if that's true, then the Devil can't inhabit the body."

The five of them made their way down to the warehouse. It was more Nigel's decision than anyone else's, but they had all agreed that something had to be done to stop all this.

Eggnog lagged behind, doing some sort of a shoop de shoop dance.

Celina wasn't comfortable with the plan of leaving the security centre at all. And she liked the idea of facing all the elves and the Devil even less. Being partly responsible for the creation of the elves, she felt extremely guilty about where all this was heading, and it was more the guilt than her wish for a confrontation that made her realize that this was the best course of action.

"It's the Santa Claus unit, you see," said Celina. "The unit was so big and required a much larger processor than what the elves needed.

Essentially, the Santa Claus unit would be the most important part of the whole project, so he would have to be the most lifelike, which we didn't know how to do. It was actually my idea to use a human brain to cohabit with an artificial intelligence processor."

Nigel looked at Celina.

"Basically, you've created Frankenstein's monster, just with a red suit and a round belly that jiggles like a bowl full of jelly? That's amazing, in a sick and twisted sort of way."

Celina, who was originally proud of her idea to create a half-human, half-robot unit, began to feel deflated.

"It's not human, by any means," she said defensively to no one in particular, "but components of its processor are human."

"Amazing," said Nigel again.

Gerald glanced back at Eggnog for the thirteenth time. The ex-penguin was highly amused by the little creature who had a tendency to dance for the majority of the time. He was currently wiggling his little hips in between running to keep up with the other four.

"Why is that elf dancing?" asked Gerald innocently.

Celina looked back at Eggnog. She'd been wondering the same thing herself.

"I don't think he was turned on with the rest of them. Maybe the Devil couldn't change his programming the way he did the others."

What none of them knew, or would ever know, was that Eggnog had simply been misplaced. When the other elves switched on programmed with the Devil's evil coding, Eggnog's lifeless body laid behind a stack of crates well away from the other elf units. He probably would have lain there all day if a string of code hadn't been flung through the stratosphere, transcending time and space, redirected through the mind of a prophetic goldfish, and then thrown into the elf. The string of code made the elf harmless and also gave him the strange yet entertaining compulsion to dance. What they also didn't know was that this same string of code was mounting itself up again inside the head of that same prophetic goldfish at this exact moment.

"So the Devil can possess the body as long as the brain is active," said Death, getting back to the subject at hand.

Celina nodded thoughtfully.

"The size of the lemon battery they've created down there is big enough to jumpstart the Santa Claus unit. Once that happens, the brain will be active."

"And the Devil can hop right in," said Nigel, finishing off everyone's thought. "If he can switch bodies so easily, then why is he still in the cat?"

"The rules of his contract are very clear; he's only allowed to possess the body he enters when he arrives on Earth. However, the rules of possession are fairly bendable, you see—"

Death didn't have a chance to finish his sentence. The three humans, one angel, and the dancing elf had just rounded the corner of a dark corridor. Before them stood twelve elves, angry-looking ones.

13m20s

The Devil had been busy watching over the assembly of the battery. He'd found good reasons, or at least any old reasons, for which to chastise a couple of the elves, and he even yelled at Big Ernie for no apparent cause. With Big Ernie and Itch's task complete, the Devil was content to let them stand around for the time being.

Itch had tried to explain to Big Ernie that going along with the cat's plan was a good idea. Big Ernie wasn't convinced.

"But he's not cute," said Big Ernie, "cats are meant to be cute. He's scary!"

"Look, Ernie, he's not really a cat, he's just using the cat," explained Itch.

"Who's using the cat?" said Ernie.

"The Devil."

"I thought the Devil was in the cat," said Big Ernie.

"He is," said Itch, his temperature slowly rising. He'd been through many similar situations with Big Ernie. "He's using the cat's body. We're helping him so that when his plan works, then he'll reward us. Got it?"

Big Ernie thought hard, calling upon every bit of his shallow IQ.

"No," said Big Ernie.

Itch sighed.

"Okay, let me try again. The cat is the Devil, got that part?"

"Yes," said Big Ernie, nodding for emphasis.

"And we're helping him because at the moment he's just a cat. Still with me?"

"Got it."

"When he's no longer a cat, then he'll reward us for helping him, okay?"

"Right," said Big Ernie.

"So you've got it then?"

"No," said Big Ernie solemnly.

Itch began to hop up and down as he always did when angry.

"You two over there!" shouted the Devil. "Be quiet and stop jumping around or I'll have you pummeled with a wooden spoon!"

Something distressing had occurred to the Devil, although it was probably nothing at all. He knew how many elves had been created at Majestic Technologies, and he was almost certain that he'd activated all of them. Then, as he counted over the little creatures, he couldn't help but notice that one was missing. With a swish of his tail and several looks of ill contempt, the Devil dispatched twelve elves to search for the missing unit.

12m11s

Nigel briefly remembered what his life had been like before he woke up this morning. A respected and renowned serious crimes detective, slight gambling problem, ate healthy. It wasn't like he was completely happy with his life, but at that very moment anything would have been better than standing in a dark corridor with twelve pairs of little elf eyes staring angrily at him.

He leaned over to Celina and was about to ask what they were doing, as none of the elves had moved yet, when one of the elves went and moved. It was one of the elves at the front, who had a jingle bell on the tip of his pointed hat that jingled every time he moved his head. He produced a walkie-talkie from his little green jacket and spoke into the microphone.

"This is Cuddles, we've found the missing unit and some other people."

The Devil's voice squawked back over the tiny transmitter.

"Other people! What other people? Who are they?"

"Three humans and something else," said Cuddles, the something else being Death.

"We don't have time for this, dispatch them all, bring me the unit."

Cuddles turned his attention back to the group.

Nigel leaned over to Celina.

"Seriously, how dangerous can they be, they're just little elves."

Celina didn't have chance to answer as the elves let forth a loud battle scream that would have made Celina's Scottish ancestors proud and began to charge.

Gerald and Celina turned to run away, Death stood his ground, Eggnog executed some form of the Can-Can and Nigel wasn't sure what to do, although two seconds later it didn't matter if he was doing anything or not as his entire world suddenly stopped moving.

A couple of miles away, in Nigel's apartment, Jeremiah's mind swam with so much information that the walls of his little castle looked like they were about to close in on him. All of a sudden, Jeremiah reached the realization that he knew exactly where to send the information and flung it all out of his head with such force that the window of Nigel's apartment shattered completely and a small crack appeared in Jeremiah's bowl. And then the information was gone.

Jeremiah wiggled his fishy little tail and swam to the top of his bowl and blew a few bubbles, completely content and totally oblivious to the events taking place at Majestic Technologies.

Nigel's last thought, which had been *maybe I should turn and run*, hung in his mind only for a moment as his brain was suddenly assaulted with a pile of information that made the corridor shake ever so slightly.

Time seemed to slow down; the only thing removed from the whole situation was Death, who leaned against the corridor wall grinning at Nigel. Behind Nigel, Gerald and Celina were running in super slow motion.

"Don't worry," said Death. "I'm good at this time control thing."

In front of him the elves, their little faces contorted with sheer rage, charged forward with extreme slowness. The information in Nigel's head was muddled, confusing, and yet completely understandable. The sheer amount of it blinded his mind's eye and made his head feel like a large construction crane had just landed on top of it, and yet, it had a sense of familiarity to it. He had the distinct feeling that he'd been drinking all night and woken up with the worst hangover ever, but he was happy about it because the severe pain in his head let him know that he was still alive and not dead from alcohol poisoning.

Everything happened in a split second, even though it felt like an eternity to Nigel. The first thing he realized was that the information he received was nothing but numbers,1's and 0's. The second thing he realized was that he knew what the numbers meant and knew what to do with them.

Doubt suddenly clouded his vision; he had no power, it was gone. As quickly as he'd received the gift, the disaster in a mini-skirt stole it from him, leaving his perfect moment crushed and his state of mind shattered.

Death, who had been happy to lean up against the wall, walked toward Nigel at a regular and normal speed; the elves were getting a little bit closer but not fast enough to worry about. Death placed a comforting hand on Nigel's shoulder and looked him in the eye.

"Nigel, I realize that getting your head around what you're meant to do might be a little difficult. I especially have no idea how you're going to pull it off."

Celina and Gerald stopped running in slow motion and instead, turned around in slow motion to see what kept Nigel and Death. Eggnog slowly kicked his little legs high in the air.

"You see, everything happens for a reason. We're all here because we were meant to be here. The Devil has possessed a cat because if he didn't, then we wouldn't be here. Years ago, you had an extraordinary gift, one that you attributed to having some sort of a perfect moment. Heinrich told me to give you two messages. They're simple ones, and I don't think you could handle anything more complicated in your current state. Firstly, he said to tell you to stop thinking so much, you know how to do whatever it is you have to do, so don't think about it, just do it. Now, I realize that all sounds like a bad sportswear commercial, but Heinrich is rarely wrong."

"And the second?" asked Nigel.

"The fiery redhead, the one with the temper."

"Celina?"

"Yes, that one. You're destined to end up together. Heinrich thought it might break down the nervousness if you already knew it." Death patted Nigel's shoulder and went back to stand against the wall. "In a moment, I'm going to restore time to its normal state, ready?"

Nigel thought about Heinrich's words, thought about his doubt, thought about the information in his head, glanced at Celina with a slightly whimsical smile, nodded to Death, straightened his tie, stuck his hands in his pockets, and then stopped thinking entirely because that's what he knew he had to do.

Celina had always had a ridiculous fear of little people, but now her fear, fully realized, lay directly in front of her. Turning and running was the first instinctive thought that entered her mind. She turned, leaped over Eggnog, who was doing some kind of a French dance, and was about to sprint down the hallway when she realized that Gerald was the only one following her. She looked back to see what happened but saw nothing, as the entire hallway filled with a blinding light that threw her backward, landing painfully on her posterior.

The walls shook slightly, the light spots in front of her eyes cleared, and she looked up to see Nigel standing calmly in the middle of the hallway and some guy in a black robe that she sort of recognized standing against the wall with a big grin on his face. Celina leaned to the side to see where the elves had gone and realized that they weren't gone at all.

They were still in the hallway, but they weren't charging anymore, they didn't even look deranged anymore.

Instead, they were all dancing in perfect unison.

7m18s

Thirty-Four.

The lemon battery was practically complete. Each lemon had a piece of copper and a paper clip inserted into it, every lemon connected to another lemon. An elf stood on either side of the lifeless Santa Claus. Each held an end of the wire hooked up to the ridiculously long line of lemons; both were careful not to touch the ends of the wire.

The Devil was busy swishing his tail excitedly; he hopped down off the Santa Claus as getting electrocuted was not part of his plan. There were few moments in the Devil's long career that he could say he was proud of. The getting kicked out of heaven thing was a bit of a downer, that guy getting nailed to a tree screwed up his plans completely, he had to take some credit for Hitler, and he was extremely proud of creating the world-wide phenomenon of Reality TV Shows, but all in all, he felt he hadn't really left his mark yet.

This, however, wouldn't just be a mark, this would be an enormous scar across the face of the Earth. He was about to gain control of the biggest holiday of the year. He would become jolly old Saint Nick incarnate—the chaos he could cause, the heartbreak, the influence, it was all too beautiful. He would practically be worshipped! Oh, how he longed to be worshipped. There was still the matter of the contract to deal with;it stated that he had only seven days on the surface, but he had a plan to change that. A magnificent plan.

"Let's get this show on the road!" shouted the Devil. "Battery ready?"

"Ready," shouted several elves in unison.

"Santa Claus prepped?"

"Prepped and ready to go!"

"All right, let's plug it in!"

Nothing happened.

"Are we plugged in?"

Still nothing.

"What the hell is going on?" snapped the Devil.

The elves stood completely motionless. The two elves holding the wires had stopped at mid-plug-in.

The Devil looked at Itch and Big Ernie for answers.

Big Ernie stared vacantly, which he always did when he didn't know what was going on. He tended to stare vacantly a lot. Itch just shrugged his shoulders.

"What just happened?" said the Devil.

"I think I can answer that," answered Death as he walked into the warehouse.

As Death led the way through the dozen or so dancing elves, Celina's mind danced with questions. One question in particular pushed its way to the front.

"How did you do that?"

Nigel stepped around an elf that was doing the Twist.

"I'm not really sure myself."

"You just reprogrammed all the elves."

"You said it could be done."

"You said you weren't telekinetic," said Celina.

"I didn't think I was!" said Nigel.

"What are we arguing about?"

"I'm not sure, you started it. Everything just sort of appeared in my head, I just had to focus on the elves," said Nigel as if it was the easiest thing in the world.

When Nigel stopped thinking, everything fell into place; he realized that the power of thought played a very little part in his ability. In fact, Nigel realized that his telekinetic power, even at such a minor level, was not controlled by his thoughts at all, it was his belief that he could do it that had thrown the information provided by Jeremiah into the elves and scrambled their programming.

A large amount of his belief had been fueled by the little goldfish, not that Nigel knew that. But then, neither did Jeremiah.

"What now?" asked Celina.

"Have I told you how beautiful you look?"

Celina stared at Nigel, turned a lovely shade of hot crimson, giggled a girlish giggle, and then quickly regained her self-control and told him with a fair amount of aloofness, "No you haven't, and frankly, I don't think you should at a time like this."

"Fair enough, maybe later, then," said Nigel and strode on purposefully. "You know, I think I have an idea. Death, could I have a word?"

"You!" shouted the Devil.

"Me," said Death. "Aww, what a cute kitty you are."

"Shut up! Shouldn't you be looking for work? I demand you tell me what you're doing here!"

"No," said Death.

The Devil looked quite put out for a moment and then a look of calm anger washed across his little kitty face.

"Plug in the unit, you ridiculous little creatures!" barked the Devil, despite being a cat.

The elves didn't move.

The Devil ran over to Death and looked up at him, pupils large and fierce, his claws extended, tail swishing as if it had a mind of its own. "All right, what did you do?"

"Nothing," said Death innocently.

"What are you even doing here? I thought you'd quit, no, I thought we had agreed that you'd quit. In fact, I quite expected you to be sitting on a beach somewhere, completely sozzled by now."

"I was for a while, but it's a bloody pain in the ass trying to order drinks when no one remembers you," said Death. "It was a good plan, though, convincing me to quit."

"I don't what you're talking about," said the Devil with feigned innocence.

"You knew what would happen if I quit, you knew the dead would stop being dead and it would cause worldwide confusion, but more importantly it would cause a distraction."

"Oh, you are very good, you've been chatting to a wine waiter, haven't you?" said the Devil and turned to Itch and Big Ernie. "You two!"

Big Ernie jumped slightly.

"Plug in the Santa Claus," said the Devil, and then turned to sneer at Death, "you can't stop me, you know? No one can."

Death shrugged. "I know I can't."

"Then what are you doing here? You're just delaying the inevitable?"

Nigel stepped into the warehouse and walked calmly over to Death and the Devil.

"Ah," said Death, "Luci the Devil, meet Nigel."

Death bristled, or rather the hair along his back bristled, and his tail puffed out. "Luci-*fer*, Lucifer!"

Nigel looked at the cat. *Remarkable, the Devil inside a cat.*

The Devil stared right back at Nigel and took a quick glance into his soul.

"And just what is it you think you can do to me, Nigel?" asked the Devil. "Shouldn't you be off gambling somewhere?"

Nigel smiled.

"I'm thinking of giving it up. Actually, I'm just here for the cat you've possessed. Oh, and to make the elves do this." Nigel snapped his fingers and the warehouse PA system came to life with a squeal.

Celina thought the plan was ridiculous. There was no chance of it working. Not even a slim chance of them succeeding. Throughout the last several hours, however, she had learnt a great many things, one of which was to trust Nigel. At first, he'd seemed sort of dull, not overly smart, and annoyingly calm. It would appear there was a lot more to him than met the eye, and she was seriously considering asking him out for a coffee or something.

"What the hell are you thinking, Celina?" asked Celina. "We're in the middle of a life and Death, in the most literal sense, situation and you're thinking of going on a date!"

"Pardon?" said Eggnog, who sat beside her on the floor of the shipping office.

Celina had momentarily forgotten about the elf who was again being used as a power source.

"Sorry, Eggnog, just talking to myself."

The two-way radio they had taken from the dancing elves buzzed to life.

"Hullo." Gerald's voice crackled over the speaker.

Celina picked up the radio.

"Almost ready, Gerald, two secs." Celina, who had several wires plugged into Eggnog, inserted a CD into the computer she was using, turned up the volume on the speakers, removed the office phone from its cradle and poised her right index finger over the PA SYS button. She picked up the radio and pressed the talk button. "Okay, Gerald, ready when you are."

3m25s

Gerald was joyously hiding behind a pile of empty gasoline drums watching Death talk to the cat when Nigel walked out. He pressed the talk button on the radio.

"Nigel's talking to the cat." He watched Nigel raise his hand and snap his fingers. "Now, Celina, now!"

Celina pushed the PA SYS button on the phone and hit *play* on the computers CD player.

The Macarena was an amazingly popular Spanish dance craze that was quickly adopted by the rest of the world, and for a long period of time, no one could go to a wedding, night club, bar mitzvah, house party, disco, or birthday party without hearing its infectious beat. It consisted of a simple techno beat, with fast lyrics topped off with *Ehhhhh, Macarena* accompanied by a repetitive sort of line dance. Instructions for the dance were as follows:

One places his/her arms forward, palm down, right arm, then left arm.

Then the dancer turns his arms over so that the palms are up, first right, then left.

The dancer puts his hands on his shoulders, first right hand on left shoulder, then left on right.

Then the dancer puts his hands on the back of his head, again right, then left.

The dancer then places his arms on his hips, right hand on left hip, then left on right.

Then the dancer's hands go onto the respective hips or rear end, right then left.

The routine finishes with a pelvic rotation in time with the line, *Ehhhh, Macarena!*

Then the dancer jumps 90 degrees counter-clockwise and repeats the same motions throughout the entire song.

This world famous song pumped out of the loudspeakers in the corners of the warehouse, and with the gentle urging of Nigel's mind the elves began to dance.

"What is all this? I demand an answer." The Devil's voice got louder. "Stop it all of you, stop it, I command you to stop!" screamed the Devil at the elves, who were all line dancing together.

"Plug it in, plug it in now!" He shouted at Itch and Big Ernie, who stood on either side of the Santa Claus.

They each plugged a wire into the Santa Claus' ears, which caused a loud electrical *crack*. The Santa Claus unit began to shake. Itch and Big Ernie ran as fast as possible back toward their side of the warehouse in order to get closer to the door, in case they had to make a quick getaway. Big Ernie didn't quite make it all the way there, as he tripped over a large black box that had a tiny clock on it.

Nigel smiled at Death, who nodded back. The plan was not an intricate one, by any means. At Nigel's insistence, Death had explained the rules of possession. If the possessor became dislodged from the body, it needed to find a host quickly. If the body the possessor had possessed died, then the possessor would die with it. The last request in Heinrich's letter to Nigel had troubled him for a while—*if you see any black cats, kick them as hard as possible*—until Death managed to clarify a few things. And so they formulated the plan: takeover the elves, thereby distracting the Devil; kick the cat to dislodge the Devil, who would then possess the Santa Claus unit.

Death had assured Nigel that he would handle the Devil from there, but wouldn't elaborate anymore than that.

Nigel had to keep looking at Death to keep from forgetting who he was, but so far it was all going according to plan.

The Devil grinned maniacally as the Santa Claus came to life in a shower of sparks and electricity.

2m 2s

Big Ernie rubbed his shin where he'd tripped over the box. Itch had returned to help the large man to his feet when he noticed the box that Big Ernie had tripped over. Itch's mind went from confusion, to fear, to blind panic in less time than it takes an albino to get a sunburn.

"It's a bomb," he whimpered.

1m48s

The Devil's plan was to have the large insipid ape called Big Ernie kick him as hard as possible in order to dislodge himself from the cat's body. His two apes looked panicked on the other side of the warehouse, and the Devil was running out of time. He turned to the elf closest to him who was dancing happily.

"You! Elf!"

The elf jumped to its left and carried on dancing.

"Listen to me!"

The elf put both hands out in front of him, and then crossed them over his chest while his little hips wiggled.

"Dammit all to hell," said the Devil, "someone kick me!"

1m27s

Nigel lined up the kick and took himself back to his secondary school days when he played forward for his school's soccer team. He wasn't exactly fond of abusing animals but the thought of telling the story of how he kicked the Devil was an amusing one. He took a few quick steps to where the Devil stood, then kicked him clear across the warehouse.

Somewhere in mid-air, the Devil's spirit separated from the cat and fell directly into the Santa Claus as the unit suddenly sat bolt upright. The cat that was once again just Fuzzbucket, and no longer possessed by Satan, wondered why it was flying through the air. It landed in Itch's arms as the two criminals turned and ran from the warehouse.

1m00s

Outside Majestic Technologies, a cab pulled up, and out hopped Chester, after paying a generous amount of money to Rupert, who had decided to call it a night. Chester was examining the damaged security gate when he was knocked over for the second time in the last hour as a large man and a small man carrying a cat collided with him.

0m31s

"I'm alive! I'm alive!" screamed the Devil's voice from the Santa Claus unit.

Nigel was back standing next to Death, observing the strange situation. Every elf happily danced to the Macarena, Santa Claus rose up on the table screaming that he was happy to be alive, and the Angel of Death stood next to Nigel.

"Okay," said Nigel, turning to Death, "what now?"

Death looked at his wrist as if there was a watch there, and smiled mischievously. "Time for me to go."

"What?" said Nigel.

Death placed a hand on Nigel's shoulder.

"It'll all be okay. But this part might hurt a little. Actually it's going to hurt a lot. See ya soon."

And with that, Death vanished in a flash of blinding light.

Gerald, upset that his friend had just vanished, ran out from his hiding place, closely followed by Celina, who had refused to sit idly in the office for any longer.

"What just happened?" shouted Celina to Nigel.

Nigel just looked at her as if someone had slapped him with a wet fish. The look of confusion was clear.

Eggnog was still busy acting as a power source to the computer, speakers, and the PA system when a new directive flung itself into his data processing unit. It was simple, straightforward, and Eggnog accomplished it in just under eleven seconds. It said, *hide in a filing cabinet.*

0m11s

The Devil climbed down off the table and stretched his new legs. Nigel, Celina, and Gerald looked at the Devil's new body. It was still a jolly-looking Father Christmas but the look of pure hatred in the eyes was unmistakable.

0m 7s

"I'm alive!" shouted the Devil. "And now you're all going to pay, the whole world's going to pay, it feels so good to be alive!"

0m00s

There was an earth-shattering *boom* and the Majestic Technologies building ceased to exist.

Nigel, Celina, Gerald, and the Devil all died instantly.

Thirty-Five.

Years later, Nigel often pondered the experience of exploding into nothingness. Being in the vicinity of a bomb was one thing, someone could get some shrapnel in the knee, lose a body part, be horribly scarred and that sort of thing. But to be so close to the bomb where people were literally vaporized was quite something else.

To Nigel, it felt like a cross between a sneezing fit and falling asleep in the sun for several hours, all compacted into one millisecond. One minute he was there, and the next minute, he wasn't. His entire body, along with Celina's body, Gerald's body, all the elves, and Santa Claus, ceased to exist in the blink of an eye.

Nigel was surprised that, although his body was gone completely, his essence, or what he presumed was his soul, could still see, hear, and feel quite well. And so the shock waves from the explosion sent his soul flying straight upward, through the clouds, through the Earth's atmosphere where he bounced off a satellite and found himself floating lazily through the dead coldness of space.

It wasn't long before Celina's soul also joined Nigel's soul, and Gerald's soul didn't want to be left out, so that wasn't too far behind. The trio's souls looked very much like their owners' bodies had in their previous life; they were just a lot brighter, sort of transparent with a luminescent glow, and instead of moving they just drifted unnaturally around.

They couldn't speak to each other, as they lacked the physical ability to do so; thinking to each other was also out of the question as there was no longer a brain to work with, but neither of these things seemed to hinder the group, as somehow the souls of the individuals found it incredibly easy to take the complete lack of sound that can only be *not* heard in space and reverse it into noise, which at first sounded like nothing but static on a television; but the more they tried, the better they all got, until finally Nigel's soul said, "Can anyone hear me?"

"Nigel?" said Celina's soul.

"Hullo," said Gerald's soul.

"Celina, Gerald," said Nigel's soul.

The lack of ears didn't appear to hinder the conversation as they weren't even speaking but naturally knew what everyone else was not saying.

"This isn't exactly how I pictured all this turning out," said Nigel's soul.

The large blue and green globe that was the Earth spun slowly beneath them.

"It is quite beautiful up here, though, isn't it?" said Celina's soul.

"Marvelous," said Gerald's soul happily. "What do you think happens now?"

"Well," said Nigel's soul as he floated through Celina's soul, "we all appear to be dead. I couldn't even begin to guess what happens next."

"I thought the dead couldn't die?" asked Gerald's soul.

"That's true," said Celina's soul, "but if we can't die, then what are we still doing here?"

Gas from a nearby planet floated by and collided with a ray of sunlight that had deflected off a bald gentleman's head in northern Cambodia, causing the gas' atoms to realign themselves and turn into a very nice mahogany door with a brass handle. The three souls floated their way over to the new phenomenon to investigate.

The door opened, and a dull light spilled out, instantly swallowed up by the emptiness of space.

Death poked his head out of the doorway.

"What are you all waiting for, get in here!"

Earlier on, in the quaint little bistro, Heinrich had taken Death aside for a chat. Gerald happily sat alone and filled up his wine glass for the third time.

"Look, I really am sorry about everything," said Death.

Heinrich nodded and grinned whimsically.

"I know. And it's okay. You know me well enough to understand that everything's going to work out in the end, right?"

"Well, it usually does."

"Have a little faith, then," said Heinrich still smiling. "You can have your job back, don't give it a second thought. But I need you to do a couple of things first."

Death was ultimately relieved to know that his job was secure and that the Creator of the universe still liked him, even though, while in a drunken stupor, Death may have inadvertently referred to him as a giant baboon's backside.

"Of course," said Death solemnly, "anything."

"Well, first, we have to get our old friend out of that poor cat and back to where he should be."

"I can take care of that."

"I know that you probably could take care of it yourself, but I have something else in mind. Firstly, I need you to deliver two messages and secondly, I need you to abandon everyone, even your newfound friend over there, at a most critical point."

Death nodded slowly, understanding absolutely nothing. He looked into Heinrich's eyes, which twinkled a bright blue and told him everything he needed to know in a matter of seconds.

"Ohh," said Death, nodding more knowingly, "that makes more sense."

Death walked across the room to Gerald and leaned over the table.

"Er, Gerald, Heinrich would like a quick word with you and then we have to be off again, okay?"

Gerald nodded with a ferocity that most headbangers would admire, picked himself up, and wandered over to Heinrich.

The afterlife was not what Nigel expected. Although when he thought about it, he really hadn't thought very much about what the afterlife would look like. But he figured that if he had thought about it, then this would not be what he expected.

"Nigel," said Death, "You're thinking far too loudly."

"Oh, sorry," said Nigel.

When they passed through the door, their souls stretched extremely thin and forced their way through some sort of long tube made of light and beautiful music. For a twinkling moment, Nigel could have sworn he'd seen, out of the corner of his eye, the San Francisco Philharmonic Orchestra floating around,

The entire thing came to a shocking and sudden halt when Nigel's, Celina's, and Gerald's souls were spewed into nothingness, which quickly turned into an Arizona desert landscape at night. Death stepped out from behind a cactus and grinned.

"Well, how much fun was that?"

Celina's soul looked stupefied. "Which part? The floating in space part? Or the getting blown into little pieces part?"

"I was thinking about the entire experience as a whole, really."

Nigel was certain that if Celina had any sort of physical presence, she would have swung for Death at that point.

"All right," said Nigel's soul, "what now? And why does the afterlife look like Arizona?"

"This isn't the afterlife. It's more like a waiting room. I pick the souls up, bring them here, and then they find out whether they go up or down. Heaven or Hell. Best place in all of eternity, or hot, humid, and swimming in a lake of fire until kingdom come."

"You paint a lovely picture," said Celina's soul.

"And it looks like Arizona right now because I want it to. Sometimes it's a big grassy meadow, sometimes the top of a mountain, bottom of the sea, wherever I feel like it, I guess."

"So we're dead?" asked Gerald's soul.

"As a doornail," replied Death.

"And there's no way around that, then?" asked Nigel's soul hopefully.

"Well, you can't really get blown up and survive, unfortunately."

"Didn't think so," said Nigel's soul.

"I know it's a bit of a downer."

"Bit of a downer!" yelled Celina's soul, "we're all dead! What kind of a plan was that?"

Death continued to smile. "Well, all the elves are gone and you three stopped the Devil from taking over the world."

"Yes, but we're dead. We can't even enjoy it!"

"Think of the people you saved. You died for a good cause. No point worrying about it now."

Celina's soul flew at Death angrily and passed right through him.

Nigel's soul eyed Death suspiciously.

"There's something you're not telling us, isn't there?"

Celina's soul, having lost control, floated upside down. "This isn't how I thought my day was going to go at all," she fumed.

Death wiggled his finger at Celina, much like people do to a baby who has just thrown her plate of spaghetti all over the floor and was gurgling happily about it. Consequently, Celina's soul flipped the right way up.

"Thank you," said Celina's soul.

"All right," began Death, "there are a couple of things I'm not telling you. The Devil has been taught a valuable and much-needed lesson about control and power and he's not going to forget it quickly. All of you helped bring that about in one way or another.

Celina here created the elves, Gerald was given the body the Devil should have had, thereby forcing him into a cat. Nigel, you found a goldfish, among other things."

Nigel had been thinking about his goldfish and had somehow felt that the strange messages he had been receiving all day had something to do with his little swimmy friend.

"You played your parts," said Death, "you saved the world from constant torture and tyranny at the hands of Satan and you all came together."

Celina's soul rolled her eyes in a way that only a recently exploded, redheaded, female genius could.

"Doesn't stop us from being dead though, does it?" she said, stating the complete and utter obvious.

"Well, that's the other thing." Death looked at his wrist where a watch was not. "I'm not back at work yet; in fact, I have a good forty seconds before I'll be taking any dead people in, so I'm afraid you'll all just have to go back."

"You're serious?" asked Nigel's soul.

"We don't have to be dead?" said Gerald's soul.

"Good, because I wasn't exactly warming to the idea," added Celina's pouting soul.

Death smiled at his new friends.

"Celina, look after Nigel and don't you dare try to tell me you're not attracted to him just a little."

Celina's soul, which was an off-pink sort of colour, managed to blush a little.

"Nigel, look after that goldfish and take care of Gerald. And Gerald," Gerald grinned. "Don't forget what Heinrich said, we'll talk again soon."

"Thank you," was all Nigel could manage.

Death smiled a truly happy smile, and another doorway appeared where a cactus used to be. The door flew open, and the three souls got sucked inside like lint up a vacuum. Death closed the door and snapped his fingers, the landscape collapsed into itself and then exploded in a dazzling display of multi-coloured sparks that settled to form a large, snow-covered mountain top that looked out over several other snow-covered mountain tops.

A doorway arose out of the snow and swung itself open. The twisted and deformed soul of the Devil trudged through the doorway and stood with his arms folded in front of him, tattered leather wings folded behind him.

Death grinned.

"Ahh, Luci, so good to see you. You caught me at a good time; I just arrived back at work. You're going to want to take the elevator down to the basement. I think you know the way."

Heinrich took his break. The bistro was quiet, so he stepped outside for some fresh air and pondered upon the day.

The world was a mostly normal place. Strange events always happened, no doubt about it, but generally people went through their lives on a day-to-day basis under the impression that the world was completely normal. Although this was an arguable point; for all intents and purposes it could be agreed that the events so far in this story had not been normal. And, as with all not normal events, there were consequences. Unfortunately, things like dead people not dying and then all of a sudden dying again, the Devil leaving the Earthly plane abruptly, a penguin becoming a man, and an Entity traveling across the world, did cause quite the rift in our normal little universe. At the exact moment that Death sent the Devil back to Hell, the culmination of all these events caused reality to turn askew for a brief moment.

The moment passed practically unnoticed by most inhabitants of Earth, and the only telltale signs of anything happening at all were as follows: in northern Canada, a man inadvertently gave birth to a large mongoose, whom he eventually named Stan, was shunned by his friends and colleagues, and became a hermit. In the deepest deep part of the ocean, a creature of terrible power and fury that had slept for six hundred thousand years woke up, rolled over, and went back to sleep.

On the outskirts of London, a professional theorist named Terrence Macklesfield, who had recently been disgraced on national television briefly, turned into a mango chutney-curried chicken-mayo-dried cranberry sandwich. Those who knew Terrence would have seen this event as the epitome of irony.

At the BBC News Studio, a young anchorman who had agreed to be shot on live television suffered a terrible bullet wound that almost killed him.

The strangest and most noticed event that took place in that particular moment was the sudden and abrupt disappearance of the entire law firm of Chatham, Chitham, and Chump; the building, and all its inhabitants, including Neville Bartholomew Snell Jr III, ceased to exist on Earth. Despite an extensive search, the building and its inhabitants were never seen on Earth again.

Heinrich headed back inside the bistro but before returning to work decided he should make a very special phone call.

Thirty-Six.

The Devil pushed his way through the line of ingrates and no-goods waiting to get into Hell. The dark gates of Hell arose ominously from the dry, hot, and generally hellish landscape. Stan the gate guardian was still at his post, refusing to open the gates as was his order. The Devil liked to make the new inhabitants of Hell wait in line for what seemed like an eternity, knowing full well that all they were waiting for was another eternity of pure suffering.

The Devil trudged up to Stan.

"Open the gate," said the Devil dejectedly.

Stan looked the Devil up and down.

"Don't I know you?" asked Stan.

The Devil put one of his talons to his forehead; he could already feel the onset of a migraine.

"Open the gate or I swear I'm going to flog you so hard you'll have no idea what hit you, and in your complete disbelief of not knowing what hit you I'll hit you some more so you know exactly what it is that's hitting you. Got it?"

Stan slowly shrank as he realized who he was talking to, and the thought of being flogged with a giant wooden spoon, which everyone knew was the Devil's instrument of choice, was not a comforting one. He quickly opened the gate and the Devil stalked through, eyeing Stan until the gate closed behind him.

The Devil was not happy to be home. His plan to inhabit a human body had been foiled the second he landed on Earth, and then to top it all off, his backup plan to take over the world had also been trashed. And here he was, back in Hell after only one extremely long day of being on Earth. Usually the sight of his fiery kingdom spread out before him, his lake of fire overflowing with lost souls, and the karaoke bar on the corner, were always enough to bring an evil grin to his leathery face. He was angry; no, not even angry, he was upset. He felt cheated, conned, taken for a ride.

"Damnit," he said.

I'm good at all those things; I should have seen it coming. At least my little apartment and my fish, Percy, will bring me some minor comfort.

He absentmindedly kicked a lost soul off a nearby cliff and made his way to his apartment overlooking his kingdom.

The demon he left in charge of his apartment, Azeal, although he had no power of speech, only one leg, half a wing, and smelled like something scraped off the bottom of someone's shoe, was still able to—

The Devil's thought process ground to a halt as he stood in front of his apartment, which was currently on fire. The Devil kicked open his door to find Azeal sitting in a reclining chair watching re-reruns of *I Love Lucy*.

"Azeal! My house is on fire, you little ingrate, can't you see my house is—"

The Devil suddenly realized what he was saying and quickly put it all down to a serious lack of sleep. Of course, his house was on fire; he was in Hell, everything was on fire. The Devil picked Azeal up by the horns.

"You've done a fantastic job of house sitting, thanks very much, Azeal, bye bye now."

Azeal responded with a series of quick burps, which prompted the Devil to throw him out a nearby window. The Devil stretched his wings, tapped on Percy's fish bowl, which Percy hated but couldn't do much about, and then lay down on his bed.

"Maybe I'll have better luck in the next millennia," said the Devil.

The Devil's phone rang. Being in absolutely no mood to talk to anyone, he let the machine get it. The Devil's answering message clicked on.

"Hi, you've reached the Devil in the very pits of Hell; unless you wish to be ravaged relentlessly I suggest you don't leave a message. Oh, and wait for the beep."

There was a lengthy pause, and then the generic answering machine *beep*.

"Hello, Luci," came Heinrich's smooth voice.

The Devil sat up and stared ferociously at his ancient answering machine, having absolutely no intention of answering it.

"God here. I realize that this whole situation must have been very trying for you. You really should learn to read our contracts a little more closely." A couple of angels could be heard giggling in the background. "But sincerely, I do wish you better luck on your next endeavor, whatever that might be. Maybe next time we can get you into something a little bigger, maybe a dog, oh, I know, how about an unusually large rabbit. You could try to take over the Easter holiday?"

The Devil became so furious he spontaneously combusted.

"Anyway, I've got some errands to run, universe to watch over, that sort of thing. You take care of yourself and give me a call sometime, we'll do lunch."

The answering machine clicked off and the Devil rolled around on the ground trying to put himself out. He lay there for a while, smoldering quietly.

The anger he felt was the painful kind and he didn't like it.

"Only one thing for it." The Devil fished about in his closet, then pulled out a large wooden spoon. He put on his best look of ill contempt and stalked off to find someone to torture.

Nigel had wanted to thank Death for everything he'd done, for the realization and knowledge he'd obtained and for making them not dead anymore, but his soul had been sucked out of the afterlife waiting room too soon. There was also one question in particular that he had wanted to ask Death, a question that played on Nigel's mind, a question he felt to bean important one and to which the only answer he could come up with was one that needed confirmation from someone who knew what they were talking about, which was, *who is Heinrich? And how did he know everything?*

These were all really inconsequential at the moment as Nigel, Celina, and Gerald quickly discovered that coming back to life after an explosion was a hell of a lot more painful than being blown up in the first place. Each of their bodies had to rebuild itself from scratch: bone, muscle, hair, skin, clothes, everything.

Later, Nigel compared the experience to swimming in a pool of broken glass and lemon juice, only ten times worse. His soul whipped out of the cosmos, back toward the Earth, and on the way down got assaulted by a great many elements. Atoms rushed toward him, rebuilding his bones, muscle, skin tissue, and hair at the speed of light. The Earth got closer and closer, the pain got worse and worse, and Nigel and his companions blacked out.

When they awoke, they found themselves lying in a pile of rubble that had once been the Majestic Technologies building. Nigel struggled to his feet and looked around. Small fires still burned, and it was impossible to see anything else because of the large dust cloud that enveloped them. The smell of crushed lemons was unmistakable.

Celina coughed a little, stood up, looked down at her fully formed body, and hugged herself warmly. Gerald had only just been getting used to his body and now felt he had to do it all over again. Sirens sounded close by.

Nigel looked at Celina. Celina looked at Nigel. Nigel, half smiled, blushed a little, and looked at where he presumed the sky would be through the dust. Celina brushed her red hair away from her face and kissed Nigel squarely on the mouth, something that took Nigel completely by surprise but made him feel warm and tingly.

"What was that for?" he asked.

Celina shrugged and grinned mischievously.

"Seemed like the right thing to do."

"Oh, okay, as long as we're both on the same page." Nigel grabbed Celina and kissed her with as much fervor and passion as someone who had just died and come back to life could muster.

The rain that had momentarily stopped became bored with doing nothing and began to throw itself toward the Earth once more, which helped clear the dust a little.

Celina and Nigel helped Gerald to his feet. The three of them made their way through the dust and rubble and emerged out onto a roadway lined with fire trucks. Police cars were just arriving and an emergency response team milled around drinking coffee and telling blonde jokes. A fireman noticed the three survivors, and they were all quickly questioned, then wrapped in blankets and seated on the back bumper of an ambulance.

None of them really had any answers to the questions asked. They couldn't rightly say what had happened, as it still all sounded completely crazy to them, let alone anyone who hadn't even shared the experience.

"What about all the other workers?" Nigel asked Celina.

A young fireman brought them all tea, which Gerald sniffed suspiciously. Since becoming human, all he'd had to drink was alcohol.

"On the security cameras it showed the elves were holding them in the storage warehouse which is over there." Celina pointed to the far end of the compound where a large steel structure sat quiet and undisturbed. "It has a reinforced structure to protect many of our old prototypes. Aside from being wrapped in bubble wrap and packaging paper, they should all be okay."

Nigel quickly relayed the information to a nearby officer who released the employees of Majestic Technologies.

The bomb site had started to attract attention and either end of the street was cordoned off and manned by the police who did their best to look menacing, daring anyone to step across the line. Chester decided to challenge the menacing looks of the police as he ducked under the yellow caution tape and ran full belt down the street toward Gerald.

"Mr. Miller! Mr. Miller!" he shouted.

Had it not been for Big Ernie and Itch running into Chester and knocking him over, he would likely have been caught up in the explosion too. The two criminals themselves, both very much wanted by the law on counts of extortion and threatening grievous bodily harm in the form of hanging people off the edge of buildings, were now in the back of a police van. Fuzzbucket had permanently attached himself to Big Ernie and had no intention of letting go.

A police constable took up the chase after Chester, who was running with his arms flailing, a bad habit he'd never been able to get rid of.

"Who's he shouting at?" asked Nigel.

Gerald went over what Heinrich had told him, very specific instructions involving a small, pudgy gentleman who would be happy to see him and refer to him as *Mr. Miller.*

"He's here for me, don't worry I'll take care of it," said Gerald.

Chester ran up to Gerald and gave him a big hug, holding him tightly.

"Oh thank the heavens," said Chester, "you're alive!"

"Umm, yes," said Gerald. "It's, uhh, good to see you again, Chester."

Chester released Gerald and looked at him.

"It's an honor to see you again, sir! What happened? Why are you here? We got a report that you were hit by a bus in Portugal."

Nigel and Celina, happily holding hands, glanced at each other and shrugged.

"Uhh," said Gerald.

Nigel suddenly put two and two together.

"I'm sorry, Chester, is it?" Nigel grabbed Chester's hand and shook it firmly.

"Yes, I'm Mr. Miller's bank manager."

"Ahh, yes, of course you are."

Nigel put his arm around Chester and gently moved him away from Gerald who was doing his best to remain calm.

"Mr. Miller has had a most trying experience. First that whole bus business in Spain."

"Portugal," corrected Chester.

"Yes, and then this whole bomb thing, it's all been quite horrifying, as I'm sure an astute gentleman like yourself can understand."

"Well, of course," said Chester, "It's just that when Mr. Miller vanished I was quite beside myself."

"Really," said Nigel, "I had no idea that bank managers took such an interest in their client's well being these days."

"Well, Mr. Miller is no ordinary client," said Chester, then whispered, "his fortune is rather substantial."

Nigel's mind clicked over; there were definitely parts of this scenario that didn't fit, but Death had told him to look after Gerald.

"Of course," said Nigel.

"Who are you anyway, if you don't mind me asking?"

"Doctor Reinhardt," said Nigel.

This caused Celina to raise an eyebrow and smile.

"After such a traumatic episode, Gerald, uhh, Mr. Miller has decided to undergo my total emergent treatment. He'll be staying with me for a little while and we'll be in contact with you shortly. Where is it you're from again?"

"Upper Ramsbottom," said Chester quietly.

Nigel gave the man a sincerely apologetic look. "I'm sorry," he said.

"You get used to it," replied Chester.

Gerald had been concentrating hard, searching the fragmented memories of Raymond Miller's mind. Something came to him suddenly like a brick to the head.

"Ba Ba Black Sheep," blurted out Gerald.

"What was that?" asked Nigel.

235

Chester nodded knowingly.

"Good to see your memory is still intact. I'll be expecting your phone call, then." Chester hugged Gerald again, bid farewell and left.

"What just happened?" asked Nigel.

Gerald took a sip of tea calmly, as if he'd been inhabiting other people's bodies all his life.

"The man whose body I have is very rich. His name was Raymond Miller I think. Raymond and Chester had passwords with which to control the flow of money from one place to another. They also had passwords for emergencies and passwords for discretion."

"So what does 'baba black sheep' mean?"

"It means *everything's fine, can't talk now, will contact you later.*"

"And you have Raymond Miller's memory?"

"I dunno, sort of. Parts of it, lots of it. Hard to say. I definitely know that I'm rich, though," said Gerald and smiled. "Not that I really understand what that means, or what money is for that matter, but I have a lot of it. And to think that all I was this morning was a penguin."

"Yeah, I've been meaning to ask you about that," said Nigel, but the words went unheard as Gerald noticed something over Nigel's shoulder and took off at a run.

"Where's he going?" he asked Celina, who also didn't hear, as she'd seen what Gerald was looking at and taken off after him.

Nigel stood there awkwardly before joining in the sprint.

Emergency crews noticed the three of them running, and saw what happened and promptly converged on the scene.

The rubble of Majestic Technologies was unmoving, with the exception of one tiny area to the far side of where the warehouse once stood. Here a tiny, grubby elf waved wildly from what looked like the remains of a metal filing cabinet. The jingle of the bell on Eggnog's hat wasn't as jingly as it normally was, but for the most part, the elf appeared unharmed.

Gerald, being the first to reach him, helped him out of the filing cabinet drawer.

The Emergency Response Team climbed over the rubble and helped dislodge the stuck elf.

"What is that?" asked one of the officers.

"That," said Celina, partially out of breath, "is my, uhh, little brother, he was visiting me at work when all this happened."

"Why's he dressed like a Christmas elf?" asked the officer.

"He's very festive," said Nigel.

"Why's he dancing?" asked the officer who was observing Eggnog doing The Sprinkler.

"He's happy to be alive, obviously," said Celina. She motioned to Eggnog. "Come here umm, Bobby."

Eggnog looked at Celina and shuffled his way over to her with all the grace that a dancing elf can call upon.

Celina picked him up with amazing difficulty, as each elf weighed approximately one hundred and eighty pounds.

Nigel helped support her, and together with Gerald, they made their way back across the rubble.

"Is anyone else hungry?" asked Celina.

"Hungry?"

"Well, all I've had to eat today was some yogurt."

"All I had was fish while I was still a penguin, and then some peanuts," added Gerald.

"Now I think about it, I don't think I've had anything all day," said Nigel.

Celina put Eggnog down on firm ground so he could walk.

"Okay, so I say we go out and get some food and talk everything over. I hardly think our lives are going to be the same after this mess. It really makes you wonder what kind of a cosmic presence moved us around all day so that we'd end up right here, together."

The four of them walked through the police line and made their way through the crowd. Eggnog was the only one who really drew any stares, but after a stern look by Celina that would have made her dead ancestors proud, most onlookers decided it was best to look in other random directions.

All the while, Nigel tried to reflect on the day as best as a rational mind could.

"You're right, the whole thing's mind-boggling," he said. "But I think a large part of it had to do with a fish."

Jeremiah swam around his little bowl, oblivious to the events of the day and with absolutely no memory of helping to influence any part of it. Jeremiah the prophetic goldfish simply swam without the knowledge that he was indeed a powerful, cosmic, spiritual, and unique creature.

He suddenly felt a stab of excitement.

"Good grief, there's a castle in here!"

THE END . . .

almost . . . .

Epilogue.

6 Months Later

The enquiry had lasted a little under six months. Although responsibility for the Majestic Technologies bomb was unofficially immediately claimed by the IRA, there was still a lot of speculation about Nigel, Celina, and Gerald's involvement. The enquiry involved several interrogations of Nigel in particular, as he infuriated his interrogators by telling them anything except what they wanted to hear which ranged from stories about polar bears to theories that the bomb was a direct result of a butterfly hitting the window of a fast-moving vehicle driven by a drunken beaver somewhere in northern Alberta, Canada.

Gerald and Celina underwent their own interrogations. They dismissed Celina as being an employee in the wrong place at the wrong time. They let Gerald go as soon as the official investigators discovered that he was none other than Raymond Miller and was consequently wealthy enough to buy their jobs out from under them.

The investigators grew weary of Nigel, who had developed a habit of giving them all a headache. Giving people headaches appeared to be the extent of Nigel's current telekinetic abilities. He could also change the channels on the TV by thinking, and while walking the street during a heavy rainstorm three months after the Majestic Technologies bomb, he had sneezed and inadvertently thrown seven cars, a bus, a small dog, two cats, and twenty-threepassersby six feet into the air. His abilities were there, he knew they were there, but he had yet to master them.

The authorities charged Itch and Big Ernie with extortion, and they were put away for a three-to-five year stretch in Strangeways Prison in Lancashire. After much pleading and appealing, Big Ernie gained permission to keep Fuzzbucket, who was no longer an unholy vessel for the Prince of Darkness, in his cell. Police tried to return Fuzzbucket to Mrs. Jones, who opened fire with an ancient shotgun, barely missing the cat but injuring a police constable so that he couldn't go to the bathroom right for many months after. Mrs. Jones was serving a three-to-five year stretch in the mental hospital wing of Strangeways Prison in Lancashire. The cat was then handed over to Big Ernie, who had grown to love the cat now that it was cute and not quite so evil-looking.

The quaint little bistro where Heinrich worked vanished from the face of the Earth. Nigel and Gerald had returned to see Heinrich not even a week after the bombing, only to find the bistro boarded up, and no one in the vicinity could ever remember there being a bistro there in the first place.

Gerald received a phone call from Death once a month to see how things were going. Gerald asked Death about Heinrich but the Angel simply replied that he didn't know what Gerald was talking about.

Celina and Nigel had become very close over the last six months, with only one big fight which had occurred when the two of them were discussing their days in college where it would seem they had both partaken in similar games of Hide the Kipper. Celina claimed her high score to be better than Nigel's and a pointless fight had erupted. The fight lasted all of three minutes, the apologies took another twenty seconds, and the making up took a little over four hours and included a large pizza somewhere in the middle.

Nigel's captain accepted a generous cheque covering the cost of the helicopter Nigel had lost at the poker tables in Vegas, and then offered him his job back. Nigel refused, claiming that he had no wish to work for a large, over-reacting walrus and he was considering opening up his own private detective firm that would soon put the entire police force out of business. This was all lies, but it sounded good at the time. Gerald had been working on retrieving the parts of Raymond's memory that he really needed, and with Nigel's help, they had managed to sort out where exactly all the money was located and how they could access it, if need be. Gerald had moved in with Nigel who triedto teach him the finer points of being human and how to play *Hide the Kipper.*

Celina decided to keep Eggnog at her apartment and see if there was any way to stop him from dancing all the time, but that seemed next to impossible without wiping his entire database, which she just couldn't bring herself to do. The little elf had developed his own personality and was very content to bounce between Celina and Nigel's apartment and, due to his size and limited knowledge, could be passed offeasily as a child with a growth deficiency.

And so, along with Eggnog, with Nigel and Celina fiercely dating, and with Gerald living with Nigel, the four became inseparable friends. Celina no longer wished to work for Majestic Technologies and had resigned, much to the disappointment of the company, which already had enough trouble as its owner had vanished into thin air, quite literally.

The problem of money, thanks to Gerald, was no longer a problem at all. Gerald had insisted on helping his new friends with any financial difficulty they were experiencing, or had experienced, or would ever experience. He asked only to be friends and that they go on another adventure much like the last one, but without the bomb at the end. After the enquiry over the explosion was laid to rest and any suspicion dropped, Nigel, Celina, Eggnog, and Gerald booked a flight to Europe with the intention of backpacking around for a while.

The Entity grew weary, many moons had passed, and it had traveled a great distance. The journey neared its end, and after swimming the English Channel, the Entity made its way toward London. It had crossed over so many miles, they were hard to count and only once, at the foothills of Tibet, had the Entity been spotted. This was no mean feat, as the Entity stood at least seven feet tall.

After much searching and sneaking around, the Entity came to find what it was looking for. It entered the building, ripping the front door off its hinges in the process, and proceeded to the fourth floor. Moments later the Entity removed the hood of its cloak and politely knocked on the door of apartment 3B.

The flight was set to leave at seven in the evening, and Celina and Eggnog had gone back to her apartment to pack a few things. Gerald ran out to buy some travel toothpaste as Nigel packed his suitcase. He tried to decide whether he would have any use for his slippers while backpacking around Europe when there was a loud knock at his apartment door.

Funny. I don't remember buzzing anyone up.

Nigel stuck a finger in Jeremiah's fish bowl and swished it around, much to the enjoyment of the little fish. Nigel had bought a good-sized jam jar, which would allow Jeremiah to come with them to Europe. Following Death's instructions, he planned to take good care of the fish. There was another knock on the door, a little less patient than the first.

"I'm coming, I'm coming," said Nigel and opened the door.

Whatever Nigel had expected to see when he opened his door, it was definitely nothing like the thing that stood before him. To call it a man would be a profound understatement, and thinking back to his high school mythology and history classes, Nigel could think of only one way to describe the thing standing in his doorway.

A Minotaur stood in his doorway. A seven-foot creature with a man's muscular upper body, the enormous legs and head of a bull, with a large gold ring through its nostrils, dark eyes, dressed in a dark cloak, with a golden chest plate, and two long horns stared down at Nigel with absolutely no readable expression.

The Minotaur snorted. It pulled a small slip of paper from somewhere withinits cloak and read in a deep gutturalvoice.

"Nigel Amadeus Reinhardt?"

"Umm, yes," managed Nigel.

"I'm here for the fish," said the Minotaur matter-of-factly.

The last thing Nigel remembered before becoming unconscious was being smashed in the head by a very large fist. Twenty minutes later, when Nigel awoke to a worried Gerald shaking him violently, the seven-foot creature was gone. And so was Jeremiah.

THE END . . .

for now . . . .

Thank You For Reading

Curiosity Quills Press
http://curiosityquills.com

Please visit http://curiosityquills.com/reader-survey/ to share your reading experience with the author of this book!

About the Author

Andrew Buckley has been writing steadily since he was six years old when he wrote a story about a big blue dinosaur and received a gold star from his elementary school teacher. He had the good fortune to grow up in England where the sense of humor is rather silly.

In 1997 he moved to Canada because the thought of a country run entirely by beavers was amusing. He attended the Vancouver Film School's Writing for Film and Television program where he graduated with excellence. After pitching and developing several screenplay projects for film and television he worked in marketing and public relations for several years before venturing into a number of content writing contracts. During this time he abandoned screenwriting altogether and began writing his first novel.

Andrew now dwells happily in the Okanagan Valley, BC with 3 kids, 2 cats, 1 beautiful wife, and a multitude of voices that live comfortably in his head. His debut novel *The Death, The Devil, and the Goldfish* is published by Curiosity Quills Press.

Stein & Candle Detective Agency: Red Reunion, by Michael Panush

For Weatherby Stein and Morton Candle – private detectives specializing in the paranormal – life normally isn't easy. They deal with cases that pit them against ferocious demons in the Tokyo underworld, Satan-worshipping teenagers in a seemingly normal suburb and lizard-men in a Lake Tahoe lounge, and they still manage to come out on top. But now one of Weatherby's ancient ancestors, the villainous Viscount Wagner Stein, has been resurrected and is looking to stir up trouble – and he's not alone.

Weatherby, Morton and their allies must make a stand to stop the evils of the past from corrupting of the future – and only one side will emerge alive.

The Kulture Vultures by William Vitka & Bill Vitka

In the black of the cosmos, the Combine rules over entire planetary systems with an iron fist, maintaining a monopoly over hearts and minds everywhere with their terrible sitcoms.

Just so happens that the best pirated culture comes from Earth. The human monkeys might not be smart, but damn if they aren't entertaining.

Earth's biggest fan, a lowly intergalactic cab driver named Zel, joins a few not-so-loyal companions in a race to prevent humanity's extinction – by resurrecting Earth's great pulp writers and scientists. The only ones with enough creative craziness to figure out how to stop the Combine.

The Department of Magic, by Rod Kierkegaard, Jr.

Magic is nothing like it seems in children's books. It's dark and bloody and sexual – and requires its own semi-mythical branch of the US Federal Government to safeguard citizens against everpresent supernatural threats.

Join Jasmine Farah and Rocco di Angelo – a pair of wet-behind-the-ears recruits of The Department of Magic – on a nightmare gallop through a world of ghosts, spooks, vampires, and demons, and the minions of South American and Voodoo gods hell-bent on destroying all humanity in the year 2012.

Dinosaur Jazz, by Michael Panush

Acheron Island is a world lost to time, home to prehistoric creatures from earth's savage past – and Sir Edwin Crowe, son of one of the world's last Gentleman Adventurers. When ruthless American businessman, Selwyn Slade, brings an army of corporate cronies and modern industrial power to conquer this world from the past, it's up to Sir Edwin to protect these prehistoric lands.

Its Jazz Age meets the Mesozoic Age in a world where cave men, gangsters, hunters, zeppelins, pirates, warlords and dinosaurs clash for a chance of survival. All that and more is waiting for you in Dinosaur Jazz, a tale of high adventure in a prehistoric world.

Automatic Woman, by Nathan L. Yocum

There are no simple cases. Jacob "Jolly" Fellows knows this.

The London of 1888, the London of steam engines, Victorian intrigue, and horseless carriages is not a safe place nor simple place…but it's his place. Jolly is a thief catcher, a door-crashing thug for the prestigious Bow Street Firm, assigned to track down a life sized automatic ballerina. But when theft turns to murder and murder turns to conspiracy, can Jolly keep his head above water? Can a thief catcher catch a killer?

The Devil You Know, by K.H. Koehler

Not only does the Devil have an only begotten son, but he's currently residing in the rural town of Blackwater in northeast Pennsylvania.

Semi-retired from law enforcement, the handsome, if cynical, Nick Englebrecht becomes quickly caught up in a local missing child case that seems mundane on the outside, but when the sheriff requests his help as a psychic detective to help find the missing girl, his off-the-books investigation quickly leads him to some terrible truths about life, love and the universe as we know it.

CPSIA information can be obtained at www.ICGtesting.com
Printed in the USA
LVOW07s1544020216

473347LV00008B/1129/P